# CAIN LAKE

## THREE

# RED DEVIL

# RED DEVIL

## CAIN LAKE

### BOOK THREE

Copyrighted Material © 2025

Cover Design by Terry Fisher – Copyright © 2025



www.terryfisherbooks.com

ISBN: 978-1-7364107-8-3

# 1

## THE CALL

H ello?”
   “Hi, it’s me. Did I wake you?”
“No. No, I was just drinking a cup of coffee. Is everything okay?”
“He’s awake. About twenty minutes ago.”
“Oh, shit, really? Okay. Okay, I’m on my way.”
“Wait! He doesn’t want to see you right now.”
“What?”
“He’s a little upset.”
“He blames me for being in a coma, doesn’t he?”
“He’s not himself right now, you know? He’ll come around. Just give him some time.”
“Yeah, sure. Okay. Keep me posted, will you?”
“Of course. Gotta go. Bye.”
“...”

# BEAT YOURSELF UP

Cody Savage kept his right shoulder back and his left foot forward. He jabbed with his left fist, once, twice, three times in a blur of speed. Each jab hit its mark, and he followed with a big right hand that landed with a thump. His target swayed back and forth from the force of his blows.

"Still punching that bag?" Daisy Torrez asked from behind.

Cody had been so focused on his workout that he didn't see her creep down the stairs to check on him. Sweat ran down his brow and dripped off his nose. "Yup," he said through gritted teeth while throwing a right elbow into the leather heavy bag.

"Keep it up, and you'll put a hole in it."

"Maybe." He jabbed again.

"Kicking the hell out of a punching bag isn't going to solve anything, you know? Where'd you get that thing anyway?"

"Garage sale down the street. Mr. Laney had ten dollars on it, so I bartered with him and mowed his lawn."

Daisy stood at the bottom of the basement stairs and watched Cody take his aggravation out on the hapless gym equipment. She could feel his anger from across the room. She could see the fire in his eyes.

She began to sit on the third step from the bottom, but then noticed the dust and dirt that covered the hardwood surface. She ran her index finger across the wood and inspected the filth that had accumulated on her skin. She gently blew most of it away and then rubbed her hands together in disgust.

Cody continued the assault he was putting on the heavy bag. Padded gloves struck the leather over and over, and occasionally, he'd throw a knee or roundhouse kick at his leather victim.

"Where'd you learn to fight like that?" Daisy asked, trying to get a conversation out of her boyfriend.

Cody just shrugged. "Don't know." Right, left, left. "Used to play superheroes with my brother when we were kids and imitate TV." Left, right knee, right elbow. "Came in handy when I had to fight for real. Never had to think about swinging or ducking—just react."

She watched him punch, kick, and knee the bag a few dozen times, hoping he'd feel better after his workout. He'd been a recluse for the last two weeks, and Daisy had hoped to get him outside. Maybe they'd go hiking along the river trail or drive to the next town and find a new diner. Maybe she could convince him to pack a lunch and go fishing downriver from the power station. She was willing to do anything that would make him forget the guilt he had for AJ Timmons' condition.

Cody was drenched with sweat and anger as he thought about Levi Thompson and Jeremy "Cricket" Morrison, the two men who put AJ Timmons in a coma. With every blow, kick, and elbow he threw, he imagined them feeling the wrath of his temper. He wanted to hurt them more than he already had. He wanted to go savage on their asses.

Daisy started to speak, decided not to fight the heavy bag for his attention, and ascended the stairwell that led out of the basement. She couldn't watch anymore because no matter how many times Cody hit that bag, she was sure the only one he was beating up was himself.

*****

Cody pulled his sweat-soaked T-shirt off and slung it over his shoulder. Removing his tight leather gloves with padded knuckles took a little more effort. He opened his new left hand and flexed his fingers and tendons. Even with the gloves' protection, he'd

4

managed to paint the skin black and blue. Stiff knuckles resisted as he worked his fingers like a pianist warming up before a recital.

He recalled the night the bruised hand had grown back and the punch that sent Levi Thompson flying across Annabel's barn. The memory brought a sly smile to his face.

Cody disliked the psychic power he'd been given by Cain Lake, but he *really* liked this new hand. When he made a tight fist, it felt like steel. And when he threw a punch, it was like swinging a golf club. He wasn't sure if it had any practical use, but it made him feel strong and capable of defending himself against anyone.

With the naked left hand, he punched the heavy bag with two light taps and stepped away.

He climbed the stairs from the basement to the upstairs laundry room. His sneakers fell heavily on the steps, echoing off the cinder block walls of the room. When he reached the top, he saw Daisy sitting at the kitchen table, staring into a short glass of orange juice. Her face was calm and serious, but she gave Cody a lightning-quick smile to hide her concern. He bought it for a second but knew there was something on her mind.

He wasn't in the mood to talk. It had been two weeks since he received the call that AJ was out of the coma, and for two weeks, Cody brooded over the events that caused so much harm to his friend. He blamed himself for everything that happened, and now AJ wasn't speaking to him. Daisy could see Cody's pain and gave him time and space to deal with the events that happened at Parson's Store the night he confronted Levi Thompson.

"Feel better?" Daisy asked.

"What do you mean?"

She stood and faced him. "You can hit that bag all day, but it's not going to help. I know you blame yourself for what happened to AJ. And I know you need time to mourn your brother. But you've got to stop beating yourself up. None of this is your fault. You were trying to do what Cody Savage does best."

"Yeah, what's that?"

"Be the hero." She kissed his lips as if it would drive the point home.

Cody's eyes glazed over, "Some hero, eh? I couldn't save my brother, and my actions nearly killed AJ. I'm done trying to help people. I'm done with all the bullshit happening in this town. If everyone wants to go out and kill each other, then let them. From now on, you're the only one worth protecting."

"I can take care of myself," Daisy said. Her deadly appeared again, melting Cody like a Hershey's Kiss on a windowsill. He pressed his forehead against hers, and they just lingered in each other's presence for a moment.

Cody pulled away, wiped away the little bead of sweat he'd transferred to her skin, and smiled for the first time in weeks. "I don't deserve you."

"You're just now realizing that? Holy shit, I've been telling you that since we met." She pulled away and sat back at the table. "Go shower, and then we'll talk more about how unworthy you are."

Cody laughed, "Yes, Princess Torrez." He poured himself a glass of water, gulped half of it down, and headed to the upstairs bathroom.

*****

Cody returned to the kitchen wearing clean clothes and a fresh attitude. The couple decided it was a perfect day to go fishing since the sky was slightly overcast and the wind was calm. They could cast a hook and bobber from shore near the powerhouse and let the current carry their fishing line in a wide sweeping arc. It was a great place to catch bass, and if they stayed until dark, they could drop a jig in the water for walleyes.

Cody gathered a couple of fishing poles and a tackle box he inherited from his uncle Bruce. The garage attic, he discovered, was a treasure trove of little goodies for outdoor sports, seasonal decorations, scrap lumber, some power tools, and boxes of books. Daisy made him throw away the stack of old Playboys before Sammy found them.

While Cody organized the fishing gear, Daisy made them lunch consisting of peanut butter and banana sandwiches, a few apples, grapes, four granola bars, a thermos of orange juice, and ten bottles of water.

When Cody returned to the kitchen to see if she was ready, she rearranged everything to fit in the Igloo cooler. "Is it going to fit?"

"I'll make it fit."

"Do we really need all that?"

"Well, I'm not sure how long we'll be, and we need enough for all three of us."

"Oh, great. Sammy's coming, too?"

Daisy shook her head to indicate that her son was not coming. She stood close to him, gently took his hand, and placed it on her belly.

Cody nearly fell backward into the kitchen counter. "Are you fucking with me? That's not funny. You're joking, right?"

Choking on emotion, she was speechless, and merely shook her head again. Her big, beautiful smile bloomed like a flower, and her eyes dripped to keep it watered.

She finally coughed up the words, "I took two tests yesterday."

Cody grabbed her by the waist and gently wrapped his protective arms around the woman he loved. With their faces pushed together, they stared deep into one another's eyes.

Since the day he'd left prison, Cody had been beaten, shot, stabbed, and tied up in a burning barn, but this was the first time he felt truly scared.

# 3
# RIVER RUNNING

River Kelly backed her 2015 Nissan Pathfinder into a shaded corner of the parking lot and killed the engine. She checked her phone—5:47 pm, no messages. She and her vehicle sat alone at Full Throttle, the biker bar and grill on the edge of Stoneville. The establishment was dead quiet, but that would change in a few hours. So, she waited for the parking lot to fill with the usual Saturday crowd. Soon, members of the Road Barons, the Zombie Riders, and the Mayhem Maidens would fill the bar and drink and dance the night away. Comprised of generous and loving people, the three biker gangs came with nothing but good intentions, mostly.

Three employees were on the clock, consisting of one bartender, a short-order cook, and a floater to go back and forth when the other two needed assistance. They all parked behind the building, out of sight from the anterior side. The bar had opened at three o'clock, but the first customer didn't arrive at 6:13.

River gulped down several cans of an alcoholic seltzer with a fruity taste, which she decided wasn't as satisfying as a fresh cold beer. But the seltzer had fewer calories than a domestic brew, and she wanted a buzz, not love handles.

After her third can of the seltzer, the alcohol tickled her brain just enough. Each gulp filled her with fervor in anticipation of what the night would bring.

The sun still hovered high over an evergreen knoll on the same western side of the railroad tracks that snaked behind the building. She needed to pass the time by considering everything that could go wrong. She'd been scouting Full Throttle for two weeks, ever since she experienced the power of the knife she twirled in her right hand.

The Azure Blade—that's what the woman in her head called it. The knife was carved from a beautiful blue stone that her professor acquaintance, Dr. Claxton, called 'chert.' The stone's shape reminded River of the kayak she used to own, and memories of her shooting the rapids of the Ausable River always splashed across her mind when she held the knife. Those were her memories, but the blade also allowed her to see someone else's. A girl from long ago held the knife in a bloody pose while standing on a rough-planked dock. She stared out over the water with terror-filled eyes and clothes soaked with blood and shame.

The little girl talked to her sometimes; "Kill 'em all. Embrace your revenge. Feed on their fear and devour their sins."

River thought she was going crazy, but when she held that knife, she knew she was holding power. She knew she had to make things right, and that it was her duty to avenge AJ.

She contemplated the knife's age. It could be hundreds or even thousands of years old. How many people had possessed it? How many people had been possessed by it? How many people had been maimed by its deadly double-edged blade?

The knife was heavy in her delicate fingers but perfectly balanced. She had practiced with the weapon for over a week, throwing it into a target and willing it to return to her hand. It was an incredible sensation. They had a mystical bond now that they'd found each other. She took it everywhere she went, kept it on her nightstand beside the bed, and even left it on the back of the toilet when she showered. A leather worker fashioned a sheath from a sketch she had provided, which fit her belt and allowed River to conceal it behind her back. But she never let the man set eyes on the blade to keep her secret.

She leaned toward the vehicle's steering wheel, re-sheathed the Azure Blade, sat back, and closed her eyes. It took four cycles of her box-breathing to calm her nerves and lower her pulse.

*Breath. In...one, two, three, four. Out...one, two, three, four.* She repeated four cycles of her breathing exercise.

She envisioned her targets, members of the Road Barons, and pictured them dropping like flies as she cut her way through the crowd.

*No, that won't work.* She needed to take them one by one. In the parking lot—that's where she'd get revenge for what happened to AJ Timmons.

Sweet, innocent AJ. All he was trying to do was keep his best friend alive. And what did he get for his bravery? A fractured skull and three days in a coma.

*The fucking Barons are going to pay for that!*

When she finished her onslaught, and her hands dripped with Baron's blood, she'd go after her most dangerous prey—Cody Savage.

Her breathing exercises imploded from the anger inside that steamed like a locomotive, accelerating her heart rate to 127 beats per minute. She could hear the train thumping in her ears and feel the steam building in her bosom. Her hands trembled, so she held the steering wheel to keep them steady. In anticipation of the night to come, she bit her lip and nearly drew blood.

The bikers seemed to arrive in groups. Motorcycle after motorcycle filled the parking lot, followed by truck after truck. One man even rode a bicycle and parked it in a row of hedges. They all parked close to the building, leaving the rusty Pathfinder alone like a sick kid on a playground.

River watched them enjoy "happy hour." They spilled into the parking lot, toasting with shots of liquor, laughing at jokes, and smoking vape pipes, marijuana, and cigarettes.

*Have your fun, assholes.*

At 8:33, the sunlight tip-toed away, letting the night take center stage.

The parking lot was dark now, with the exception of a 125-watt floodlight over the bar's entrance and a similar light in the backyard, where a rowdy game of corn-hole was being played.

The parking lot was full of large trucks with oversized tires, toolboxes, ladder racks, and winches. They were the perfect cover for her when she was ready to approach.

One more shitty seltzer drink and she'd be ready.

She pushed the Pathfinder's door open but stopped when a sharp pain grabbed her temples. She slammed the door closed as if the sheet metal and plastic would shield her from the attack. A buzzing sound lit her mind on fire, like a radio squawking, searching for a clear station. A disembodied voice finally tuned into the right frequency. Frantic, she rotated the volume knob to zero, hoping the sound was emanating from the speakers. Her effort was in vain. A mature female voice rang with the clarity of an alarm clock, and now she could make out the words as the buzzing dwindled away.

*"Are you going to kill them all?"* The voice asked.

River didn't answer. She turned to check her back seat for the source of the voice, then looked outside. She was sure she was alone.

The buzz hit her ears again to gain attention and the voice spoke again. *"I know you can hear me, dear. Do you intend to kill them all, or do you have a specific target?"*

River gave in to the conversation, speaking in a loud whisper, "I...I, don't know. I want to kill them all. No, not all. Just the Barons. The Road Barons."

*"Once the blade tastes blood, there will be no stopping. Vengeance will consume you."*

"What am I doing? I should stop, right?" River asked the female inside her head. Her eyes tingled as she fought back tears. She knew what she was doing was wrong, but this must be done. She was compelled to inflict revenge on the Barons.

*"No."* The voice answered. *"Don't stop. Kill the sinners, and bring the blade to the lake when you've finished. I'll show you how to purge your sins in the water."*

"How do you know this? Why should I listen to *whoever* the fuck you are?"

*"Because the blade you possess belongs to me, and I want it back. I know its history and will answer all your questions when we meet.*

*Bring me the blade, and I will give you what you want."*

"What do I want? Tell me because I don't even know."

*"Cody Savage. You want revenge on Cody Savage. I will give you that or get it for you. But you must soil the blade, feed on the sinners, and bring the knife to me."*

"Are you the little girl? The one I've been dreaming about?"

*"I was,"* said the voice. *"But that was long ago."*

The voice went silent, even though River tried to ask more questions. The static stopped, and River was alone once more. She rolled her window down to allow fresh air into the car, and breathed deep to calm herself.

A woman inside the bar sang an amazingly accurate karaoke version of "Zombie" by the Cranberries drawing everyone from the parking lot back inside.

River pushed the car door open, pulled her hood over her red hair, and jumped out, hoping the voice wouldn't follow.

As if on cue, the front door of Full Throttle opened wide, and a burly biker stepped outside. Larry Larson wasn't any taller than River. He wore a black leather vest with all the Road Baron insignias and patches. He whistled as he staggered into the parking lot while quietly singing the lyrics to a 3 Doors Down song. The volume of his voice erupted when the lyrics mentioned New York getting too damn cold. Larry was no Bob Segar, but his glossy voice surprised River.

Larry walked to the far side of the parking lot, 300 feet from the building. River crisscrossed from vehicle to vehicle, ducking low and staying in the deep shadows of the tall trucks and SUVs. She could smell stale beer and antifreeze that had soaked into the gravel over the years. The high school physical education teacher was light on her feet—quiet as a wave crossing the lake.

She followed Larry through the parking lot and crossed in front of a Dodge Ram with a rooftop tent folded down in a hard plastic case. She peeked around the truck's front fender and lost sight of her prey. She crept along the truck and stood tall when she reached the back bumper.

A small shadow crossed the ground in front of her. She turned toward the bar and noticed a black crow had settled on a fiber optic wire that crossed over the lot. The solo crow cawed twice but stayed perched on the thin wire. River felt a tingle down her spine and couldn't help but feel like she was the one being hunted now.

*Where the hell?*

"Hey," Larry whispered behind her, trying not to startle the huntress. "Looking for me?"

River spun 180 degrees. *How the fuck?*

The exterior light illuminated Larry's round face, and his red beard stretched from his broad smile. An adrenaline explosion hit River like a water balloon to the face.

*"Strike him, now!"* Flesti Thaed's voice screamed in her ear.

River felt her arm muscles spasm out of her control. Someone else was in command of her reflexes.

Larry felt a sting in his belly, like the time he wrecked his Harley-Davidson, and the mirror mounted to the handlebars pierced his abdomen. That was before he gained sixty pounds of extra fat and the injury hurt like hell. The Azure Blade had done nothing more than slice the thick layer of fat that threatened Larry's chances of doing a perfect push-up.

River was uncertain what she had done until Larry jumped back and doubled over.

There was little blood on the blade. The wound wasn't fatal, but her mistake was.

"What the fuck, lady?" Larry winced. He began to run—a moving target that River had never anticipated. She thought this would be like the ninja movies she used to watch with her ex-boyfriend, where the victim just fell dead. They weren't supposed to run or move; she'd only practiced throwing the blade at a stationary wall.

*Fuck, fuck, fuck!*

Aiming at the dodgy biker, River let loose with the Azure Blade once more. This time, she threw the deadly blade at Larry, who was much quicker than he appeared. The knife tore through another layer of fat on his ribs.

He screamed more in fear than pain.

River reached out with an open hand, calling the knife back to her. On its return, the knife grazed Larry's shoulder, drawing blood as it tore through the meat.

River caught the knife with ease. She'd mastered that skill, at least.

Larry zig-zagged through the vehicles, trying to reach the safety of the building.

River chased after him, stepped on the bumper of a Land Rover, launched herself over to the bed of a Silverado, and then leaped off the roof. In mid-air, she picked her target—the exposed vertebrae in Larry's neck—and let loose with the deadly weapon.

It stuck deep in Larry's flesh, and he screamed in agony as he fell to the ground. The stone parking lot scraped away skin along his elbows and ground dirt into the open wound on his belly.

"Jesus! You stabbed me in the ass! What the fuck is wrong with you?" Larry extracted the blade with his left hand and held it in the light to examine the weapon of his attacker.

*"Pathetic!"* Flesti spit the word into River's brain.

*How is she seeing this? How does she know what's happening?*

The crow swerved around River, landed on the Silverado's rear view mirror, and bounced up and down while cawing in laughter.

River gestured for the blade to return. The Azure Blade spun in Larry's hand, tearing and cutting through his palm, and returned to its master's open fingers.

Larry bellowed in agony. The cut to his hand was the most painful injury the blade had yet inflicted. He scrambled to his feet again, left hand holding his buttocks, right hand holding his gut. He was just twenty feet from the door. Twenty feet from safety.

River aimed with fierce concentration. This had been sloppy, and she hated herself for being so careless. The onslaught had to end now with one good strike. She pulled her arm back, stepped forward with her opposite foot, and focused on Larry's spine.

She stopped, frozen from the sound that erupted from within Full Throttle—a gunshot. Two more. People screamed. The front door flew open, nearly ripping off its hinges, and slammed against the wall. The ground vibrated as a stampede of people erupted from the building and spilled into the parking lot. Chaos in the crowd as they all scrambled to find their vehicles. They ran past River, blurs of motion as she tried to focus on her prey. She needed to keep Larry in her sights and make sure she finished the job. But the shadowed faces blurred together as everyone ran past, stopping and starting, zigging and zagging, confusing the woman with the knife hidden under her arm.

Motorcycle engines fired up with ear-shattering decibels. Vehicle lights erased the dark of night. Tires flung gravel in all directions, and horns honked.

Larry disappeared in the mayhem. River decided to do the same.

She struggled to catch her breath, making it impossible to scream like everyone else. All she could do was run. She bolted for her car. The crow flapped by her head, scaring her even more. The bird landed on the Nissan's roof rack, squawked twice, and then took flight to disappear in the night sky.

She took refuge inside her vehicle, fumbled the keys until she found the correct one, and cranked the engine. She spun the Pathfinder's tires, merged with the frantic traffic, and never looked back.

# 4
# THE TAILRACE

The water of Cain Lake was channeled through a narrow bedrock chasm just beyond South Bridge before entering another large section of the lake. At the southernmost edge of the lake, a 422-foot dam held back the lake's hefty volume. Thirty-seven feet high, the dam funneled most of the river's water through a penstock pipe connected to a concrete powerhouse. Inside the powerhouse, the water-driven turbines generated megawatts of electricity, supplying Stoneville and many surrounding areas with sufficient energy. A chain-link fence ran the perimeter of the powerhouse to deter trespassers and vandals.

The water that exited the concrete structure gave birth to the Cascade River. The Cascade had been flowing over and around glacial boulders for eons, eroding the sharp corners and edges until the rocks were smooth as giant marbles.

Some of the best fishing in town was located just below the powerhouse, provided you knew how to access the isolated area. Cody Savage knew the way well.

He guided Daisy down a dirt road that challenged the Subaru's suspension. The vehicle weaved and dodged potholes, rocks, and tire ruts as it journeyed a half-mile down the one-lane road. They parked in a small open area beside an abandoned burgundy Chevy truck. The truck was unoccupied, so Cody assumed another fisherman had the same idea—spend the day hooking bass from the shoreline.

The couple exited the car and collected two coolers, a tackle box, two lightweight lawn chairs, and a single fishing pole. They hiked a narrow trail that led toward the Cascade River. After three-tenths of a mile of fighting mosquitoes and dodging poison ivy, they arrived at their destination, the rocky shore of the Cascade River.

Daisy smiled as they stepped from the shade of the evergreens and into the hot summer sun. The bedrock beneath her feet was smooth granite, like the counter top in her apartment without the polish. Boulders of all shapes and sizes were strewn about. She picked a flat-topped rock and sat. She could feel her stress melt into the rock below. She kicked off her white tennis shoes and enjoyed the serenity of the landscape.

The water's surface was smooth and calm, and despite the partly sunny sky, it appeared dark. The only indication that the water flowed came from the occasional leaf that floated past. Tiny eddies formed on the down-current side of boulders, and Daisy watched them spin hypnotically as they slowed and dissipated. It had a dizzying effect on the twenty-five-year-old woman.

"It's pretty here," she said. "And quiet."

"Give it a few minutes," Cody said with a smirk. He opened the cooler and grasped two cold bottles of water. Parched from the hike, they both guzzled half of the refreshing beverage.

Cody set his water on the ground and tied a medium-sized hook to the mono filament line of his fishing pole. He retrieved a large worm from a container they'd purchased from the general store on the way, tore the creature in half, and threaded the hook through its writhing body. Daisy's face scrunched with disgust as she watched the poor bug's torment.

After attaching a red and white bobber, Cody cocked his arm and then cast the line up the river and let the slow current bring it back.

Nothing happened.

He reeled in the line and tossed it again, aiming slightly to the right. The worm, hook, and bobber landed with a light splash and began their slow drift again.

Nothing happened.

"Well, this is exciting," Daisy laughed. "I hope we're not counting on you to catch dinner."

"Would you like to try?"

"No. I'm good sitting right here soaking up the sun." She moved from the rock to the Coleman folding chair and leaned back to face the light clouds. "What are you fishing for?"

"Bass mostly. But we could catch a perch if we're lucky."

Cody cast the line nine more times without a bite. He set the pole on the ground, fetched a couple more waters, and sat beside her in the other chair. They talked about the baby to come, where they might live, and possible names. They kissed in the heat of summer, and Cody felt more happiness than he had since stepping off the bus that delivered him from prison.

He'd forgotten about AJ, which was Daisy's goal for the day.

And then he remembered the picture that Roshan had drawn. It was only in a psychic meld with the boy that occurred weeks ago, but the image was still fresh in his mind. It was a picture of Cody, Daisy, Sammy, and a little girl. Roshan tore Cody from the picture, and the two sides turned to ash and blew away.

The ten-year-old's prediction had Cody worried. What could cause Daisy to lose him? Only death could tear him from their lives. Lately, he'd been having fewer and fewer psychic visions—a blessing—but sometimes, he wished he could see the future.

His thoughts were interrupted by a muffled, single-bang noise from within the powerhouse. Cody jumped to his feet, "This is it!"

Daisy sat up straight, unsure what the hell he was talking about. "What's that sound?"

A rumble came from the bowels of the concrete structure, growing louder and louder.

"That's the dinner bell for all the fish," Cody said. He was already on his feet with the fishing pole in hand. He pulled the rod back, then gently whipped it in a forehand cast that sent the line and bait in a sweeping arc that landed precisely where he intended.

The water at the edge of the powerhouse erupted with turbulent violence, transforming the still reservoir into a raging river. The tail race, as it was called, was created by all the water released through the powerhouse after the steel gate had opened at the dam.

The dark water turned white, filled the reservoir, and crept up the rocks to Daisy's feet. She jumped up and pulled her chair backward to evade the encroaching waterline.

"Holy shit, the water's rising—fast." She needed to shout over the sound of the rushing river that sounded like a wave that never stopped crashing. She moved up the rocks and onto the soft soil that the water never reached.

Cody laughed. "Yup! This is the tailrace, and all that water means fresh food and oxygen." As he spoke the words, his bobber disappeared from the surface. Cody pulled the rod upward and felt resistance on the end of the line, followed by a frantic tug. He began to reel his bait and hook back to shore and lifted a fat bass from the water.

"Wohoo!" Daisy exclaimed. She gave Cody a thumbs-up. "Good job." She already had her phone ready to snap his picture. She waded through the cold water until her knees were almost submerged and kissed him. It was a little win that he needed to distract himself from the self-doubt he'd been feeling lately.

Cody stuck a thumb in the bass's mouth and held it by its lower jaw. The fish, unable to kick or resist, waited for Cody to work the hook free. Once he released the fish back into its habitat, he re baited his hook with the worm's other half and cast again. He knew the powerhouse would only produce this opportunity once every thirty to forty minutes—maybe less.

They spent the rest of the day at the reservoir, enjoying their surroundings and each other. The powerhouse opened and closed a dozen times during their escapade. After eating a late lunch, they walked along the shore, looking at the various geographic anomalies in the old river bed, and collected some driftwood that Daisy wanted for decoration.

Every new experience with Cody, every lesson about nature, and every skill he taught her emphasized his natural and caring personality, and Daisy knew he would be a wonderful father.

A pair of bald eagles flew up the river and passed just fifteen feet over their heads. The birds of prey were so low that Daisy was in awe at the sound of their powerful, thick wings beating the air. The eagles followed the water, flying side by side until they were out of sight.

They didn't want the day to end, so Cody talked her into staying until dark. "That's when we'll catch the big ones."

"How big do bass get?"

"The bass will stop feeding before dark. But after dark," he held his hands in front of him, two feet apart, "That's when the walleye will start to feed. We can catch them right off the bottom of the river, next to the powerhouse."

"You'll have to show me. But this time, I get to fish."

They were almost a half-mile from the powerhouse when they turned and began to make their way back to the chairs. Night floated into the valley, and the air temperature fell thirteen degrees. Cody collected a small amount of dry driftwood—careful to keep it separate from Daisy's collection—and started a small fire on the bedrock shore.

They stared at the stars, and Daisy pointed out all the constellations she knew.

"How do you know so many?" Cody inquired.

"Growing up in the desert, the sky was so much bigger and darker, and you could see them all."

A meteor streaked across the sky, burning green and orange from the friction of the earth's atmosphere, and disappeared as quickly as it had appeared.

The powerhouse was idle, so the water was calm and quiet. Crickets, frogs, and the fire crackling broke the still night air until another sound emanated from Stoneville. Blaring sirens from emergency vehicles carried across the lake and down the riverbed. The sirens started softly and grew in volume as they blasted their way through traffic, then faded as the vehicles drove north. With the cacophony of noisy emergency sirens, they knew the parade consisted of police, fire trucks, and ambulances.

"What the hell do you think that's all about?" Cody asked.

"I don't know, but we'd better go find out. I'm sure my boss will be calling me any second." She looked at her phone. The cell service had been weak all day and was now completely absent. "I've got no service. Mom's going to be worried when she hears those sirens."

"Sure, okay, let's go. Let's just put the fire out first." Cody hurried to the edge of the water with an empty water bottle. He plunged the plastic into the river to fill it up. A tiny blue light submerged in six inches of water caught his attention. He stared at the blue glow. It was small and faint. He placed his left hand into the Cascade River.

A colony of blue micropods clustered around his hand—his new hand that had regrown two weeks prior. Cody held his fingers just below the surface, and the micropods took refuge below his palm. They mimicked the shape of his hand as he moved it, like a living shadow. He made a fist, and the micropods clustered together. He opened his hand wide; they fanned out like a turkey's tail. He made a V with his index and middle finger, and they copied that, too.

He wasn't sure if he was controlling them or if they were just imitating his movements.

Unexpectedly, his vision flickered. His mind went dark. And then flashes of a scene appeared in his brain. A man is trying to get up from the floor. Lights flashing. A billiard table. Two gunshots in his abdomen. He stepped over another man lying on the floor and fell onto the pool table. Billiard balls, freshly racked, were scattered across the green velvet. The eight ball dropped into a corner pocket.

He recognized the man slumped on the pool table. It was Aaron Bristol, one of Levi Thompson's rogue gang members. Which meant the man on the floor was probably his cousin, Duke.

The vision was over as quickly as it had begun. Cody didn't pass out this time or get a nosebleed. He remained calm and focused, but most importantly, he was aware. He heard Daisy's shoes scuff across the granite toward him. The micropods went dim, like a power switch had been adjusted, and in a fraction of a second, they were gone.

"You all right?" Daisy asked casually.

"Yeah. I'm okay. Just trying to wash the fishy smell off my hands." He resumed filling the plastic water bottle, not wanting to concern her with the vision he'd experienced, but he was sure it was related to the sirens they'd heard in the distance.

He stood and poured the water over the dying fire, which released an angry puff of steam as it died.

"Let's go."

23

# 5
# BACK IN TOWN 

Cody and Daisy walked the trail from the river to the car in the darkness. It was difficult to distinguish their path from the animal trails that crossed in front of them. Daisy was at the mercy of Cody's natural compass and knowledge of the local geography. Her palms were sweaty, and her heart raced, hoping they were going in the correct direction. Their steps were quick as they scrambled to make it through the woods. The thick cedars and tall pines canceled all light, so Cody used her cell phone to light the way, guiding them through the trees and illuminating the narrow, overgrown trail.

She carried the beach chairs with one hand and swatted at mosquitoes with the other. "I hate the woods at night."

"Nothing changes about the woods just because the sun went down. It's exactly the same place it was today."

A little brown bat fluttered by her head. "What the hell was that?"

"Just a bat. He eats mosquitoes, not people."

"Yeah, well, I don't remember any bats out when we came in. And the mosquitoes are pretty close to my hair."

"Do you think an animal that can accurately pick a tiny insect out of mid-air in the dark can't avoid your head?"

She had no choice but to trust him, and kept pace.

They reached the beat-up Subaru without getting lost and stowed their gear. She turned the key, and the Outback sputtered to life. Once she turned the car around, they sputtered up the rough dirt road. The Subaru bounced and rattled, shaking the two passengers inside, but Daisy was glad to be in the protective metal of the SUV. She raked her fingers through her hair as she drove, hoping no insects were crawling around her soft dark locks.

She looked inpatiently at her phone every ten seconds. "Shit! I've got no cell service. How am I going to know what's going on?"

"You should get a signal once we get north of the lake."

"I hope so."

They merged onto the blacktop near the South Bridge.

"Do you want me to take you home?" Daisy asked. She stomped on the gas pedal, and the boxer engine fought to get up to speed.

"No." Cody thought about his vision—Aaron Bristol shot, Duke on the floor. "I'll go with you. I'm not letting you out of my sight if there's been a shooting."

"I'm a big girl," said the 115-pound woman. "And what makes you think there's been a shooting? I'm sure it's just a house fire or something."

"But what if it was a shooting?"

"Cody Savage, did you have a vision?"

"No. It's been weeks since my last vision," he lied.

They turned onto Lake View Drive and headed toward town, riding in silence, and worried about the incident that was drawing so many sirens north.

Daisy's phone finally came to life as the cell service returned. Text and voice messages dinged one after another—her boss eight times, her mother four, and her landlord twice.

She called her mother first and informed her that they were okay. Then she tried her boss, but he didn't pick up.

The landlord could wait for her explanation why the rent was late again.

The Subaru weaved through town, unsure of which direction to go. A motorcycle with two riders passed them as they headed down Main Street and merged into their lane. They stopped at a red light. Daisy brought the Subaru to a stop behind the bikers and waited for the light to change.

Cody stared at the girl on the back. Her arms were wrapped around a tall, skinny driver. They both leaned forward as he revved the motorcycle's engine. It wasn't a Harley-Davidson, the trite brand of the Road Barons. From the posterior, it appeared to be a retro Triumph Scrambler from the 1960s. The operator and passenger wore medium blue helmets that matched the color of the gas tank. However, the part that intrigued Cody the most was the female riding on the back.

She had black hair that escaped her light helmet. She had a thin waist and square shoulders, visible even with the black leather jacket that covered them. The jacket failed to cover her lower back. Her legs were muscular, covered with tight jeans, and finished with Adidas sneakers. Silver thong underwear peeked out from her jeans, drawing Cody's eyes like a trout to a spinner.

*Damn, I'd recognize that ass anywhere. Alyse, who are you riding with tonight?* He kept the boorish thought to himself.

Daisy watched the couple on the motorcycle as well. She sat up straight at the steering wheel. "Is that Alyse? That is Alyse. I'd recognize that ass anywhere."

Cody fought his devilish smile. "You think so? Shouldn't she be working tonight?"

"No, remember? She's leaving town. Honestly, I'd thought she'd left already."

"Haven't you been in touch?"

"No. She's been keeping an eye on AJ when River's not around, which has been quite a bit lately. She quit working at The Mineshaft a few days ago."

Daisy let her foot off the brake and pulled into the left lane. Cody already had his window down, waving his hand for attention before the couple on the motorcycle could speed away. The driver of the Triumph ignored the green light and stayed parked on the road, but there was no traffic behind them to protest.

"Alyse! Hey!" Cody shouted.

The girl on the bike lifted her visor, and for a moment, Cody thought he was mistaken. The dark deadness in her eyes was uncharacteristic of the Louisiana beauty.

"Hey, stranger. How have you been? Hey, Daisy." Her words were slurred, and she was slightly unsteady.

"We're Good. Where are you headed?"

"Anywhere but Full Throttle. We just left there. There was a shooting there tonight in the back billiard room. We got the fuck out of there as fast as we could. It was fucking crazy!"

Cody shot a concerned look at Daisy. She mirrored his expression.

"I gotta go. This is big. Friggin huge." Daisy's words were quick; she wanted the story, but she'd have to get there soon.

"I'll get out here." He kissed her. "Go get your story. I'll see you at home."

He jumped out of the car, and she accelerated toward Full Throttle through the intersection as the traffic light turned red. Alyse and her companion didn't move. The driver politely waited for Cody and Alyse to finish their conversation.

The intersection was quiet. There wasn't a single vehicle on the street other than the Triumph sitting at the traffic light. A single street light above lit the scene, and a few lights glowed from several apartments above the closed businesses.

"I've gotta go, Cody," Alyse said. "I'm heading back to AJ's now. He's throwing me a little going-away party. Then I'm leaving in the morning."

"You said that two weeks ago."

"Yeah, well, I couldn't leave with AJ in a coma. I just stayed to make sure he was going to be okay. That you two were going to be okay."

"We're not. At least, he's not. He still won't speak to me."

"I know. Give him a little more time. He'll come around."

Cody stepped closer. The guy on the bike was as patient as a saint. Cody was glad for the moment.

"Will I see you again?" He asked.

"I don't think so. But, I've learned to never say never."

She kissed him on the lips and mouthed three little words. Her kiss was fire in the cool night air. Then she slapped her visor down and rode away with a stranger.

Cody stood in the middle of the road, alone. A part of him was glad Alyse was leaving. He hoped she'd find happiness somewhere she would fit in, somewhere with more culture, more job opportunities, and good weather. With her gone, he could build a life with Daisy and the family they were about to become.

He could focus.

Maybe he'd forget about AJ, too. Forget about everybody except Daisy. She could move in with him, and he'd get a job. And maybe a dog. Kids need a dog.

*****

Cody had four choices: go home, head to The Mineshaft, check out the incident at Full Throttle, or crash AJ's party.

He wasn't tired, so he quickly crossed the option of going home off his list. The Mineshaft would be too crowded on a Saturday night, especially if the Full Throttle crowd transferred there—maybe some other time. Full Throttle was a three-mile walk from his current location—too far. Plus, Sheriff Jo Hassett was likely to be there, and he was trying to avoid her.

He wasn't a fugitive of the law any longer and had been cleared of the shooting death of Jesse Lewis at Cain Lake. The gun used to kill the Sin Eater turned out to be a .30 caliber rifle, which nearly every hunter in the county possessed.

Sheriff Hassett squeezed Amos McGrath a little, and the big man popped like a can of Pillsbury dough, giving Hassett the truth about Andrew Mills' death. According to Amos, they kidnapped Andrew Mills, hoping it would draw Jesse Lewis and Cody Savage to Parson's old store. When it didn't work, the Bristol cousins—Duke and Aaron—killed him and dumped his body across the lake where Bourbon found him.

After Andrew proved to be of no use, Levi realized they needed a victim with closer ties to Cody, and it just so happened that Michael Savage was in town to reconnect with his brother.

Sheriff Hassett was trying to build a case against the Bristol

29

cousins to prove they killed Andrew Mills and aided Levi Thompson in the death of Michael Savage. Unfortunately, she just didn't have the physical evidence. But she knew, with time, the cousins would eventually pay for their crimes. If Cody's vision was correct, and Duke and Aaron were the victims of tonight's shooting, then Sheriff Hassett wouldn't have to worry about them anymore.

## 6

# PARTY CRASHER 

Cody walked with purpose, heading west until he reached the edge of town. He stopped at the bottom of a long driveway that navigated a tall hill. AJ's house was nestled at the top of the drive, lights on, and by the sound reverberating from within, AJ's party for Alyse was in full swing.

Cody began ascending the steep grade, his steps in time with a Dr. Dre ditty. By the time he reached the top of his asphalt driveway, his legs burned with exhaustion. He sucked the sultry night air into his overworked lungs in an attempt to catch his breath. A thin layer of sweat evaporated from his forehead as he turned to admire his achievement. The driveway looked much more impressive from the bottom than his present location.

*Damn, I gotta start hitting the gym more.*

His lungs thanked him for the break as he stood atop the hill and watched AJ's house. Music escaped through the Sheetrock and wood walls. A rap song was playing, the beat as fast as Cody's pulse, and then he heard a chorus of voices from within the dwelling shout in unison to the song's catchy vibe.

Cody couldn't refrain from whispering the lyrics as he approached the door.

AJ's home was a modern two-story design with plenty of glass on the back that overlooked his pool. The roof was a combination of hip and gable trusses protected by course after course of architectural shingles. The vinyl siding was medium blue, and black shutters hugged the windows. The long winding driveway Cody had just climbed—460 feet—led to the garage's sixteen-foot-wide door. On the way up, he passed a couple dozen cars parked in the driveway. Cody surmised that approximately forty people were in attendance.

He looked for the Triumph motorcycle, wondering if Alyse had made it to her party. It wasn't there. Cody felt satisfied, hoping her ride to the party was nothing more than that. He hated to admit it, but seeing her riding on the back of the bike—legs straddling the frame, arms wrapped around a stranger—had made him a little jealous. Perhaps she decided to skip her party or took a detour.

The sidewalk, a pattern of sand-colored pavers, was bordered on both sides by a short hedgerow. He rapped two knuckles on the front door and then rang the doorbell. Typically, he would enter AJ's house without invitation, but circumstances were different now. He heard an unfamiliar voice yell over the music, "Pizza's here!" The volume of the music dropped a few decibels.

It wasn't long until AJ opened the door. He wore a colorful button-up shirt with a neatly folded collar and short sleeves. Framed in the doorway, he kept one hand on the door while the other grasped a half-empty bottle of Corona. A drowned slice of lime lay at the bottom of the beverage. He took a slow, long sip of the beer and studied Cody momentarily.

"Hey, pal," Cody said. "I just stopped by to see how you were doing."

AJ took another sip. "You weren't invited." He began to close the door, but Cody stuck his foot forward to stop it.

"Still pissed? I get it, buddy. Look, I'm so sorry about what happened to you. I know I got in over my head again. This time, it nearly killed you."

AJ let the words sink for a moment, recalling the beating Levi Thompson had put him through. He nearly shuddered but fought it. He refused to show weakness.

Cody continued. "Say something, man. I've been going crazy wondering how you're doing. Tell me to fuck off if you want, or punch me in the face, or tell me you just need some time to put all this behind you. Anything, please."

AJ set his beer on the hallway console table. The bottle rested dangerously close to the edge of the Crate & Barrel furniture.

Cody was hoping for a big man-hug. Instead, he received a big knuckle roundhouse that landed square on his left cheek. He saw the blow coming and could've ducked or blocked with ease, but if this helped AJ relinquish some of his resentment, he'd sacrifice a moment of pain for his best friend. He heard the crunching sound echo in his ears and hoped AJ hadn't broken his hand.

*Go ahead and get it out of your system.*

The blow had power behind it.

*Jesus, you could've pulled your punch a little, buddy.*

The taste of blood and copper filled Cody's mouth. Water filled his left eye and prevented him from seeing the second punch. It landed with just as much force.

Up went down. Left went right, and Cody's world swirled like he'd been caught in a clothes dryer rolling down a hill. He stumbled backward, the hedge row grabbed his calves, and he tumbled over the top. The music cut out. Cody wondered if he'd blacked out for a moment, and then he heard the voices—whispers mumbling in a foreign language. As his senses returned, he saw the silhouettes of party guests funneling through the door to witness the front yard commotion. He felt surrounded, vulnerable as he lay there. Getting up would have provoked AJ's anger further, so he stayed on the ground.

AJ loomed over him and finally spoke, "That's how I'm feeling, bitch! That's how I feel." He rubbed his knuckles. "Your apology doesn't mean shit to me. I'm done backing you up, Cody. You want to run off and play hero—get yourself killed—every fucking time you have a vision? Go ahead. Leave me and River out of your little adventures." He started back toward the house, turned with a middle finger aimed at his victim, "I don't give a fuck, anymore. You're on your own because you're not going to stop until you get yourself or someone else killed."

*He's probably right. He's so right.*

AJ entered his house, and everyone else fell into line, following their beloved, wealthy party host. Whispers escaped the line, and rumors had already arisen from the incident. Cody could only hear bits and pieces of the voices, but it was enough to reconstruct what they were saying:

"Cody hit AJ."

"AJ hit Cody."

"Cody was being an asshole."

"Got what he deserved."

"Fighting over River, I think."

"I thought AJ and Cody were a couple?"

"Probably come back with a gun."

As the little crowd poured back into the house, it parted to allow the guest of honor to make her way out. Alyse Burns urged everyone inside, "Head back inside, people. Fights over. Just a couple of friends hashing things out. No big deal."

She stood over Cody with her hand outstretched. "Come on, handsome. I know you can take more of a beating than that."

Cody took her hand, soft and strong, and stood. He brushed dry leaves and dirt off his jeans. "He's never going to forgive me, is he?" A pounding sensation within his left ear worsened as he stood. Blood pumped through swollen arteries somewhere in his head. He rubbed the side of his face, attempting to soothe the pain.

"Ahh, he'll come around—just bad timing. I don't think things are working out with him and River. She's been kinda distant lately—preoccupied with something. AJ thinks she's trying to let him down easy."

"She's not here?"

"No. He hasn't seen her in, like, two days."

Cody stretched the tight muscles in his neck. "I didn't know that. No wonder he's so pissed off. Well, I hope she shows up tonight. Maybe that will soothe things."

"Truth is," Alyse explained, "I don't think AJ is having this party for me. He's just having it to distract himself. He feels he's lost everyone he cares about—you, Daisy, River, and even me. It's just all kinda sudden."

"Yeah, well, I'm here making an attempt."

"True, but he's losing everyone else *because* of you. Plus, he's still angry about the whole Levi situation." She lowered her voice, "He talks about having him killed in prison. I can't tell if he's joking or not."

"Jesus. Nobody wants Levi dead more than me. Not after what he did to my brother. Hell, I'd pull the trigger myself if I could make this all go away."

Alyse put a hand on his shoulder. "I think that's part of his anger, because neither of you finished the job."

"Only because Bourbon stopped me. Luckily."

"I'd better head inside."

"You're really leaving tomorrow?"

She grabbed him by the shirt. "Not if you tell me to stay." She snared him with her big green eyes full of tears. She moved closer. They shared the same breath. Two more inches, and they welded together in a passionate kiss. Her tangerine lip gloss mixed perfectly with the faint taste of vodka on her tongue, and Cody found himself drunk on her elixir.

They gently broke apart, and Alyse whispered in his left ear. "Come with me. If you don't want me to stay, then come with me. Let's get out of here. Just you and me, like we used to be. A fresh start."

Cody stared at his shoes in silence. A part of him wanted to say, "Let's go." There was something about Alyse that reminded him of his wife Willa. Every time he was near her, it was like his deceased wife was back in his life. He knew it was a illusion, but as fake as it was, he lingered in it as long as possible. He couldn't run away with this woman, who was a reflection of his wife. Everything he loved was right here in Stoneville, even if he'd only brought misery to the town he loved.

"Daisy's pregnant," he blurted.

Alyse smiled, partly because she was happy for him and partly because it made her decision to leave easier. Space formed between them as she stepped backward. Water from her eyes was pushed to the side, transferring black mascara to her knuckles.

"Sammy's going to be such a good big brother," She conceded. Her right hand covered his heart. "And you're going to be an awesome dad. I'm happy for you—both of you—all of you. Really, I am." Her feelings were genuine.

"Will you stay in touch?" Cody asked.

"Of course." Her lie was almost believable. She stepped back toward him and they hugged for a long moment. And then she turned and vanished through the door.

Cody sucked in a big breath and then exhaled slowly. He stood alone, in the dim light, as the music inside began to rise.

*Well that was a shit show.*

He began the long, dark descent down the driveway, forcing one foot in front of the other, his cadence like a man with chained ankles. He had nowhere to be, no destination, and no one waiting on him. Walking killed time, and he had a lot of time to kill.

As he approached the bottom of the hill, the air temperature dropped from the cool, damp convection currents that drifted around him. The day's heat finally gave way to night. Goosebumps formed on the skin of his arms like little Braille dots that seemed to say, "You're not alone." The distant noise of the party died away, but there was a faint beat that mimicked his footsteps.

Thump. Thump. Thump. Thump.

He thought it was the blood-swollen ear, but in truth, he was hearing the beating sound of bird wings above the tree tops.

*****

A thick cloud pushed east on a breeze, revealing the pale glow of a quarter-moon. The light reflecting off the moon's scarred surface was just enough to light Cody's way, illuminating the rough edges of the cracked asphalt. He walked toward town with only his thoughts to keep him company. Occasionally, he'd stop to listen to the creatures of the night: tree frogs, barred owls, crickets, and a lonely coyote.

*I hear ya, big guy.*

He was a mile from AJ's house when an unnatural sound approached from behind. An engine sputtered a half-mile from his current location and he knew that sound as well as he knew his own voice. The headlights from the approaching vehicle began to illuminate the tops of the trees, and as it grew closer, the beams of light intensified and lowered. The car slowed as the driver kept a watchful eye for deer, raccoons, and skunks.

The bright lights hit Cody, and the car pulled beside him and idled. The passenger-side window lowered with a groan as the electric motor struggled to perform.

Daisy sat behind the steering wheel of her little Subaru station wagon with a smile just for him. "Need a ride, sir? I don't usually pick up strange men, but you're kinda cute."

Cody felt the weight of the world lift a bit. She had that effect. He squeezed into the passenger seat and buckled his seatbelt. The dome light above revealed the shiny new bruise on his cheek. Daisy reached toward the mark but refrained from touching it, not wanting to cause more pain. From the look on his face, she also knew the real pain was in his heart.

"Party didn't go so well?" She asked.

"How'd you know?"

"Alyse shot me a text message. Said you might need a ride."

"It's a nice night. I didn't mind walking." He reached behind her seat, flipped the lid on a small cooler, and retrieved their last water bottle. He put the cold bottle to his warm cheekbone. "Did she tell you what happened?"

"Just that AJ wouldn't let you inside." She squeezed his hand. "I already called Mom and told her I wouldn't be home tonight. She didn't mind. Sammy's already in bed, and she has no plans tomorrow."

He snapped the cap off the water and offered her the first drink. "Shouldn't you be writing about the shooting at the bar?"

Daisy took a sip and handed it back. "No." She took her foot off the brake, and they accelerated down the road. "Trena Cutlass got the story. She's the new journalist who keeps getting the big scoops."

"Scoops? Do people still say that?"

Daisy ignored his question. She rolled through a stop sign on the edge of Stoneville, turned right, and bypassed the hospital. "By the time I arrived, WKED was already interviewing Sheriff Hassett."

"So, no story?"

She shook her head in defeat, "No story."

"I'm sorry. We shouldn't have stayed at the river so late."

"No, don't apologize," she squeezed his knuckles. "It was worth it."

They drove silently until they reached Cody's house, and neither brought it up again. They went straight to bed and held each other for some time. They talked about the baby, Sammy, and how they'd never see Alyse again. Their thoughts and emotions were scattered like butterflies in a windstorm. It was a restless night, but they finally succumbed to exhaustion and slept until the sun peeked in on them.

# 7

# THE NAZI

"Can I show you something?" Daisy asked as she poured Cody's morning coffee into a mug.

Cody finished pulling a clean shirt over his freshly washed hair. "Of course. What is it?"

Daisy walked to the living room, retrieved her computer bag, and returned to the kitchen table. She dug into the black canvas bag and came out with a dossier on a story she'd been working on.

"What's that?"

"I've been working on this project in my free time. I've been collecting old photos and articles to write a book on Stoneville's history. Maybe I can make a little money from it, but it's kinda for Sammy when he gets older. Plus, I was curious about it myself. I couldn't find a single resource to learn about the region. It's been a total scavenger hunt."

Cody smiled. "That's cool. Where'd you get all this?"

"Some of it's from local people I've met. Some of it's from the Internet, the museum, and old newspapers." She displayed a few old photos on the kitchen table. They had small Post-it notes, color-coded for efficiency, attached to the back with handwritten dates and names. Some of the names were the owners of the photos, so she'd know where to return the images, and some of the names were the subjects in the composition.

"This is just one of the folders I've compiled. There are three more."

She had grouped old tintypes, photos of paintings, and black-

and-white drawings. There were pictures of loggers and trappers in the 1700s, miners working in the 1800s, farmers from every century, and soldiers from the 1900s. There were also businessmen and women, children in schools, and construction photos.

"These are amazing," Cody said. "I could spend all day looking through these."

Daisy reached for a small print, "Well, this isn't what I wanted you to see. Look at this photo." She dropped a five-by-seven picture in front of him. A former journalist had photographed an old painting. "Recognize it?"

Cody held the photo, "Sure, everyone in town's seen this. It's a painting of Laramie Cain, his wife, and their four children. This painting used to hang in the school lobby, but they moved it to the museum during construction in the late 1990s."

"Okay, so you've seen it. The Cains went on to have five more children after this painting. Nine total." She dug into a bright yellow folder, seemingly picked to stand out from the rest. "Now, look at this photo. This was taken during a ribbon cutting ceremony when the airport opened in 1963."

Cody scanned the photo of a woman with an oversized pair of novelty scissors ready to cut a ribbon. Three men in suits flanked her side, and she smiled at the camera. She was attractive, probably in her mid-fifties, with blonde hair pulled in a bun. As she leaned forward, a necklace dangled from her button-up shirt, with a symbol engraved in stone—a triangle pointing downward and three wavy lines on each side.

Cody instantly recognized the accessory, "Holy shit, that's Flesti."

"Yup, but read the names under the photo."

"Marion Castor. Is that her real name?" He reread it with the full description, "Marion Castor, distant great-granddaughter of town founder Laramie Cain."

Daisy shuffled the photos and placed another in front of her lover. The photo was notably older, with frayed corners and stained edges. It lacked detail, and the contrast was so strong that the shadows appeared almost pure black. "This is a photo taken when Harry S.

Truman came to town. He vacationed in the Thousand Islands six months after an attempt on his life at the Blair House in Washington, DC. But he stopped in Stoneville and ate lunch at the Cascade Diner, accompanied by four secret service agents."

Cody stared at the picture of the thirty-third president of the United States. "Okay, so what am I missing?"

"The waitress. Who does she look like?"

"Flesti, I guess, but that could be a coincidence, right?"

Daisy presented another photo from the newspaper, printed in 1951. The staff of the same diner stood in front of the glass double doors. A burly man in a T-shirt and an apron was flanked by three women dressed as waitresses. The man and his wife, presumably the owners, were presenting a check for a fundraiser to benefit war widows. The paper listed the employees, including the same waitress who resembled Flesti Thaed. Her name, according to the paper, was Marion Rackley. She looked exactly like Marion Castor, who cut the ribbon at the airport.

"Okay, call me intrigued," Cody admitted. "All these women look alike and have the same first name. You think these women are all related?"

Daisy put one more print on the table. A copy of the original, but no doubt a mugshot of the same woman they knew from Cain Lake. It occupied the front page of The North News, the first newspaper printed in Cain Falls, later to become Stoneville. Flesti wore an elegant dress, and her hair was pulled to the back of her scalp with an intricate clip. Her facial expression was blank, and the headline above her portrait read "Wanted" in bold type.

Daisy read the sub headline printed in smaller text below the photo, "Marion Ducane: Wanted for the murder of her husband." She went on to read highlights of the article—how Marion Ducane killed her husband with an ice pick. She later escaped police custody while being transferred to the courthouse after a flock of crows attacked the escorting officers. The crow incident had convinced the residents that she was a dark witch.

"A witch?" Cody said with a laugh. "Did she eat any children she chased down on her broom?"

Daisy elbowed his shoulder, "Look at the newspaper's print date, wiseguy." She lay the photocopy flat and placed an index finger in the top right corner.

Cody leaned in to focus on the blurry number, "Holy shit. This can't be right. 1887?"

Daisy nodded with a smile as she moved to the kitchen counter to check on some eggs cooking in a pan. "Marion Ducane disappeared and was never apprehended. Her 'doppelganger' showed up sixty years later, after World War II. Of course, by that time, everyone was focused on recovering from the war, starting new lives, and returning to some sense of normalcy." Daisy pushed the eggs around to keep them from burning. "No one gave a shit what happened to Marion Ducane. She was probably dead of old age by then, right?"

"So, you think she's been hiding out in the woods of Cain Lake ever since she escaped?"

Daisy turned the heat of the stove top down a few notches. "No, I don't think so. My money's on Europe or Germany, maybe Canada."

"A Nazi. I knew there was something about her."

"Try to keep up, Indiana Jones." Daisy chided while flipping eggs in the pan with a silicone spatula. "She fled to Europe somehow. She must have. That would have been decades before the First World War. She probably changed her name and started a new life, only to have the European conflict destroy everything. She was probably trapped there until the end of World War II. She could have easily come back to the U.S. as a refugee of war. Then she returned to Cain Lake, thinking no one would ever recognize her."

"That would explain why she's such a recluse. But why risk coming back here?"

Daisy added salt and pepper to their breakfast. "That's what I want to know. What's her story?"

"The lake water. The same way it's healed me, it's kept her young."

Daisy pointed the spatula his way, "Who knows how long she can live if that's true?"

Cody stood and fetched a carton of orange juice from the refrigerator, poured two glasses half full, and took a sip from one. "Bourbon said that Flesti was looking for something." He took another sip. "What would be so important that she would risk coming back here? What's she looking for?"

Daisy set two plates of eggs on the table. "That's what I want to know. I want her story. I've got to talk to her."

"Oh, fuck, no. She's crazy, Daisy." Cody sat across from her and looked her in the eye. "I told you what she did to me—how she controlled me, somehow, to shut the door on my parents when I was fourteen. She made me kill them."

Daisy took his hand. "That's why I need to know. What drives her? What does she want? Maybe if I know, I can stop her from hurting anyone else. Maybe she just wants her story out."

"No, you can't pursue this. You'll get yourself killed."

Daisy pointed her fork at him, "I love you, but this is not your decision. I have to do this. I have to find her. Bourbon spent three days in the woods with her. She didn't harm him."

"Bourbon wasn't trying to reveal her true identity!" Cody pushed his plate aside. "Think about Sammy and your mom. What if something happened to you? They need you—I need you. For God's sake, you're carrying our baby."

"Then come with me—"

"No. Take this information to Sheriff Hassett, the FBI, or someone who can do a formal investigation. But if you approach her by yourself, she will kill you, or worse."

Daisy wasn't sure what would be worse than death. She began shoving the photos back into the folders, unconcerned if they were in the correct file. When the paperwork had been cleared from the table, she ate her eggs in silence. She thought Cody would back her up—take her to find the elusive mistress of the forest. But now, she could see that he refused to let her interview Flesti Thaed. She couldn't change his mind, but that didn't mean she needed to obey his wishes.

# 8
# THE NEWS

D aisy! Daisy, check this out."

She sprinted down the stairs. "What is it?" A toothbrush was stuck in her mouth, and her hair was still wet from a shower.

Cody thumbed the television's remote control, cranking the volume to level thirty-five. An attractive anchorwoman was talking while a headline on the bottom of the screen read: "Person of Interest in Night Club Attack."

The seasoned anchor, Bethany Smart, began reading the teleprompter. "Last night's gruesome attack on patrons of a popular Stoneville establishment, Full Throttle, has a new twist. Not only were two members of the biker gang killed inside the building, but another patron was attacked outside with a knife. Let's go live to Carl Mason, who's standing outside Full Throttle, with the details."

"Turn it up," Daisy said through a mouth full of toothpaste.

The camera switched to a medium-built man standing in front of Full Throttle. His light brown hair was receding too far for his age. He pushed his wire-rim glasses into their proper position, looked up to the camera, and began to speak. "Thanks, Bethany. I'm standing outside the location of last night's attack at Full Throttle, here in Stoneville, where police state that two male victims were found after a series of gunshots. But simultaneously, a man outside was being attacked by a woman with multiple throwing daggers." Carl peeked down at his iPad and then continued with his description. "Fortunately, the victim of that attack has survived, and has been treated and released from the local hospital. He has

45

been identified as twenty-seven-year-old Larry Larson, a native of Stoneville. Larson is expected to make a full recovery after suffering multiple lacerations from the knives used in the attack. WKED has also learned that Larson recognized his assailant. She has been identified as twenty-seven-year-old River Kelly, who is vacationing in town during the summer months. Bethany, back to you in the studio."

Bethany Smart was sitting in the studio with an inset photo of River Kelly in the upper left corner of the screen. The image, clearly not a mugshot, was a picture the news channel had stolen from her social media page. The candid portrait of River flashing a white-toothed smile was a sign that AJ's girlfriend was still on the loose.

Cody's legs felt weak. He lowered himself onto the sofa, and Daisy mimicked his body language, although her rear landed on the couch's arm. She could feel a tingle in her eyelids and a lump in her throat, but resisted letting the waterworks flow.

Bethany Smart continued her commentary, "Thanks, Carl. Back in the WKED studio, we've learned that the suspect, River Kelly, is the daughter of renowned District Attorney Dale Kelly. WKED personnel have tried to reach Mr. Kelly for comments, but have not yet received a response. River Kelly is still on the loose and is presumed armed and dangerous. The Stoneville Sheriff's Department is urging the public to be vigilant and not approach or confront Ms. Kelly under any circumstances. If you have any information that could lead to her apprehension, call 911 or the sheriff's office.

"The identities of the two shooting victims inside the popular bar have not been released. WKED will stay on this story and post updates as they come."

Cody hit the power button on the remote control, and the TV went blank. He and Daisy sat in silence for a moment. Daisy rubbed Cody's shoulder with her right hand and brushed her teeth slowly with her left. She finally stood and returned to the bathroom to finish getting ready.

When she returned, he was sitting on the front porch steps watching four starlings pick their breakfast from the grass. Daisy sat beside him and leaned against his muscular shoulder. She pushed her freshly washed hair to one side as a warm summer breeze tried to push it back.

"This is going to devastate him," Cody said.

"I know. Maybe it's not true. There must be a mistake, right? How can they just take the word of some drunk biker who was attacked in the dark?"

Cody shook his head, "I don't know. The sheriff must know more than the media's revealing. The victim—what was his name?"

"Larry Larson."

"He must know her somehow. Maybe through her father."

"Why would she do this? It doesn't make any sense. AJ needs her right now, especially since Alyse is leaving town and he's not speaking to you. What's her game?"

"I don't think it's a game, Daisy. I think she attacked Larry because he is a biker. Maybe she wants vengeance for what happened to AJ."

"So, she's going after the Road Barons? They held a charity ride for AJ when he was in a coma. They raised $4500 for his medical expenses."

Cody shrugged and gave a little laugh. He did a little math in his head, "AJ probably makes that much money in two days. $4500 wouldn't mean much. But it was still a kind gesture."

Daisy swallowed hard as if the large numbers were stuck in her throat. "Holy shit, really?" She pushed the information out of her mind, trying to keep the subject to the problem at hand. She thought about the night AJ was put in a coma and the beating he took at the hands of Levi Thompson while Cricket watched and laughed. She reflected on the night AJ went into Parson's General Store and how lucky Cody was to be alive. AJ had gone there to save his best friend.

"Oh, shit," Daisy jumped to her feet and faced Cody. "Cody, she might be going after the Road Barons because she blames them for what happened to AJ."

Cody looked up confused, "Yeah, that's why I said she's going after the Road Barons. She's blaming all of them, but it was really Levi and Cricket who were responsible."

Daisy knelt back down and grabbed his face. "She's going after everyone responsible for what happened that night, which means she'll come after you, too."

Cody let the revelation ferment in his mind for a moment, then stood and pulled Daisy up to her feet. The wind blew through the yard and scattered the quartet of starlings. He held her loosely and shook his head, "She won't have to come looking for me...'cause I've got to find her before the police do."

# 9

# BEER FOR MY HORSES

Cody left the house on foot, heading to town to find more information on River Kelly's attack on Larry Larson. There was little Daisy could do to convince Cody not to go looking for River, and she couldn't do much to help him. This was some biker bullshit business that he had to take care of himself. It was only, he insisted, to restore his friendship with AJ.

Once he was gone, she waited twenty minutes to pack her files, photos, and laptop into a soft case. She carried the case to the car and set it in the backseat. She started the engine. The Subaru sounded even louder when she was trying to be stealthy. She idled slowly down the road, heading in the opposite direction Cody had taken, hoping he wouldn't hear her leave.

A brisk morning wind, rattling all the leaves and scattering sound waves, produced just enough noise to cover her escape. Once she cleared a couple of blocks and knew there was no turning back, she sped up.

Her phone, mounted to a plastic holder on the dashboard, displayed her destination. It was on the southwest side of Stoneville, a few miles from the lake, on the Cascade River. She drove along Lake View Drive, turned right onto Peacock Street, and followed that until she ran parallel to the Cascade.

The Cascade River flowed south once it left Cain Lake, but made a wide-sweeping arc west, then a sharp bend north at Powder Falls. This confused Daisy because she thought the river kept flowing south. She never studied a county map or realized how the mountains affected water flow. Being a native of a desert state, her sense of direction was often muddled by northern New York's rugged terrain and winding rivers. She passed overgrown fields and a campground nestled in the pines. The road meandered as much as the river until it reached a straight stretch of asphalt with a large sawmill. Daisy pulled over and stopped the car, zoomed out on her map, and regained her bearing.

Happy she wasn't lost, she continued driving another mile and found the gravel driveway that led to the house she was looking for. She parked the car in front of a double-door garage and admired the log cabin-style structure for a moment. It was a modest-sized home, no bigger than Cody's house. From her perspective, the garage appeared to be the same size as the house. The decks that surrounded the cabin's perimeter made up most of the floor space.

She exited her car and was immediately hit by the fresh smell of pine that reminded her of yesterday's trek through the woods to fish at the powerhouse. She raised her nose and inhaled the wild air, and her olfactory senses introduced her to scents she wasn't accustomed to. A hint of lilac merged with the pine smell.

At the front door, she rang the doorbell three times, but no one answered. She could hear a radio playing from behind the house. Toby Keith's voice boomed through the speakers, although Daisy couldn't identify the country singer. She had to listen for a moment to be sure she was understanding the lyrics correctly.

Why would anyone sing about giving their horses beer?

She followed the sound waves around the house to find their source. The radio was perched on the rear deck facing away from the cabin.

"Hello? Anyone home?" She continued walking around the back of the house, under the deck. The country song ended, and there was silence before the next song began to play. During those three seconds, she could hear the faint sound of a small waterfall.

The Cascade River pushed through the small meadow at the back side of the property, only eighty yards from the house. The view from the cabin was nice, probably even more so from the second-floor balcony. The backyard had fewer trees than the front of the house, presumably to preserve the vista. A light breeze played in the field, twisting and tickling the long stalks of wild grass that seemed to bow to Daisy as she approached. A walking path, freshly mowed, cut through the tall grass. She strolled down the path, occasionally stepping on flat stones used to pave over mud holes where the trail's natural drainage was poor.

Frogs darted across the trail to elude the woman intruding on their peace. Dragonflies hovered over stalks of timothy grass, occasionally landing to rest with their mates. She thought she saw a grass snake disappear through the weeds, and a woodchuck scurried across the trail ahead. There were species of birds she didn't recognize and flowers she'd never seen. There was more wildlife in that meadow than she had seen all summer.

She was instantly in love with this place.

A man's head appeared over the riverbank and disappeared again.

*There you are.*

Daisy approached, unsure of what his reaction would be, hoping for a warm welcome.

From the river, the sound of a shotgun fired, and Daisy wasn't sure if she was hit or if her heart had nearly exploded in fear. Her adrenal glands fired a retaliatory shot of adrenaline into her bloodstream. She crouched in the middle of the path, hidden from view by the tall grass. Sweat formed on every inch of her skin as she lost control of her lungs. Her breaths were short and fast, and the idea that this was a mistake clouded her mind.

She was halfway to the river and equally as far from her car. There was only one thing she could do, so she stood.

"Bourbon!" Daisy yelled across the field.

The man's head by the river reappeared.

"What the hell are you shooting at?"

Jeff Bourbon climbed the riverbank carrying a short pump-action shotgun. He wore a blue T-shirt, black shorts, and a white ballcap. "Daisy?" He pumped the last two shotgun shells out of the gun's tubular magazine and leaned the weapon against a dead tree trunk. "What the hell are you doing out here, kid?"

Daisy marched through the path, her pace a little quicker now that she was in fight-or-flight mode. She hopscotched across a random pattern of flat rocks, missed one, and landed in two inches of thick black mud. When she pulled her foot out, her sandal was left behind. She groaned in frustration, retrieved the footwear, and opted to leave it off her freshly pedicured foot. She stripped the other foot naked and carried her sandals in her left hand.

The texture of the fresh-cut grass along the trail massaged her tender feet, and she relished the sensation of the soft green grass. Red toenail polish contrasted with bright green grass. The adrenaline high dissipated, and the warm wind dried the sweat from her skin as she walked facing the wind. The scent of the pine returned, and her pulse returned to normal. She'd read about the effects of the earth on human energy levels and people's Chi and how walking barefoot helped to ground a person's energy, but this was the first time she was aware of the experience. She'd nearly forgotten why she came here as she enjoyed just existing in nature for a moment—Even if shotgun pellets were flying by.

Bourbon met her partway, "What brings you out here? Everything okay?"

"Yes," Daisy sighed. "No. I don't know."

Bourbon smirked. "Come on. If we're going to chat, let's get a cold drink in us." He turned back toward the river and descended the bank. Daisy followed, a little slower, as the terrain changed from soft grass to rocks and sticks. Once she reached the water, she was surprised to find that the river bottom and shoreline were composed of flat, solid stone. The slate, with large and small layers splitting apart, created sharp edges and acute angles. She stepped cautiously to avoid slicing her feet. At the edge of the river, she rinsed her muddy sandals and set them in the sun to dry.

Bourbon opened the lid of a white cooler and extracted two cold beers. He handed one to Daisy and then dropped into an empty camping chair. He gestured to the cooler for her to sit.

"What the hell were you shooting at?" She asked as she brushed some dirt off the cooler lid and sat.

Bourbon took a drink and pointed behind her with the bottle. Daisy turned around to see three dead crows lying on the ground.

"Smart little sonovabitches," Bourbon said. "Probably won't see anymore for a while."

"You're shooting the crows?"

Bourbon held back a belch, nodded, and took another sip.

"Is that even legal?"

"Nope, and I don't care, 'cause I don't trust the little friggin spies."

"Spies? For who?" She already knew the answer.

Bourbon parried her interrogation. "So, what brings Stoneville's finest journalist out here? Looking for a story?"

Daisy sipped the icy Sam Adams summer ale more out of courtesy than thirst, but found it satisfying, "Something like that. Did you hear about the incident at Full Throttle?"

"Nope."

"A couple of bikers were gunned down inside the bar, and another was attacked with a knife outside the bar. The funny thing is, both attacks happened simultaneously."

"Lotta nut jobs out there these days," Bourbon said while adjusting his cap. "Police have any leads?"

"Just one. The guy attacked in the parking lot identified his attacker: River Kelly, the DA's daughter."

"The redhead?"

She nodded, "She's been dating AJ Timmons for three or four weeks."

"Sounds like AJ has terrible taste in women." He washed the statement down with a long gulp. "So, you've got questions. Why did she do it? Who's going to stop her? Sorry, kid, but if you're looking for answers, I've got nothing."

"No. I'm not looking for answers. In fact, I'm not even reporting the story. Another journalist got the story, and WKED is covering it. I'm here on another matter."

She told Bourbon about her discussion with Cody and how River might target him next. Then she went into detail about everything she'd assumed about Flesti Thaed. Once she finished, she set her empty beer bottle back in the cooler.

"So," Daisy continued, "I want to interview Flesti and get her story."

Bourbon turned in his chair to face her, "So, you believe Flesti is, like, two hundred years old?"

She shrugged.

"Have you been doing drugs or something? Getting enough sleep?"

She stood, slipped back into her sandals, and paced along the shoreline. "I don't know what to make of it all. But I'd like to find out. Maybe I'm crazy, but she has a story—secrets."

"And you think she'll give it to you?"

"I hope so. I thought you might be able to help with that. You know? Help me find her and convince her to talk to me. You know her better than anyone."

"Kid, that fucking nut job is too dangerous. You should just let it go. Go back to your cubicle—or wherever the hell you work—and write something else."

She started biting a thumbnail, thinking of a way to convince him. She turned toward the dead birds. "Are you going to shoot them all? Or would you like to ensure you get the right one? You're right, Bourbon. Flesti is dangerous, and someone needs to stop her. You can sit here and shoot every damn crow that flies by, but you know it won't make a difference. You're just hiding from the truth, out here in your pretty little cabin, getting drunk on the river. Help me find her, expose her if we must, and you'll never have to shoot another bird again."

Bourbon stood and stepped toward the river. His feet were just inches away from the water. He squatted to pick up a bottle cap lying on the rocks. His knees popped and cracked, especially the one he'd injured weeks ago while walking through the woods with Flesti. Cain Lake had nearly healed the knee, but now the pain and inflammation were returning. The lake had given him a newfound energy he hadn't felt in years. He missed that sensation. Now his back ached, and his hips were tight. Each knuckle on his left hand felt stiff, and he couldn't remember the last time his feet didn't hurt. He felt old.

"I don't know how to stop her without putting a bullet between her eyes or cutting her damn head off. I've been racking my brain about it for weeks. I just sit down here by the water, shooting the fucking crows and trying to think of a way to stop her. Or scare her away. I was beginning to think she was good until she had me nearly kill the Bristol cousins in Annabel's barn. She was in my head, trying to control me, and it almost worked."

"She's hurt a lot of people, including Annabel, Willa, and Cody—"

"And Andrew," Bourbon interjected. "His death is a result of her madness. The Bristol cousins killed Andrew Mills to lure Jesse Lewis out of hiding. It's all tied together. Flesti's powers come from the lake, and she'll do anything to retain it."

"She's never going to stop hurting people. Are you going to let her? Everything bad that's happened in Stoneville this summer all leads back to her."

Bourbon's voice softened as if he'd already been defeated, "It's not that simple, kid. She can control anyone who's ever been in Cain Lake—Anyone who's been exposed to those little blue water bug things. We're all puppets to that bitch."

Daisy squared up to Bourbon. "Jeff Bourbon is no one's puppet. So, if there's anyone who can stop that 'bitch,' it's you."

"I see what you're doing. Trying to build me up and convince me to take you out there so that you can get what you want. If we do this—If we do this, then we should have Cody with us. He's got some mystical voodoo shit going on with Cain Lake that I don't under-stand. He might be our best shot at stopping her without anyone getting killed."

"Nah, he's too preoccupied. He's hellbent on finding River Kelly before the police. He's afraid that if the police find her first, she'll wind up dead. Plus, he feels he owes it to AJ. This might be the only way to mend their friendship. It's just you and me on this one."

Bourbon stood, picked up his shotgun, and gave her a stern look. "Okay, kid. We'll give this one shot and one shot only. But understand, this could backfire, and shit could go sideways real quick. You prepared for that?"

She gave him a gentle nod, trying to look brave.

"Okay, then. We'll head out in a couple of hours. Give me time to pack my gear. Meet me at," he peeked at his phone to check the time, "Two o'clock at the South Bridge; there's a gravel parking lot just past the bridge. Pack a bag for a couple of days' hike. We'll find Flesti if we can and try to get her story. And hopefully, we won't die in the process."

# 10

# LARRY LARSON

Cody walked to the north side of town. He didn't have a plan and wasn't sure where to start looking for River Kelly or who to talk to. He'd only had one vision in the last week: last night at the river when he witnessed the two men who resembled Duke and Aaron Bristol with gunshot wounds sprawled on the floor beside the pool table. He hadn't seen it again, and he didn't want to. What good were his clairvoyant powers if he couldn't actually help anyone? He learned that the hard way when they found his brother Michael deceased.

He summarized everything that had happened lately: AJ was beaten and put in a Coma, Levi and Cricket went to prison, River was hellbent on getting vengeance, and Larry Larson was her first victim.

But who shot Duke and Aaron Bristol in the bar? And why? Did River have something to do with that, too?

A phone would have saved Cody from miles of walking and a lot of wondering. But AJ had disconnected Cody's device, so he was out of touch with the rest of Stoneville. After forty-four months in prison, Cody was used to the disconnect. It also made communicating with Daisy difficult, but on the plus side, she was at his house more often.

Cody found himself in front of the Stoneville Public Library, a cobblestone structure with massive fluted pillars painted white that ascended from the concrete foundation to the decorative gabled dormer. Heavy double doors with large glass windows showed their weather-worn age.

57

Cody climbed the ten steps two at a time until he was standing at the doors. He pulled the right side door open and entered. The cool library air greeted him, relieving his skin of the exhaustive summer heat. His feet hit the soft, low-pile carpet that had been recently installed to muffle voices and noise. The rug's scent was still fresh in the air.

He made his way to the front desk, which was staffed by a gentleman who resembled Abraham Lincoln. He was wire-thin and well over six feet tall. He had a balding scalp and black hair that formed little waves behind his ears. Wire-rimmed bifocals balanced on his nose, with a black cord attached to each side that drooped downward and back around his neck. The man pounded a computer keyboard with strong fingers, staring intently at the screen.

Cody patiently waited for his attention. When the librarian finally finished typing, he gave Cody a warm smile, dropped his glasses from his nose, and let them hang against his chest.

"May I help you, sir?"

"Do you have computers for the public to use?"

"Of course," the librarian answered. He stepped from behind the oak counter. "Right this way." Cody followed him toward the back of the building, turned right into a short hallway near the bathrooms, and then right again into a small room with eight workstations. Each workstation was partitioned off to form a cubicle. Each cubicle had a gray office chair, a Dell monitor, a keyboard, a scratchpad, a pen, and a computer mouse. Cody wasn't sure where the physical computer was located, but assumed it was hidden behind the cubicle's partition to prevent tampering.

The librarian tapped a couple of keys, waking a sleeping computer, and then entered four digits on the number pad. "Please sign in over there." He pointed at a legal pad near the door they had just entered.

Once Cody signed in, he thanked the man and sat at the computer to begin an online search. He looked for Larry Larson first, found his address—just three blocks from the library—and wrote the information on the scratchpad. Larry had a couple of misdemeanors, and an article popped up about him saving a drowning boy at South Bridge seven years ago.

*Way to go, Larry.*

Another article appeared in *The Stoneville View*. Cody's face twisted in disappointment as he read the author's name, Trena Cutlass, not Daisy Torres. The article, dated yesterday, described the incident at Full Throttle. Cody gave them a quick read. The article was brief at the time, as the police had limited information to release to the public. There was no mention of the Bristol cousins.

*Maybe I was wrong.*

Next, he searched for River Kelly. He was curious to see if AJ's girlfriend had been in trouble before the incident at the bar. The same article also appeared regarding Full Throttle and Larry Larson. He also found a few old sports reports that touted River as a high school and college star athlete. He discovered two other women with the same name in Albany and a few reports about her father, Dale Kelly, the District Attorney.

Once he'd gotten the information he was seeking, he tore the first page from the scratchpad and stuffed it in his pocket. He signed out of the computer room and thanked the friendly librarian as he passed his desk.

*****

Larry Larson's house was on a hillside, with half of the base-ment exposed to the street and the other half underground. A Toyota Rav-4 with a cracked windshield leaked antifreeze onto the ground. The yellow house was losing some of its vinyl siding, and the exterior basement walls contained patches of mildew. Faded little garden gnomes hid in the tall grass, hiding whimsically within the overgrown lawn. Small birds occupied a single apple tree, chirping in disapproval of the empty birdbath in the middle of the yard. The tree, though striving, struggled to support the weight of all the yellow fruit growing in hefty clusters. Its boughs bent with gravity's force nearly to the point of breaking.

59

If it hadn't been for the motorcycle parked in the driveway, Cody would have guessed he had the wrong address. He took the note out of his pocket and read the number he'd written, then compared it with the house numbers. It was a match. He stepped over the little stream of antifreeze and approached the modest home.

He climbed a hazardous set of steps that ascended parallel to the house and made a right angle to the front door. He gently pushed the dangling doorbell, hoping it wouldn't fall off the thin wires holding it in place. He heard the bell chime inside the home, and a small dog began to bark immediately.

No one answered the door, so he rang the bell one more time.

He was about to give up when the door opened, and a woman inside yelled at the barking dachshund to get back. She was two inches taller than Cody, with strong arms and a thick neck. If she hadn't been wearing a dress, Cody might have guessed she was a man. She had long, gray hair loosely pulled behind her ears with barrettes, glasses with frames that matched the door, and faded, wrinkled tattoos adorning her arms.

She opened the door, "May I help you?" Her voice was soft and angelic, a stark contrast to her rough appearance. Her smile transformed her stone-cut face into an amiable, grandmotherly figure.

"Hi, ma'am, I'm looking for Larry Larson. Is this his residence?"

"I'm sorry," the woman said. "No, Larry moved a few months ago. I'm not sure—"

A male voice interrupted her from the living room. "Ma, it's okay, Ma. He's not a reporter. Let him in."

"I'm sorry. We haven't had a moment of peace all day. Come in, please, Mr—?"

"Savage. But please, just call me Cody." He stepped inside and was pleasantly surprised by the clean, nicely decorated interior. The caramel-colored dachshund barked a few more times and then worked up the courage to sniff Cody's pant leg.

"That's Weenie," the male voice said from the living room. "Weenie, go lie down."

Weenie ignored his owner's command.

Larry Larson was propped in a vinyl recliner, wearing a green tank top and several bandages, and a couple of pillows awkwardly shoved under his right hip. He was leaning to his left to keep his weight off the stab wound in his butt. He remained seated with his feet up as Cody entered the room.

"You must be Larry," Cody said with an extended hand. "I'm—"

"Cody Savage," Larry said with a firm grip and a smile. "All the Barons know who you are, brother. You want a coffee or a beer. Ma, get Cody a coffee or something."

Cody declined the offer for the beverage.

Larry made a hand gesture to a leather sofa. "Have a seat, brother. Take a load off."

Larry's mother disappeared into the kitchen.

The two men spoke about Larry's early days as a Road Baron, and Larry bragged about the motorcycle parked in the driveway. Bikers always talked about their motorcycles. Then Larry complained a little about the pain in his hand from the damage River's knife had caused. He stared at his left hand, wrapped with thick, clean bandages to protect the damaged appendage. It reminded Cody of his own hand weeks ago and the miracle that had returned it to him.

"Well, that's why I'm here," Cody said. "I'm trying to find the woman who did that to you." He nodded at the bandaged hand.

"The police are already looking for her. Crazy bitch was trying to kill me."

"Do you know why she attacked you?"

"Hell, no, brother. I stepped outside to take a leak and get a fresh dip, and I see a shadow behind me. Then I notice her in a truck mirror following me. So, I think she wants a little ride on the Larry-go-round, you know what I mean? So, I go around my truck and a couple more vehicles and end up behind her. Playin' a little cat and mouse. Then the psycho bitch just attacks. Stabbed me in the stomach." He raised his shirt to reveal more bandages. "Good thing I'm sportin' a little extra protection." He slapped his fat abdomen gently but winced in pain. "Kept my vitals from gettin' carved up. Then she hit me in the ass and nearly tore my hand off. Jesus, brother, it was insane. I've been in a lot of scraps in my life, but brother, that was the only time I've been truly scared."

"How did you know who she was?" Cody asked as Weenie jumped on the couch beside him. "The news channel said you were able to identify her."

"River Kelly? Shit, brother, I've been in love with that girl since high school. And I seen a recent photo of her at her father's house. See, I'm a 'tin-knocker.' Installing heating and air conditioning ducts in people's homes and businesses. I was working at Dale Kelly's place last spring and seen all the family photos. Recognized River right away."

"Are you sure, Larry? Sure it was her?"

"You ever seen River Kelly, brother? Guys don't forget a girl like that. I'd bet my Harley on it. Why are you looking for her? You helpin' the police or something?"

"She's a good friend of a good friend. I'd like to find her before the police do."

Larry fought the pain from his lacerations, put the recliner upright, and leaned toward Cody. His voice was low as if he didn't want his mother to hear, "Can't you just, you know, use your mind powers?" He was holding an index finger from each hand to his temples.

"My what?"

"The psychic stuff you do. Can't you just find her with your mind?"

Weenie climbed on Cody's lap for attention. Cody scratched behind his ear. "It doesn't quite work that way, Larry. I wish it were that simple, but no, I can't find her like that."

Larry leaned back, disappointed by Cody's admission. "Well, brother, when you do find her, you watch yourself. That knife she's carrying is some crazy shit."

"What do you mean?"

Larry leaned forward again, holding the wound on his stomach. "When she threw that fucking thing, it would come right back to her. Like a damn boomerang-knife. It was some fucked up shit."

"How does a knife come back to you?"

"It beats the hell out of me, man. The funny thing is, I'm not even sure it was a knife. It was made of stone like it'd been carved from a rock."

"Are you sure? Seems like stone would break, wouldn't it?"

Larry held his bandaged hand up as evidence, "I pulled the fucking thing out of my ass. Held it in my hand. So, yeah, I'm sure. One hundred percent, brother."

Mrs. Larson returned with a prescription bottle and handed it to her son. "Take two." She rubbed his head gently. "Coffee's almost done, Mr. Savage, if you've changed your mind."

Cody gently nudged the dachshund off his lap and stood. "Thank you, Mrs. Larson, but I really must be going. Get some rest, Larry. I hope you feel better."

Weenie followed Cody to the door but stopped when Larry started talking again.

"You watch yourself, Savage," Larry advised. "Watch yourself real good. Oh, and I almost forgot—you'll know that knife when you see it. When she threw it, it glowed with a blue light, like it had momentum-activated LED lights inside. Freaky." He shuddered from the memory.

Cody turned on his heels to hear the statement again. "I'm sorry, it did what?"

"Blue, brother. The fucking knife glowed with blue light."

<h1 style="text-align:center">11</h1>

# TARGET PRACTICE 

*Shit! Shit, shit, shit, shit.*

The information Larry provided had Cody riled and scared. The knife, which could somehow return to the person who threw it, glowed blue.

*Friggin blue!*

He knew a glowing knife had to be connected to the micropods swimming in Cain Lake, meaning Flesti Thaed was somehow involved in this mess. If he were going to stop River and save her for AJ's benefit, he'd have to find Flesti again.

"Flesti," he whispered. The name was like battery acid on his tongue. He spit.

She was a plague on Stoneville, and no one even knew she existed except an esoteric group of his friends and a couple of sheriffs. If the knife in River's possession was related to Cain Lake, then it was possible that River was being worked like a puppet. He had to find her and cut the strings before anyone else was harmed.

He pointed his boots toward Washington Street and began walking. He took significant, eager steps, anxious to check out Dale Kelly's seasonal rental property. He'd never been to the house, but everyone in town admired the bright red home with a view of Cain Lake. It stood out among the other weather-worn homes that were painted in dull hues with no imagination, and hadn't changed since the day they were constructed. Dale Kelly had purchased one of those homes in the early 2000s, renovated it, and painted it red. His wife picked the color after River came home crying because some other girls at school had teased her about her ginger locks.

"Let's give them something really red to talk about," Mrs. Kelly told her daughter. Sitting on the hill, the house became a landmark, centered among the dull row of abodes. As the town fell in love with the primary-colored house, the teasing diminished, and the mean girls at school realized that people—like houses—were more beautiful when they were unique.

The Kellys retained ownership of the home, even though they later moved to a large house across town. Now, it was a favorite vacation rental for tourists who enjoyed visiting Cain Lake for its serenity and cool summers.

Cody walked almost two miles before reaching the narrow street that followed the Cascade River through town. This little part of town seemed lost in time, with narrow homes perched on hillside lots. It was prime real estate that would have been worth millions in other parts of the country, but here in northern New York, the market was still sensible, and the large river lots were somewhat affordable—if you could find one for sale. Most people here were elderly Stoneville residents who refused to move to overcrowded southern states or nursing homes. And who could blame them? The houses all had river access, although on a steep grade, and the river created a valley that offered stupendous views of Cain Lake, a few miles away.

The street was quiet. He felt instant relief from the noon heat as tall maple trees provided a thick canopy above, shielding him from even the most intense sunlight. The mighty trees, hundreds of years old, dwarfed the homes. The mighty roots that anchored the old wood heaved the sidewalk and split the road's surface, making for a treacherous path.

He'd been walking uphill for the last half mile, and now his legs burned from the effort. He stopped to rest his weary muscles and huffing lungs. A light breeze flowed up from the river and evaporated sweat from his skin. He tilted his head back, hands on his hips, and enjoyed the relief momentarily, almost forgetting why he'd come here.

A glimpse of red beckoned him further up the hill. He put his legs back to work, attracted to the red like a hungry trout. When he reached the property, the Kelly house looked vacant. A vehicle had created fresh tire tracks beside the road, in the small front yard, and across the road, but there were no vehicles in sight, and the home lacked a garage. The police had been here, probably numerous times, looking for the accused assailant. She was nowhere to be found.

He climbed the stairs to the side porch, enjoyed the view of Cain Lake in the distance for two full seconds, and tried opening the side door. The unlocked door surprised him until he noticed a boot print on the surface. Someone had kicked the door in, destroying the jam and bolt. The cheap doorknob and flimsy pine gave way without much resistance, and the broken lock was now useless to secure the door.

As Cody entered, the room to his right was the kitchen with a couple of bay windows that offered a view of the street. A small round table with four chairs took center stage in the kitchen. He walked around the table and checked the counter and sink. There was nothing to note, and he wasn't sure why he was even looking.

He entered the living room. A narrow staircase led to a loft. Cody checked the coffee table, which held a few empty Michelob bottles and a wooden bowl that appeared to be used for popcorn. Again, nothing out of the ordinary.

The far wall beside a bedroom door intrigued him the most. It was decorated with numerous photos, taped to the wall with blue painter's tape. He moved closer to inspect the irregularity.

A dusty white powder coated the hardwood floor below the pictures. Within the dust, small feminine footprints with a narrow width were visible. The photos on the wall were torn and jagged; some had been destroyed beyond recognition. There were photos of models from magazines, felt coasters that once belonged on the coffee table, a printed Red Baron's logo from the Internet, and more. But one was very clear. It was a picture of him, torn along the side as if someone else once occupied the image.

Cody knew the picture well. It was taken on the first night he'd left prison. Alyse had taken a shot of him and AJ at The Mineshaft. AJ had the photo printed at a local Walgreens Pharmacy and pinned it to a bulletin board in his garage. The bulletin board was filled with old photos and memorabilia that AJ added to every month or two.

The bottom of the photo appeared to have been chewed by a dog. But the concerning issue was the one-inch gash between Cody's eyes and across his face. The hole in the photo went straight through the paper and into the drywall. He looked at the rest of the images. Rage had marred them all. The wall was perforated with narrow one-and-a-half-inch holes produced from a dagger blade. Most of the holes had little paper burrs from the blade's extraction. He came to understand what River had been doing in her spare time.

*Target practice.*

He took a step backward, leaving his footprints in the Sheet-rock dust. He'd seen enough. He knew she was pissed, armed, and dangerous, and that he might be her next target.

A light wind pushed the door open, creating a slight creaking sound that broke his train of thought. Cody held his breath and listened intently. He could hear soft footfalls coming up the side stairs. Someone was coming.

He picked up an empty beer bottle, his only option for a make-shift weapon, and hoped it was enough if River attacked. But judging by the damage to the wall and Larry Larson's description, he knew her knife was much more deadly than a brown bottle.

# 12
# BOBCAT TRAIL

Daisy crossed the South Bridge in her Subaru and pulled to the right to park beside Jeff Bourbon's truck in the gravel lot. He'd beaten her there by nearly fifteen minutes and looked ready to get started.

Bourbon was dressed in blue jeans and a fresh T-shirt. The green color blended with the trees in the background. His light boots looked durable and comfortable, even though they appeared to have a million miles on them. He was sitting on the tailgate of his truck. A military-style backpack, a natural camel color with multiple pockets and buckles, sat beside him. An embroidered American flag, stitched with black thread, adorned both sides.

"Ready to go?" Bourbon asked as Daisy stepped from her vehicle.

"Almost." She opened the back hatch and retrieved a pink backpack with a purple Columbia logo silk screened on the front. The bag's seams looked like they would burst if they were fuller, but she unzipped the top and stuffed a light jacket inside. The seams held miraculously.

Bourbon watched her inspect the zippers and double-check the list she'd written herself. Then she tried to choose a pocket to hold her car keys clipped to a gold carabiner. She jingled the keys and the bulky keychain, searching for sufficient space.

Bourbon sighed, took the keys away, bent over, and tucked them inside the car's fender. "Pack light. You'll just end up losing them in the woods. No one in Stoneville is going to steal this piece of—" He cut himself off. "What the hell is that?"

"What?"

He spun the backpack around to reveal a plastic dinosaur toy hanging from the side of Daisy's pink pack. "That." The toy looked like a six-inch version of Godzilla.

"That's Greenie—Greenie the Meanie—Sammy's second favorite toy. He gave him to me as protection from the wolves and bears."

"Okay, does he know there are no wolves in this area, and the bears are more afraid of you than you are of them?"

"He's four, so he thinks there are wolves and bears in Walmart. He was worried about his mom. I thought it was cute."

Bourbon shook his head. As a man with no children, the gesture didn't seem practical. "Okay, princess, are you ready now? It's a long hike to the top of the hill, and then we need to get past Turkey Alley to find a place to camp for the night."

"Almost. Oh, I almost forgot," she moved to the back seat and retrieved a brown paper bag with a small bottle inside. She handed it to Bourbon, "This is a little token of my appreciation. Something for the trip."

Bourbon pulled out a bottle of Dr. McGillicuddy's Mentholmint schnapps—his favorite. He smiled at the gesture and slid the bottle back into the bag. "Thank you, but let's save this for when we get back, okay? We'll celebrate. I don't want my mind clouded out there. It's too risky in such rugged terrain."

Daisy hoisted the pink backpack and slid her arms through the straps. She followed Bourbon up the road with a hefty weight on her shoulders and mind. They veered to the right and stepped off the road onto a smooth sand trail lined with tall grass and weeds. The Bobcat Trail ascended gently for the first five hundred feet until intersecting a small brook. The snowmobile association had built a wooden bridge across the water, where they paused to adjust the straps on Daisy's backpack. Once they passed the little bridge, they turned left. Their path became more rugged, and the hill's incline was daunting.

For six hundred feet, they marched in unison, Bourbon leading the way. They stepped over washouts and navigated around boulders. It was a slow, meticulous climb, as each step was carefully planned and placed. The overgrown briar bushes, which spilled onto the trail during the summer months, grabbed their skin and clothes. Bourbon stopped at a couple of the bushes and loaded a plastic Ziploc bag with blackberries.

"Is it going to be like this the whole way?" Daisy whined while pulling a thorny branch out of her triceps. "This is terrible."

Bourbon laughed, teasing her, "No, it gets harder toward the top."

She huffed, thinking about the dirt stains on her new Adidas sneakers. "I'm starting to think this was a mistake."

"Flesti Thaed walks around this lake continuously. If she can do it, so can you."

"Yeah, but she was raised in these woods—on these hills. I was brought up in the desert—a flat desert." She panted. "Near a shopping mall."

"We're almost to the top."

Daisy forced her legs to work, trying to ignore the lactic acid burn that was building in her thighs and glutes. She didn't want to show weakness, but the climb was more arduous than anticipated. Her lungs struggled to keep up, causing her throat to go dry, and then a light cough began to torture her. She did her best to stay moving and keep up with her older guide, but she noticed him stopping and pausing to keep from pulling ahead.

Bobcat Trail was rugged. Rain had washed the trail's surface clean of soft soil, exposing boulders and smooth rocks that threatened every step. It was an easy climb for a nimble ATV but proved too exhaustive for an inexperienced hiker.

Daisy found herself zig-zagging from one side of the trail to the other, increasing the distance of her journey. Bourbon preferred a straighter route, stepping over large ruts and stones rather than going around. They stopped to rest every few hundred feet, but only long enough to let their heart rate drop to a comfortable tempo.

Sweat made their clothes uncomfortable, and Daisy wished she had worn shorts. They forged on for over an hour before the incline eased, and the land seemed kinder.

Once they reached the top of the hill, she found a dead log to sit on and began gulping water to satisfy her thirst. The cold liquid eased her dry throat, and the cough subsided.

"Go slow," Bourbon advised. "Small sips will help you hydrate—"

Before he could finish, she turned away, bent over the log, and vomited clear liquid. When she finished, she wiped her mouth with her hand. "Ugh. I'm dying, Bourbon."

"No, you're not. Just slow down. Take a moment to catch your breath and let your heart rate return to normal before drinking more water. Take your mind off your thirst."

"How am I supposed to do that?"

"I don't know. Try enjoying the view." Bourbon looked over her shoulder with a smile.

Daisy had been staring at the stains in her shoes, contemplating a cleaning strategy. She hadn't taken the time to look back at the direction they'd come. She turned to see if they were making any progress. Below, she could see Cain Lake and the South Bridge. The sun glittered off the water, sparkling like fine diamonds floating on the surface. The gently rolling hills of Stoneville were adorned with a variety of green colors created by evergreen and deciduous species of trees. An eagle soared through the sky below them, and Daisy found it funny that she was above the raptor. She watched the eagle swirl in figure-eights, catching updrafts to rise higher for a better view. After a minute, she tilted her head back to view the circling hunter as it gained elevation. Now, the eagle was looking down at her.

It was the third time in two days that she fell in love with Stoneville's natural splendor. It was a raw beauty she thought only existed on National Geographic programs. She wished Sammy and her mother were here. Cody had been here before. She could feel it in her heart. She hoped they would come back here someday. A day when they had nothing to do and could casually hike without feeling a sense of duty or pressured by a clock.

"So pretty," she heard herself say.

Bourbon stood over her shoulder. "It looks like it was painted by

God himself, doesn't it?"

"Hmm," Daisy nodded. "I'm more of a Monet girl, but yes, there is so much beauty from this perspective."

"What I like most," Bourbon said, "Is the lack of detail. You can't see your job from here. You can't see the traffic lights or the parking lots. You can't hear horns honking, construction vehicles, or anyone arguing. The whole is greater than the parts."

Daisy agreed in silence.

She took a sip of her water, swished it through her teeth, and spit out the taste of stomach bile. She took another satisfying drink, swallowed, and then another. The thumping in her chest subsided, and the perspiration on her skin dried quickly. Less than five minutes into her break, she was somewhat rehydrated.

"Ready to go?" Bourbon asked after ten minutes.

She answered by standing and pulling her backpack over her shoulders.

"Okay, then, let's get off this hill. It flattens out around the corner, and then we'll be walking downhill for a while. Hopefully, we'll start to see signs of Flesti."

"Why doesn't she just get a phone? I could pick up the phone and give her a call." She held her hand to the side of her head, pinky down, thumb in her ear, "Hey, Flesti, it's me, Daisy...Yes, the famous reporter. I'm good, how are you? No...I just had some questions for you if you got a minute...You do! Great. Would you mind meeting me at the coffee shop? Awesome! I'll see you there." She dropped the imaginary phone. "But no, I've got to trudge through the fucking jungle to find her." She slapped at a deer fly as it landed in her hair. She missed, and the pesky insect orbited her head, mustering the courage for another attack.

Bourbon hid his smirk. "This was your idea, princess, remember? We can turn back if you want—before we get too far."

Daisy stopped and considered the option. Other than school, she'd never pushed herself very hard. This was a challenge, and she didn't want to give up so soon. She tried to reassure Bourbon that she was up to the task, but he wasn't too convinced.

They stayed on the trail until it appeared they had summited the small mountain. The trail ahead was clear and flat. Four-wheelers and dirt bikes had worn shallow ruts on each side of the path, leaving a grassy line down the middle, like a long green snake slithering down a dirt road.

"This doesn't look so bad," Daisy said. Her hopes were as high as the mountain they occupied.

"We're going this way," Bourbon informed her while pointing through the woods on his left. "Flesti doesn't typically stick to the trails. She bushwhacks most of the way around Cain Lake."

"Why the hell does she do that? There must be a million acres to search between here and the lake." She swatted at the persistent deer fly, missed, and beamed herself in the skull instead.

Bourbon pointed down the path, "The Bobcat Trail goes away from Cain Lake. You stay on that, and you'll end up in Higley. If we cut back through the woods, we'll be heading northwest, toward the lake. She hikes the forest to avoid people as much as possible. Plus, she can forage for food in the woods." He stepped off the trail and disappeared in the thicker foliage.

Daisy followed with reluctance. Her backpack felt like a thousand pounds now, but it was her doubt to find Flesti that really weighed her down.

# 13

# DALE KELLY

Cody held his breath and listened to the footfalls coming up the short stairs of River's summer apartment. There was nowhere to hide and no way to escape. He'd have to stand his ground when they entered the house. He'd either have a hell of a time explaining his trespass or a hell of a fight coming.

The steps stopped just outside the door.

Cody cocked his shoulder and elbow back, ready to fire the beer bottle if necessary. He counted the bottles on the table—seven. He'd have seven more projectiles to fire in desperation, and hopefully, the coffee table was suitable as a shield against the blue knife River possessed.

A Force was exerted on the outside of the door, gently pushing it further inward. For a second, Cody thought it was just the wind making an entrance, but then he saw a hand nudging the heavy wooden door. And then Deputy Dave Simpson's face appeared in the door frame.

Cody's shoulder and elbow relaxed.

"Savage? That you?"

"Yeah, it's me, Simpson."

Simpson stepped inside as Cody returned the beer bottle to the coffee table. His right hand rested on the grip of his 10mm Sig Sauer.

"What the hell you doing here, son? A neighbor down the street saw you come in. You know there's a manhunt out for River Kelly, right? Everyone is watching this place."

"Yes, sir," Cody answered. "I'm sorry. I'm not trying to mess up your search. I just wanted to help. River is AJ's girlfriend, and he's pretty worried about her." Cody stepped toward Simpson and peered out the sliding glass doors that led to the balcony. "AJ asked me to help find her," he lied.

"Well, I get it. I do. But you can't just break into someone's house because you're looking for them. That's what I get paid to do."

"I didn't break in. The door was open."

Simpson's torso swirled around and examined the broken door. "Yeah, that's my boot print on the door." He rubbed the rubber scuff mark with his fingers. It had no effect. "We've already been here searching. This was the first place we looked. I'm sure that girl's long gone by now. Authorities in Albany will probably have her in custody by the end of the day."

"I'll just see myself out. I won't get in your way."

Simpson threw a hand up like a traffic cop stopping a car. "Actually, I need you to come with me."

"What? Why? I didn't touch anything—"

"Relax, son. I've been patrolling the streets for thirty minutes trying to find you. There's someone who wants to speak to you regarding Ms. Kelly."

"Who?"

"Dale Kelly, the District Attorney. He's worried sick about this whole situation and wants to find his daughter as soon as possible."

*****

Deputy Simpson drove Cody out of town, past the golf course. They pulled into a paved driveway where two wrought iron gates welcomed them in anticipation of their arrival.

Dale Kelly lived in a large white house with a deck that spanned the entire front of the two-story structure. The hedges lining the driveway and surrounding the house were neatly trimmed. A five-acre pond to the left of the house teemed with ducks and geese that quacked and honked when Deputy Simpson's patrol vehicle drove by in the long driveway. The ducks took flight and landed on the

76

opposite side of the pond. The geese just swam shyly toward the middle. An octagon-shaped gazebo was constructed on the edge of the water, making it an ideal shelter to view the wildlife. An older man dressed in black watched the playful waterfowl from within the structure. Cody was surprised when a loon popped to the surface. Its head protruded like a periscope while its body barely showed. The bird floated on the surface for less than ten seconds before diving again to chase small fish to fill its belly.

"Nice place," Cody said.

"Mmm hmm," Simpson agreed. "District attorney does well for himself. Ten years in the Army, passed the bar at twenty-three, retired as a military lawyer at fifty, and now our admired District Attorney."

"Impressive."

They drove past the man in the gazebo, who paid no attention to the Chevy Tahoe easing down the drive. When they reached the front of the house, the driveway formed a circle, allowing them to leave without having to back the vehicle.

Cody watched the wind play with the red, white, and blue banner of the United States attached to the top of a flagpole that served as the centerpiece of the circular drive. The flag settled into a motionless droop as Cody and Deputy Simpson exited the truck. Below the US flag, the state flag mimicked its big brother.

They approached the front double doors constructed of thick mahogany and heavy black hardware, but before they reached the porch, the left door opened inward.

Dale Kelly met them at the door. He sat in a wheelchair, dressed in an impeccable white shirt. His tie hung loosely around his neck—red with diagonal blue stripes and a silver clip that Cody identified as the scales of justice.

The DA stuck his strong hand out, excited to see Cody. "Mr. Savage, I'm Dale Kelly. Thank you for coming on such short notice."

They locked hands. The district attorney had a powerful grip, with calloused palms that Cody surmised were the result of decades of pushing the tires of his wheelchair. He was clean-shaven, with bold shoulders and a square jaw—handsome and polite—and Cody could immediately see why people would vote for him as District Attorney. He was very likable.

Dale Kelly invited the two men inside, but Simpson opted to stay outside and wait. He was more interested in the pond than the DA's agenda.

Inside, Cody was led to a room he imagined Kelly called "The Study" or "The Library." The room had two walls comprised of bookshelves, full from floor to ceiling. One side of the room appeared to be fiction, the other nonfiction. He wondered if the DA had read every book in the room, but judging by his success, he guessed the answer.

Cody was gestured to an overstuffed leather chair. When he sat back, he felt like the furniture was swallowing him. Uncomfortable, he chose to sit on the seat's edge and lean forward away from the hungry chair.

Dale Kelly took a couple of laps around the room, collecting a file and his thoughts. When he finally made a pit stop in front of Cody, he was balancing two short drinking glasses and a manila envelope that looked like it was stuffed with paper. He placed everything on the mahogany coffee table that matched the front doors.

"I'll get right to the point," The DA said, backing his wheelchair up.

Cody preferred it that way. The District Attorney's environment made him feel small—insignificant even. He looked at the clock on the wall sandwiched between two taxidermy deer heads: 1:55.

Dale Kelly separated the two ornate glasses. He opened a small ice cooler at the center of the table. The little walnut grain cooler blended so well with the rest of the room's decor that Cody hadn't even noticed it until now.

Dale Kelly worked a set of tongs to fish three ice cubes from the bucket and dropped them in Cody's glass, producing three crystal notes. He repeated the process, filling his glass, but accidentally pulled out a fourth cube and put it back in the bucket.

"Gotta have the perfect ratio of ice to drink." He smirked, turned to a stout liquor bottle, twisted off the cap, and poured two fingers over the ice cubes.

Cody guessed it was an expensive brandy—something he'd never have the luxury of buying himself. He thanked Dale Kelly and raised his glass to his mouth. A whiff of spices made his mouth water. He took an anxious sip and was surprised by the blend of fruity flavors married with caramel and butterscotch. Each second the liquor was in his mouth, a new flavor unfolded on his tongue. By the time he swallowed, a smoky taste formed, and all of it dissipated with a mild burn of alcohol descending his throat.

*Fuck that's good.*

"Hennessy X.O," Dale Kelly said as if he could read his guest's mind. He took his first sip. He read Cody's face like a newspaper headline. "The 'XO' stands for extra old. Quite good, wouldn't you agree?"

"Not bad," Cody replied nonchalantly.

The district attorney took another drink and set his glass on the table. He slid the envelope to Cody's side of the table. Cody lifted it and peeked inside.

"Two thousand dollars," Dale Kelly answered the question Cody was thinking. There's two thousand dollars to find my daughter. I'll double that if you can do it within the next twenty-four hours."

Cody set the envelope back on the table. "Mr. Kelly, you don't need to pay me to find your daughter. I'm as concerned as you. I'm doing my best to find River. Really, I don't need your money."

"Mr. Savage," Dale started. "I know everything about you. I've reviewed your files and public records and had numerous conversations with my colleagues about you. I'm also aware of your financial situation. But what really interests me is the rumors."

"The rumors?"

"Yes. The rumors about this alleged psychic ability you possess. Normally, I don't believe that type of shit. But River assures me it's true. She told me how you found Darcy Poole and how your ability led you to save Annabel Thompson—before she took her life."

"Finding Annabel was just dumb luck, honestly. And Darcy Poole—" He cut himself off, trying to remember how exactly he'd done that. He thought Willa had directed him to her, but that might not have been the case. Darcy appeared in his visions, locked in a basement, and he knew she was still alive. He was lost in thought when Dale Kelly interrupted:

"I'm also aware how you cut off your own hand to save my good friend Jeff Bourbon. What I'm not aware of is how you seem to have it now."

"That's a little tricky to explain."

"I suppose it is. I also assume you know what it feels like to be so desperate to save someone you love. Willing to cut your own hand off? That takes fucking balls—balls and bravery. Right now, I'm desperate. I'd cut off my hand to find River, although I don't believe it would have the desired outcome. So I need your bravery, and your balls, and that special gift of yours to find my daughter."

Cody felt his face flush, unsure if the subject of their conversation was making him uncomfortable or if the brandy was infiltrating his brain. "It's not really a psychic ability, and it's nothing I can control. In fact, I haven't had a vision in weeks." He didn't want to admit he'd seen the shooting victims at Full Throttle in his mind when he and Daisy were fishing.

"Do you know how I wound up in this wheelchair?" He asked, taking a snip from his glass and enjoying the mild burn. "Of course, you don't. When I won my first election, I had a public press conference to give my acceptance speech as the new district attorney. River and her mother were at my side—she was just six years old then—and it was a moment I had dreamed of for years. A crowd of almost 200 people was in attendance. The day was perfect, and I couldn't wait to take office."

Dale finished his drink, poured another, and topped Cody's glass off before continuing his abridged story. "A former soldier I'd helped prosecute decided it was the best time to exact revenge. He and a couple of local punks drove by in a beat-up minivan. The door flew open, and they opened fire on the podium. Of course, I jumped in front of River. When I squatted to pick her up, a bullet shattered my spine. The bullet that hit me would have killed her if I hadn't reacted. Saving my daughter costs me my legs, but I thank God every day that my sacrifice saved the life of my little girl."

His eyes were teary, but he never broke. "So, my point is: I'd give anything to save my daughter: my legs, my arms, my money, my career, or even my life. She's all the family I have left. I'm not sure what she's going through right now, but we need to find her before she gets hurt. I'm asking—begging you—please, find her before she hurts anyone else."

Cody slid the envelope across the table as he stood. "I'm trying to find her, Mr. Kelly. I will find her. But I won't do it for your money. I'm doing this for AJ Timmons. He's the greatest guy I've ever known, and he's in love with your daughter. And she's in love with him."

"I'm aware of her motive. I understand she wants revenge against Levi Thompson and Jeremy Morrison, but they're untouchable—locked away until their trial. Then they'll probably never eat a meal outside of prison again."

"She has another target, too."

Dale gave him a reassuring nod, "I heard your picture was pinned to the apartment wall with a few holes in it. She'll be coming for you at some point."

"I think there's another factor at play. I'm certain River is being controlled, and I can't explain how right now. But I will when this is over. I promise."

"Young man, people who make promises to me had better keep them. You wouldn't want the county's most powerful man on your bad side, would you?"

"No, sir."

"If you find my daughter by the end of the day, I could be a powerful ally to you and your friends. But, Cody..."

As the DA finished his thought, he leaned forward while Cody hid behind his glass.

"Cody, if anything happens to River, I can make life in Stoneville very difficult for an ex-convict." He poured another round into his glass. "So, tell me everything you know and why you believe she's being controlled."

They discussed what Cody knew so far. Cody told him about Cain Lake's secret, how Flesti Thaed might be centuries old, how she could control anyone infected by the water, and how his psychic abilities came to be. When he finished, Dale Kelly was silent.

He rolled his wheelchair to the window and nodded at Deputy Simpson outside. Simpson was on his cell phone. A serious look adorned his face.

"See that deputy? He's a good man. We've been friends for decades. But I wouldn't count on him to find my lost dog. He does the job for the money, not out of passion."

He spun the wheelchair around to face Cody, who stood to see the view from the window. "Our new sheriff, Hassett, well, I'm not sure about her yet. She's understaffed, over budget, and still unaccustomed to our ways of dealing with the shit that's filling these streets. She's too unpredictable. Too damn much of a straight arrow."

Cody set his empty glass on the coffee table. "You're worried about what Hassett will do if she finds River."

Dale nodded. "Her and the state troopers. Those boys are a bunch of trigger-happy heroes. They'll gun her down the second they think she's a threat. Fuck, I wish Jeff Bourbon were still the sheriff."

Cody nodded in agreement.

They regarded each other for a moment. Cody wondered what it must be like to have so much power, money, and resources, and yet feel helpless to save your own daughter. Dale Kelly pushed the wheels on his chair and rolled toward the door. Cody followed.

Cody thanked Dale for the drink. Dale thanked Cody for his time, and the two men shook hands again.

"If she kills again," Dale said, "Even I won't be able to keep her from being buried by the Judicial system."

"Then I'd better find her before she does." Cody opened the door and stepped outside.

Deputy Dave Simpson was jogging toward the door as Cody crossed the porch. He'd run from the pond to the front steps and stopped at the top. He took three exasperated breaths before he could speak.

"Everything okay, David?" Dale Kelly asked as he rolled through the door.

"Sheriff Hassett just called me. Someone found a dead biker in town," he huffed a few more times, desperate for oxygen. "It looks like he was stabbed to death last night."

# 14

# BLOOD & A TRUMPET

Smoke erupted from a tire as it fought for traction, and Deputy Simpson's Chevy Tahoe painted a single black rubber streak down the pavement as they exited the DA's driveway. He drove the Tahoe like it was his 1974 Mach I Mustang. Riding in the passenger side, Cody felt the force of acceleration pull him into the black vinyl seat until the vehicle slowed when it approached an intersection.

Both men were silent, but the patrol vehicle blared a warning as it sped down the street. The red flashing lights atop the SUV flashed bright enough that Cody could see them reflecting off everything, even in the daylight.

They made their way to the north side of town and continued until acres, rather than fences or hedges, separated the houses. The truck turned right and began winding up Redmill Road, a curvy back road with no painted lines. Tall trees, a mix of hardwood and evergreens, shaded the area in dim light.

The vehicle slowed as they approached the crime scene. "Someone found a motorcycle on the side of the road and reported it as an accident," Simpson said. "Hassett thought the motorist just abandoned the bike and went for help, but she decided to search the woods. She found a trail of blood from the accident scene that led her to the victim."

Simpson parked the Tahoe. Cody stepped out of the vehicle and saw seven first responders, but not Hassett. Emergency flares burned in the roadway, and a short firetruck created a roadblock on the opposite end. Despite the flashing lights and numerous emergency vehicles, the personnel at the scene were strangely calm. Perhaps because the victim was already dead, and the realization that he was beyond saving weighed heavily on their shoulders. Now, their only responsibility was to collect evidence, remove the body, and clean up the scene.

"Wait here," Simpson instructed Cody. He left Cody by the patrol vehicle while he went to a wrecked motorcycle on the right side of the road. The bike was a twisted mess of metal and rubber, partially swallowed by a steep roadside ditch. Cody could only see the rear tire and handlebars sticking up. He watched Simpson step into the ditch to study the wreckage.

Once Simpson climbed back to the road, he talked to a couple of EMTs at the scene, then turned to a man dressed in casual clothes and a fire helmet. The volunteer firefighter pointed up the hill to the opposite side where the motorcycle had landed. They were out of earshot to Cody, who guessed they were pointing toward the body.

Simpson nodded to the man, turned, and motioned for Cody to join him.

Cody broke into a slow jog until he reached the deputy. "Where's the body?"

"Over there." Simpson pointed in the same direction as the fire-fighter. A stream of orange ribbon led into the woods. "The motor-cyclist ran uphill and dropped about seventy yards in."

They stepped over a row of burned-out flares and dropped into a ditch opposite the motorcycle. Cody followed Simpson's footsteps through matted grass. A path had already begun to form as emergency crews came and went from the scene. Cody scoured the ground for the blood the victim had lost. If he were stabbed, he must have been bleeding. But the ground was dry and clean.

"I don't see any blood. How'd she find him?"

Deputy Simpson stopped and pointed south, "Blood trail is probably ten yards downhill. We can't have everyone trampling any evidence left behind."

*Makes sense.*

They walked another thirty yards, climbed over a rusty barbed wire fence, and pushed through a tight row of cedar trees. Simpson hopped over a small stream of flowing water but lost his balance and stepped into the cool spring with his right foot. He cursed a few times but kept moving. Cody athletically jumped over the water and followed Simpson over a stone wall that he was sure had been constructed over a hundred years ago.

Once across the stone wall, they entered an old farm pasture, overgrown with tall grass, weeds, and groups of alder trees. It was apparent that the field had not been mowed or occupied for decades. Sheriff Hassett was standing twenty yards away, engrossed in a phone conversation. She looked aggravated by Cody's arrival but kept listening to the person on the other end of the call. When she finally finished her conversation, she pocketed her phone and approached her deputy and his tag-along.

"I bet you can guess who that was, can't you, Simpson?"

"I've got a pretty good idea, yeah. Dale Kelly?"

"You're goddam right. The district attorney seems convinced that Savage can be useful during this investigation. Wants him to be a 'consultant.' You believe that shit?"

Simpson knew it was a rhetorical question and let his boss vent.

She pushed her sunglasses to the top of her head and let them rest there before going on, "I'm putting you in charge of babysitting this ex-convict, Simpson. If he gets in the way or screws this up, then it's on you. Understand?" Her voice wasn't loud or demeaning, but her tone was serious.

Simpson shrank, but nodded that he would accept the responsibility. "So, do we have an ID on this guy? Is he one of the Road Barons?"

"No, he's not local. He's with another gang from downstate—the Zombie Riders." She shook her head, "Who the hell comes up with these names? Anyway, that's our assumption based on the logo on his jacket. ID in his wallet says his name is Anthony Chavez. Address on his ID is listed as Onondaga, NY."

Cody walked ten yards toward a small clearing of patted grass and saw the victim lying on his side. His arms were crossed at his chest, nearly hugging himself. Cody guessed he must have felt especially cold as the blood left his body, taking his natural warmth. Dry blood stained his shirt and the waistband of his jeans, but the ground was still relatively clean. He'd already lost much of his blood by the time he reached this area.

Chavez was still wearing his motorcycle helmet, painted retro blue with two white stripes down the middle. Cody remembered the helmet from the night before. He felt a punch to the heart. He began a visual scan of the area to be sure Chavez was alone.

"Sheriff?" Cody asked.

She took two steps closer.

"Was the victim riding a 1960s Triumph?"

"How the hell would I know? Do I look like a motorcycle expert?" Hassett barked back.

Deputy Simpson stepped closer and cleared his throat. "Looks like a 1961 Triumph—TT model, I think. Competition models are relatively rare in the US. Probably a 650 cc engine, V-twin. A classic beauty." He gloated when he finished speaking.

Hassett rolled her eyes. "I don't understand why you keep that information in your brain, Simpson, but thank you." She turned to Cody, "So, yes, I guess it was a trumpet."

"Triumph," Cody and Simpson corrected in unison.

"Fine," Hassett conceded. "It's a friggin Triumph. Can we get to your point, Savage?"

"I saw this guy riding last night, but he wasn't alone. Alyse Burns was riding with him. He dropped her off at someone's house and left."

"Alyse Burns? Wasn't she the woman who dragged two motorcycles down the road the night we arrested Levi Thompson?"

"And she tends bar at The Mineshaft," Simpson added.

"So," Sheriff Hassett started, "If he dropped her off, then we know he was alone."

"I don't think so," Cody said. "Look at his jacket pockets. They're turned inside out like someone pulled their hands out quickly.

Wasn't him because there's no blood on the pocket liner."

"So, just because his pockets are inside out means he wasn't alone?"

"Well, it got a little chilly last night, especially if you're on the back of a motorcycle. A female passenger could've had her hands in his jacket pockets to keep them warm—best place for a passenger to hang on. She would have yanked them out instinctively when they were about to crash. That's probably how the pockets turned out."

Deputy Simpson, with raised eyebrows, nodded silently in agreement. He looked at the sheriff to measure her reaction.

"Was there a second helmet strapped to his bike?" Cody asked.

"No. The only helmet is on his head."

"When I saw this man last night, Alyse was wearing a matching helmet. So, where's the second helmet?"

"Well then," Hassett retorted, "She must have walked away. We've been all over these woods—no other victim."

"Maybe she was picked up?" Simpson contributed.

"Or she walked back to the party. AJ only lives about a half mile up the hill."

Before any of them could say another word, a fire department member yelled out. They heard other first responders begin to yell. The scene erupted into chaos as all the fire department and rescue squad members jumped into action.

A young firefighter scrambled through the woods until he reached the pasture.

"What's the commotion?" Hassett asked.

"Sheriff," he huffed, sucking air to catch his breath. "Sheriff, we've got a female victim…," he huffed some more. "…Across the road."

Hassett was already in motion, light as a gazelle as she zig-zagged through the tall grass, hopped the stone wall, and disappeared through the cedars. Deputy Simpson followed like a bear with bad knees, unable to keep up with his athletic boss.

*Alyse. No, please, not Alyse.* Cody struggled to breathe. He wasn't out of breath, and he didn't over-exert himself. In fact, he hadn't moved a muscle. The trees blurred, and he lost track of direction, unaware that his legs gave way to gravity. He caught himself on one knee as he fought to keep himself from collapsing to the ground. He didn't want to go to the other victim. He didn't want to see Alyse Burns lying dead beside the road. He tried to follow but couldn't take a single step. The thought of seeing her dead or in pain terrified the hell out of him.

The seconds seemed like minutes. The minutes passed in slow motion. And then, he began walking back to the road, in the direction of the female victim.

# 15

## REDMILL ROAD 

Cody's legs were like two cement pillars, incapable of moving to follow Sheriff Hassett and Deputy Simpson. The two law officers had a forty-second head start to reach the second crash victim. He watched them vanish in the woods, and finally forced himself to follow at a slower pace. He walked alone, his steps slow and deliberate. His head was down, carefully selecting his steps so he wouldn't sprain an ankle or twist his knee on an exposed tree root or rock. He lost the trail of ribbons and cut too far north. Turning south again, he was cut off by a small marsh the size of a tour bus formed from the little creek. He circled the soupy area to avoid sinking up to his knees in thick black mud. As he doubled back, he listened for the rescue team shouting directions to save the woman they'd found. Their frantic reactions and shouting were good signs.

*She's alive.*

The Stoneville firetruck's red paint and flashing blue light finally came into view. He headed straight toward the roadblock.

When he finally reached the road, he was on the north side of the firetruck blockade. All the commotion of the rescue occurred downhill from the wrecked Triumph motorcycle. Everyone was in a circle, ten yards off the road, on the opposite side of where Chavez had been found. Cody slid down an embankment through a patch of wiry blackberry shrubs, their thorns grabbed his clothes and skin in a vain effort to keep him from proceeding. It slowed his approach, but he was determined to see if the woman was Alyse. He stepped on briers to flatten them to the ground. He broke through the brambles and finally reached the team of rescue personnel encircling the female. He kept his distance, respecting the EMT's space to work on the woman in the ditch. There were too many people to see the hurt woman's face.

"Her pulse is weak," he heard one EMT say.

"Watch her neck," another said.

"Bring us a stretcher board," a female called out.

Two men came over the embankment, downhill of the briar patch, carrying an orange stretcher board. A few of the busy rescuers moved back, forcing Cody to step back as well, as they laid the stretcher board on the ground and began working it under the injured motorcycle passenger. They strapped her to the board, counted in unison, and then lifted as a team. Cody got his first view of her face.

It wasn't Alyse.

She must have ditched Chavez at the party—or Chavez ditched her. Either way, she wasn't here; that was all that mattered. She must have made it out of town by now. She must be on her way to wherever the hell she thought she was going. She was alive and safe.

The group of EMTs, along with the sheriff and deputy, formed a single line as they followed the stretcher board with its hapless victim. They made it up the embankment, across the road, and slid the woman into the ambulance. It took a few more minutes before the vehicle sped away, as Cody, Sheriff Hassett, Deputy Simpson, and three firemen watched.

As the ambulance rounded the first corner, it braked aggressively as it passed a vehicle approaching from the opposite direction. Just seconds after the fleeing ambulance took the corner, a silver van drove onto the scene with large gold letters on a black horizontal stripe. The van arrived on the scene and came to an abrupt stop behind Simpson's Tahoe. Shari Kapoor, the Stoneville coroner and pathologist, stepped out of the driver's side.

*****

Shari Kapoor squatted beside Anthony Chavez, zooming

in and out with a digital SLR camera and whispering notes into a small handheld recorder. The camera's shutter clicked away as Shari moved from the victim's helmet to his feet. With gloved hands, she gently removed the helmet and snapped several more shots from different angles.

Cody, Sheriff Hassett, and Deputy Simpson stayed twenty feet away to let Shari work and gather evidence. Three EMTs waited by the stonewall. They were engrossed in a conversation about installing swimming pools in their backyards as if the dead man lying in the grass was no concern. Cody decided they weren't callous, but more accustomed than he to these deadly scenes.

It didn't take Shari more than twenty minutes to complete her tasks and collect evidence. She put her equipment back in the gray toolbox and called out to the EMTs to transport Chavez's body to her van. The three men abruptly abandoned their conversation. They swatted away the flies congregating on the corpse and loaded the deceased, Anthony Chavez, into a burgundy body bag. The body bag zipper made a long ripping sound as it sealed him inside, and then he was slid onto one of their orange stretcher board. They carried him in absolute silence through the woods. The sobering experience made everyone aware of their mortality, and suddenly owning a swimming pool didn't seem so important.

They trekked over the stone wall and barbed wire fence, and across the running stream without complaint as the cold mountain water filled their boots. When they reached the road, Chavez was gently slid into the back of Shari's van.

Shari had a brief conversation with Sheriff Hassett, then climbed behind the big van's steering wheel. The big Ford van slowly accelerated, taking Anthony Chavez on his last ride down Redmill Road.

The rescue vehicles departed the scene one by one, and soon only the two sheriff department vehicles remained.

"Any idea who the woman is?" Cody asked Sheriff Hassett.

"I was going to ask you the same."

Cody just shook his head. "Such a shame. I don't know why River would do this. These people aren't—weren't—

members of the Red Barons. Hell, they weren't even locals."

"We don't know it was River Kelly yet. Could be a freak accident, but I'm pretty sure those were blade marks in Chavez's chest. Simpson, take your sidekick back to town and check in with Shari in about an hour or so. Grab a late lunch to kill time; I know you haven't eaten yet. Stay on this. I'll check with some witnesses from Full Throttle, then I'll go to the hospital to see if I can identify our 'Jane Doe'. Hopefully, she'll pull through, but it doesn't look good."

Cody and Deputy Simpson jumped back in the Tahoe and followed Sheriff Hassett in her Jeep Gladiator. Once they reached the railroad tracks, Sheriff Hassett turned left toward Full Throttle. Cody and Simpson went straight, cutting across town toward the hospital. It was too soon to check on Shari's progress, so they stopped at a local sandwich shop and devoured a couple of French dips.

Cody borrowed Simpson's phone and punched Daisy's number into the keypad. The call went straight to voicemail.

She must be working. Well, at least she's safe at home.

They sat in silence, sucking down the last few ounces of their sugary fountain drinks. Simpson slurped the last of his Dr. Pepper, held back a belch, and gave Cody a serious look. "Do you think you can find her?"

"Me?" Cody replied. "Isn't that, technically, your job?"

"Yeah, but this is a big town, and she could be anywhere. I think Dale Kelly thought you could speed things up with your—you know?" He tapped his temple with an index finger.

"My what?" Cody knew what he was implying, but wondered if Simpson had the courage to say it.

"Your psychic ability." He whispered as he stacked wrappers and napkins on his plastic tray. "I mean, whatever Cain Lake did to you—whew—man, you got to admit that you're a pretty lucky sonovabitch to have that power."

"I don't feel lucky. I feel cursed. I can't control my visions. Hell, I haven't even had one since the night Levi and Cricket nearly killed me. I think that near-death experience changed me. Maybe even cured me, if that's the right word."

"Well, if we don't find her soon, I think there's going to be more bloodshed—more victims. Ya know?"

Cody knew. He knew River's anger flowed like the Cascade's tailrace, and she wouldn't stop until she killed him. He was the problem. He was the target she wanted. Maybe he needed to give her the chance to kill him. Draw her out of hiding.

"Well, we should probably get over to the morgue and see what Shari's found out. She probably wants to wrap things up and get home to her family by dinner."

Cody froze in place. Then he turned to Simpson with a slight smile. "I've got an idea. I think I know somebody who might be able to find River Kelly."

# 16

# SHAKE THINGS UP 

Daisy and Bourbon picked a flat area with little undergrowth and tall, deciduous trees to camp for the night. They cleared the rocks and dead limbs from the ground to ensure the area was clean and smooth.

Bourbon suspended a long log across the site, held up by two trees on each side. He unfolded a plastic tarp and draped it over the log. The tarp was pulled back and down until it reached the ground, where he secured it with four metal tent stakes.

Next, he pulled the front of the tarp up and out, until it was nearly parallel with the ground, and tied the corners to two more trees with a length of parachute cord. He smoothed a second, smaller tarp on the forest floor for them to lie on. The makeshift lean-to was open on each side, but the weather forecast was mostly clear skies.

Daisy was assigned to build a small fire pit in front of the tarp, just past the edge of the roof line. She dug away all the dry debris—leaves, moss, and dead sticks—and lined it with a few small stones she'd found. She used larger stones around the outside, keeping the burning area the size of a large pizza. She then went to work searching for suitable fuel for the fire. She made two piles: one stack of dry kindling wood and another of larger wood that she hoped would burn slowly.

"There," Daisy smiled and brushed her hands together to clean some of the dirt and dry bark. She checked her fingernails and noticed two had noticeable chips, but shrugged off the damage when she looked at her finished project. "I think we have enough wood for a while."

Bourbon emerged from the woods carrying an armload of thick, dry wood cut to forearm length. Each piece was perfectly sawed on the ends and nearly the same length. Setting the results of his work on the ground, he rejoined Daisy at the fire pit.

"Where'd you get that? The hardware store?"

Bourbon chuckled, undid his belt, and slid a black nylon sheath free that held his folding bucksaw. "Cut it myself," he said, waving the saw.

"Cheater."

Bourbon handed Daisy a Zippo lighter, "Wanna do the honors?" After she took the lighter from his hand, he moved to a nearby group of evergreen trees, inspecting the bark.

She flipped open the top of the lighter and gave the flint wheel a spin. The lighter sparked, and a flame was born on the first try. She held the lighter low, hoping to ignite the small kindling and bring the fire to life. The pile of kindling, resembling a crisscross mess of pencils, charred and smoked, but refused to stay lit.

"Dammit!" Daisy cursed as the lighter grew hot. "I think the wood is too wet."

Bourbon watched her out of the corner of his eye as he dug into the bark of a balsam tree. "Everything seems pretty dry. Where did you get the kindling?"

"Off the ground," Daisy answered. "It's everywhere, but I think the last rain soaked it."

Bourbon poked at the evergreen tree some more while Daisy sat defeated at the edge of the shelter. She pulled her knees up to her chest and swatted at a half-dozen mosquitoes set to feast on her ankles.

Five full minutes went by before Bourbon returned. He was holding a piece of tree bark the size of his open hand. He showed it to Daisy. The flat bark was covered with a thick, sticky liquid, the color of burnt honey. Little bugs, specks of dirt, and debris were stuck to the surface.

"Gross," she said. "I'm not eating that?"

Bourbon chuckled again. "You really need to spend more time in the woods, you know that? It's pine pitch from that balsam tree." He lifted the pile of half-burned kindling and placed the sticky bark underneath. He then neatly restacked the pile and added some more wood on top of that. "Try it now."

Daisy reached into the little wooden hut that Bourbon created for his sticky bark. She held the blue flame of the lighter on the pine pitch. Almost instantly, the pitch bubbled and boiled and smoked until a twelve-inch flame erupted.

"Holy shit!" She jumped back. "What the hell is in that? That's friggin amazing."

"Pine pitch is highly flammable," Bourbon informed her. "That's why pine trees burn so fast in forest fires. Between the dead pine needles covering the ground and the pine pitch inside the tree, there's virtually no way of stopping it. One little spark, and poof—" he threw his hands upward, fingers splayed like he made something disappear. "Whole forest is gone in minutes."

Watching the fire's hypnotic flames lulled them into a sense of calm. Daisy yawned. They settled into comfortable positions under the tarp, their heads leaning back on rolled-up sleeping bags. Thirty minutes of daylight still needed to burn before darkness consumed the forest, so they left the fire to settle with them, knowing they could easily bring it back to life while the embers were hot. They nearly dozed off but talked occasionally about Cain Lake, Stoneville, Cody, Annabel, and Sheriff Hassett. Daisy filled Bourbon in on everything she had discovered about Flesti—or Marion Cain, if that were her real name.

He digested the information and chased it with a bottle of water.

They finally unrolled their sleeping bags and climbed inside. Neither zipped their bag to avoid overheating in the warm summer air. As tired as they were, both struggled to fall asleep. As the night snuffed out the remaining daylight, Bourbon stoked the little fire, rousing the flames to dance and flicker. The light gave them comfort and security. They didn't need the heat. It was summer, and the temperature outside was still in the upper seventies, predicted to drop to sixty-eight. It would have been a perfect night to sleep outside if they could clear their minds.

Daisy placed Greenie-the-Meanie on a rock beside her. The firelight bounced off his sharp plastic teeth in a terrifying look to ward off danger. It made her smile.

Eventually, they dozed off with Greenie standing guard.

*****

Bourbon and Daisy jumped to their feet inside their tent. Daisy put a bruise on her forehead as her head hit the supporting timber that held the tent's cover.

"What the hell is that?" She asked.

The ground rumbled, and they could hear the trees shaking as the sound approached them like a freight train. Dead leaves and debris began to shake and bounce across the forest floor, although they couldn't see the chaos in the darkness.

"Earthquake!" Bourbon answered.

When the shock wave hit them, it reverberated through their bones, shaking them in unison with everything around the campsite. Several dead tree limbs fell to the ground, just missing their tent and heads. The vibrating wave rattled through them, not around. Daisy felt her teeth and bones rattle as much as the trees and ground. There was no way to avoid being shaken. Another wave came behind the first, smaller in magnitude and duration, but the sensation echoed the effects of the initial shock wave. More tree limbs dropped, and Greenie the Meanie fell off his perch.

The earthquake's fury lasted less than ten seconds, and then calm returned to the woods. Not far from their campsite, an owl screeched in confusion, and a coyote howled at the bottom of the small mountain. The night was alive again with the sound of wild animals and insects.

"Haven't felt an earthquake in about eight years," Bourbon said. "That was a pretty good one."

"Is that normal here?" Daisy jumped to her feet. "I never knew New York had earthquakes."

"Yeah, there are fault lines in the Adirondack Mountains that run north-northeast. We get a few rumbles now and then. Nothing to worry about." Bourbon hobbled to the fire, feeling the hard ground's effects on his body during his short slumber. "That might be the only one you feel in the next decade."

Daisy wasn't convinced.

They spent ten minutes picking up the dead limbs that had fallen around them, tossing some of the small dry timber into the fire. The fire came back to life, illuminating the area around them. Bourbon shined his flashlight to the tops of the trees that circled them, looking for any large limbs that may have been shaken loose and ready to drop. He confirmed they were safe and could resume their positions in the lean-to.

They settled back into their sleeping area. Bourbon lay on his side, pitching back and forth in a desperate attempt to find comfort. He kept his back to Daisy, hoping for no more interruptions so he could get some rest. Daisy watched the fire burn, resting her hand on her belly to give the growing baby inside her extra protection. Once her fear of the earthquake subsided, she began daydreaming about her life after giving birth. She imagined she'd move in with Cody now, and they could become a family rather than just a couple.

As the orange and white flames danced in front of her, throwing their amber light upon the trees and ground, movement seized her attention. She focused on the edge of darkness, twenty yards beyond the fire pit, where the light died. Her heart skipped, and she nearly forgot how to breathe when she saw two green eyes staring back at her.

# 17

# SIN EATER

Cody followed Deputy Simpson into the coroner's office. Shari Kapoor wasn't at her desk, but as usual, her son Roshan sat at his desk in the corner, drawing away, waiting for his mother to return. His artwork adorned the wall by the door, months of sketches and illustrations. The wall had a different feel now, and once Cody had a chance to study it, he realized that new drawings covered the old. Roshan completed about two drawings daily and insisted that his mother put them on the wall. He was even particular about their placement, directing her in silence with his index finger until she found the perfect place to pin the paper. Once she had it where he was satisfied, he'd give his approval with a thumbs-up.

"Hello, Ro," Cody greeted the young artist. Roshan only glanced at Cody and gave him a four-finger wave without his thumb letting go of the green pencil it grasped. Cody knew the autistic boy wouldn't speak—not aloud, anyway.

As Cody watched Roshan draw black calligraphic lines, he thought about his vision the night his hand was healed in Cain Lake. At times, he and Roshan had an uncanny psychic connection, and Cody was the only person in the world to hear the boy speak. Something his parents would give anything for, he imagined. Ro was intelligent, mature, and polite in their conversation. He'd created a picture—a glimpse of the future—of Cody, Daisy, and their two kids. But then he tore the picture in half, dividing the family, as the pieces turned to ash and drifted away.

Cody's thoughts turned to Daisy, pregnant and happy. He could never tell her about the psychic interaction he had with Roshan. He never told her that they had a boy in the picture or that Roshan believed their lives were in jeopardy. The less she knew, the better. He didn't want her scared about what was to come. They just needed to take each day one at a time.

"Good evening, gentlemen," a female voice announced, breaking Cody's train of thought. "I've finished up my preliminary examination of Mr. Chavez." Shari entered the room, wearing a white jacket and carrying a gray folder under her arm. She smiled politely as Cody and Simpson turned to greet her.

"Hello, Shari," Deputy Simpson said. "I was afraid we were too soon."

"Like I said, it's preliminary. I'll have to do a more thorough exam tomorrow. Toxicology reports will be ready in a few days."

"We appreciate you dropping everything to work on this one, Doc," Simpson said. "We need to know as much as we can about these victims if we're going to stop River Kelly."

"I hope you do it quickly," Shari replied. "Have you heard what the press is starting to call her?"

"I have," Simpson responded.

Cody looked confused. He hadn't heard anything about a nickname for Stoneville's newest fear. Then again, he'd been walking the streets all day following leads, exempt from the barrage of news, online articles, and social media bias.

Simpson side-eyed Cody, knowing River Kelly's nickname would have a little sting.

"The Red Devil—that's what they're saying," Shari cringed. "I'm sure Bethany Smart from Channel 3 News came up with that. What the fuck is wrong with these people? This is a young woman in pain. She needs help, not damnation."

"Anything to drive sales and clicks, I suppose," Simpson said. "The District Attorney is going to blow his top when he reads that—Or sees it on the news. He'll probably try to sue the paper and WKED."

"Good! He should. Poor Dale, I can't imagine watching something like this unfold involving your child." She watched Roshan innocently draw.

The room was silent as they all contemplated River Kelly's fate, only Roshan's scratching pen cut the silence.

Cody spoke for the first time since entering Shari's office, "So, was this guy shot or stabbed? There were wounds on his body that didn't appear to be from an accident."

Shari shed her white jacket, hung it on a small hook under a bookshelf, and sat at her desk with the gray folder. She opened the folder and flipped through the pages, "Mr. Anthony Alexander Chavez. Lives in Onondaga, NY—near Syracuse. Age of the victim is thirty-three, according to his license. Mr. Chavez is also a member of—" she leaned toward her notes, "Aw, yes, the Zombie Raiders—"

"Riders," Simpson corrected. "Zombie Riders."

Shari glared at him over her bifocal glasses, "Zombie Riders. I wonder if Bethany Smart came up with that one, too."

Simpson held back his chuckle.

"Occupation unknown," she continued.

"Cause of death?" Simpson asked.

"Aw," she closed the folder. There was no need to refer to her notes for that. "Stabbed twice. One stab wound to the upper chest. The blade was retracted, and then he was hit by a projectile from behind—probably the same instrument. The second attack went straight through his body from behind. One attack from the front— one attack from behind."

"That seems odd," Simpson responded. "He was traveling forward. A knife thrown at his chest would have had a greater impact. I'd guess the force would have been like a bullet fired from a gun, depending on his rate of speed."

Shari nodded, "I think you're right. But the first wound was nonlethal, as if River just wanted to throw him off guard and cause the crash, which seemed to work. The second attack—from behind— was the fatal one."

"Are you sure the weapon was thrown?" Cody asked.

"Like I said, it went all the way through his body. It couldn't have done that if she had been holding it."

Simpson's face twisted, "Two attackers?"

"No," Cody answered. "The first throw was controlled. River knew Chavez had a passenger sitting behind him. She didn't want to harm the woman—just the driver. After they crashed, she released the second attack as Chavez ran away."

They all nodded that it made sense.

"So, she's picking her targets, just like we theorized," Simpson remarked. "We need to warn all the bikers in the area. They're all being targeted, and it appears that she's improved her aim since attacking Larry Larson."

"Maybe not all the bikers," Cody added. "She might be selecting them based on their history or criminal records."

"Punishing them?" Shari asked. "Do you think she's getting their criminal histories from her father? He'd have access to all that."

Cody walked toward Roshan, then turned to Shari Kapoor, "Shari, does Chavez have a criminal record?"

"Yes," she answered. She reopened the folder and turned a few pages. "He was a convict at Dalton Correctional Facility for three years for domestic violence. He put his live-in girlfriend in intensive care about ten years ago. Several traffic violations since, but nothing worth locking him up."

Cody rubbed his dirty blond beard, "I'm not 100 percent sure, but she might be targeting bikers with criminal records."

"Why bikers exclusively?"

"Because she wants revenge for what happened to AJ Timmons."

Shari closed the folder and stepped out from behind the desk. "Then why not go after the men responsible, Levi Thompson and that grasshopper fellow?"

"Cricket," Deputy Simpson corrected. "Because they're untouchable. They're both locked up in prison. She can't just waltz in there and start throwing a dagger at convicts."

Cody studied one of Roshan's drawings on the wall. At first glance, it appeared to depict a woman kayaking across Cain Lake. The forest in the background was dark. At the bottom of the lake, several motorcycles rested in a mangled mess underwater. Everything in the picture was out of scale, and the perspective was utterly skewed, as if Picasso and Salvador Dali had collaborated on the piece.

He leaned closer. A small, shadowy figure stood in the woods. The character was so dark against the dark forest that she was almost imperceptible, like Roshan had drawn over a mistake. But Cody knew who it depicted. The second figure in the drawing was the woman in the blue kayak, which resembled the knife Larry Larson had warned him about. The woman paddling the boat wore a black sweatshirt with the hood pulled over her head. He imagined it hid her distinctive hair color.

Cody knelt beside Roshan. "Ro?" He tapped his arm, and Roshan looked at him blankly. He blinked several times and studied Cody's face. "Ro, do you know who that is in the picture?"

Roshan didn't respond.

Shari stepped behind her autistic son and placed both hands on his shoulders, "Cody, he can't—"

"Ro, who's the kayaker in this picture? Is this supposed to be River Kelly?"

"Cody, stop, please. He can't answer you. He won't answer you."

"He can, Shari," Cody assured her, looking up at her and then at the picture. "He knows. He sees it in his mind. Remember how he directed me to Parson's Store? He pointed out the store in his drawing."

"You don't know what you're talking about. That was just a coincidence. Please, stop. You're scaring him."

Cody was sure Roshan wasn't scared and that his drawings were more than just random illustrations that popped into his mind. They were glimpses of a world he saw coming, incidents that hadn't occurred yet, places he'd never been.

Cody pushed a little more, "Ro, I need to know what you see. I need you to help me find the Red Devil. You can write it on paper, buddy." He was talking fast, and his words came quickly. "Is that River Kelly?" He pointed to the kayaker. Ro stared at him with no expression. Cody pointed to the shadow in the woods, "Is that

Flesti? The shadow in the woods? Is it her?"

Shari had enough. "Stop it, now! Deputy, get this fucking man out of my office and away from my son."

Deputy Simpson grabbed Cody's arm and pulled, and Cody only resisted a little. He arose from his kneeling position as Simpson urged him to the door.

Cody braced himself against the door casing and made one last attempt to plead his case. "Shari, Roshan is more special than you think. He's connected to Cain Lake, like me."

"He's nothing like you, Savage."

"Shari, please, we must know if he can find her. I don't think we're just dealing with a pissed-off woman hellbent on revenge."

"Then what are we dealing with?"

Simpson relaxed his grip on Cody's arm. Cody took one step back into the room. "I think River Kelly is being affected by Cain Lake—by the micropods and Flesti Thaed. I think she's being controlled and that we have another Sin Eater on our hands."

"I'm a scientist," Shari responded. "I won't be infected by all the woo-woo, hocus-pocus, stupidity that you've convinced Jefferson Bourbon and the rest of your friends to believe. The micropods in Cain Lake are probably nothing more than a species of bio luminescent diatom with no classification. Nothing more."

"Maybe you're right," Cody said, "I hope you're right. But maybe I'm right. The cost is too high if we ignore this, and I think Roshan is the only one who can track down the killer."

"Get him the fuck out of my office."

*****

"Well, that could have gone better," Deputy Simpson scoffed as he and Cody entered the patrol vehicle. "I'm sure she's probably on the phone with the sheriff right now, telling her about your theory."

"Good," Cody said.

"No, not good. She'll send you home, and then I'll be out all night trying to find River Kelly by myself. I need your help. Dale Kelly needs your help, and you need my help. This gets solved a lot faster if we all work together."

"So, now what?"

Simpson stared out the windshield, waiting for an idea to splatter across the glass. His mind was as blank as the window. "Well, if nothing else, we can drive around looking for River Kelly and hope we get lucky. Maybe someone will see her and call it in."

Simpson's phone rang before he could start the vehicle. Sheriff Hassett was on the other end of the call. Simpson pushed the speaker button on the phone so Cody could hear their conversation.

She'd been at the hospital, checking with the woman who was Anthony Chavez's passenger when his motorcycle crashed. Her name was Ellie Cruz. She'd woken up in the ambulance during transport from the accident scene. Ellie had moved from Plattsburgh to Stoneville less than two weeks ago and took a job as the new bookkeeper for a local car dealership, Ludlow's Family Auto. She met Anthony Chavez at AJ Timmons' party. Ellie described how some woman at the party refused to leave with Chavez—a beautiful girl, according to her description. They all knew she was referring to Alyse Burns.

Ellie and Chavez struck up a conversation. They stayed late at the party until she let her love of motorcycles and exotic men get the best of her and decided to accept his offer for a ride home. She was a little scared, racing down Redmill Road because the Triumph motorcycle had a single, shitty headlight.

According to her account, Ellie Cruz and Anthony Chavez were driving down a winding road when they saw a figure walking along the pavement. There was a blue flash of light; Chavez lurched back, almost sending Ellie off the back of the bike. The motorcycle veered sharply to the left, then cut right to avoid the pedestrian. That's when Ellie was thrown. She rolled off the road and down the embankment. She couldn't remember or didn't see what happened next.

Sheriff Hassett hung up after divulging everything she had learned from Ellie Cruz and told Simpson she was going back to

AJ Timmons' house to see if she could get more information about Anthony Chavez or find out when he left the party.

Deputy Simpson and Cody sat in silence, letting the new information gel. Cody thought about the night he tried to attend AJ's party. At least a dozen witnesses saw him leave AJ's house and head down Redmill Road. It was just a matter of time before Sheriff Hassett found out and put him on her list of suspects.

# 18
# DEVIL EYES

B ourbon," Daisy whispered.

The former sheriff was sound asleep and unresponsive.

"Bourbon." This time, she threw a marble-sized rock over the fire. Though the soft sleeping bag cushioned the impact, it was enough to get Bourbon's attention.

He rolled over. "What's up? I was finally falling asleep."

"We're not alone. Look," she pointed to the green eyes watching her. The eyes blinked and disappeared.

Bourbon sat up, rubbed his forehead and eyes, then tried to refocus. "I don't see anything." He lay back and shuffled inside the sleeping bag, struggling for elusive comfort.

The dark animal had crept five feet to its right, and then the eyes reappeared—firelight reflecting off the beast's retinas.

"There!" Daisy yelled. "Right there."

Bourbon sprang back to a sitting position and followed Daisy's finger. The eerie glow of two eyes watching back was unmistakable against the dark canvas.

"I think it's a wolf," Daisy whispered with a squeak. She sank deeper into her sleeping bag, as if it would provide some protection. She was squeezing Greenie the Meanie with both hands, "I think it's getting ready to attack." She pulled the sleeping bag up to her chin, ready to duck inside for safety. "Do something. Do something!"

Bourbon sat up and saw the creature watching them. He rolled to his right and reached into his backpack. His left hand explored the interior of the pack.

"Did you bring your gun?"

"No. I got something better."

"Better than a gun to kill a wolf? What's better than a gun?"

When he finally brought his hand out, he was holding a piece of beef jerky the size of a bookmark. "This guy's on our side," referring to the intruder in the dark. He held the dry meat up and gave a faint whistle. "Hetzen, come here, boy."

A medium-sized dog stepped into the firelight. His fur was black as coal, concealing him in the night. He reluctantly stepped into the light at the sound of Bourbon's voice and the sight of the treat. A wet pink tongue wiped excess drool from his muzzle. A thin tail began to whip in a frenzy when the scent of the spicy meat reached his powerful nose.

"Hetzen?" Daisy asked. "Who the hell named their dog 'Hetzen?' Sounds like a butler."

Bourbon laughed. "That's what I thought, too. The earthquake must have spooked him a little, so he came looking for companion-ship. Come here, boy. Come on, Hetz."

Flesti's dog padded over to Bourbon and gently accepted the meaty prize. He lay down at Bourbon's feet and began to chew, savoring the taste of the dry jerky. Bourbon stroked the dog's fur. He would never admit it to anyone, but he was glad to see the roving canine. Three things made a man feel safe in the woods: an accurate firearm, a warm fire, and a loyal dog. Tonight, he had two of the three.

"She's close," Bourbon informed Daisy. "Flesti can't be too far. If Hetzen found us, then she will, too. She won't be moving in the dark, but I'll bet we'll be eating breakfast with a crow."

Daisy had heard about Poe, the black crow that seemed to fly reconnaissance for Flesti Thaed. Cody described the bird to her as a feathered harbinger of trouble. But she was reluctant to believe that Poe was anything but a wild bird that came to enjoy the old lady's company. She scanned the tree branches, wondering if the scout was there now, watching, spying on them as they tried to sleep. There was no movement amongst the branches. The trees were still as headstones—not even the leaves moved.

Bourbon rubbed his sore knee. The pain was a reminder of his hike with Flesti a couple of weeks prior. It was the last time they were together. They had swum across Cain Lake in a desperate effort to save Cody Savage and stop Levi Thompson. The blue micropods, under Flesti's control, pulled them through the water to hasten their speed. Bourbon felt like he was flying through the cool water, speeding to the old Parson's General Store.

Later that same night, he felt her manipulating his thoughts and actions. In the hayloft of Annabel's barn, he held a pistol on Duke and Aaron Bristol, and he nearly shot the men dead because Flesti was toying with his brain. What was her motive? To turn him into the next sin eater? He knew—feared—that once he'd been exposed to the blue micropods, he was under her control. He hadn't visited the lake since, hoping that the effect would wear off with time and distance. He wouldn't know until he confronted her again, so he agreed to bring Daisy to the woods.

Leaving his pistol behind was a caution. If Flesti wanted him to sin, he'd be less dangerous without his sidearm.

Daisy sat and watched Hetzen chew his treat. His tail wagged in a slow, hypnotic motion, brushing leaves from side to side until a bare patch of dirt showed. As Daisy watched the tail, she closed her eyes and gave in to a yawn. She let herself fall back into a lying position, turned on her side, then her other side. She couldn't decide whether to keep her back toward the dark or face it. It was too quiet to sleep, so she lay awake for what seemed an hour, listening to the noiseless night. The nocturnal animals had settled and gone mute since the earthquake. The small fire with little pops and hisses was the only thing that disturbed the placidity of the night.

Bourbon had fallen asleep like he was staying at the Marriott, and Daisy was envious. She had hoped to doze off first, but the big man didn't realize how anxious she was about sleeping in the woods. She tossed a couple more times and ultimately decided that facing the fire made her more comfortable.

She felt a presence behind her and turned to see Hetzen had

moved from his position at Bourbon's feet. The dog sniffed her hair, instinctively spun in two circles, and lay with his back against hers. The dog's body heat was nearly as intense as the fire.

Hetzen wiggled and grumbled a little, trying to steal just a few more inches of her sleeping bag. Grateful for his company, Daisy let him have it.

With the fire at her feet, the wolf to her back, and the bear in his sleeping bag, she felt protected from anything else the darkness could muster. Her hand gently caressed her belly, knowing the little human growing inside her was safe for the night. She propped Greenie the Meanie back on his rock, thinking about Sammie, Cody, and her mother. Her cell phone had no signal, preventing her from calling home to tell everyone goodnight. So, she would have to be content with a telepathic message sent from her heart.

She was uncomfortable on the hard ground, and a rogue tree root poked her thigh. She wished she was home lying in bed—any bed. But she couldn't give up on this opportunity. She needed Flesti's story to prove her journalism skills were still sharp. Her recent canon of work lacked substance, and she was bored by the content she'd been given. How many articles could she write about school fundraisers, police citations, and community charities? She wanted a story with teeth, to show her boss—and that bitch Trena Cutlass, that she was worth more. If she couldn't, then maybe it was time to move on. Maybe Cody's idea to go into television broadcasting wasn't so ludicrous. She had the credentials, but chose the written word over the spoken. She knew she was too shy to speak to a camera, knowing how many viewers were watching—judging. Staying in the background, anonymous, writing news was more her comfort level. But she didn't want to write stories that seemed like gossip or dry news reports. She wanted stories that sang to the readers.

Her thoughts became mottled, and soon, it was hard for her to distinguish her ideas from dreams. They blended together like two flavors of a twist cone melting in the sun. Eventually, the dreams overpowered the ideas.

# 19

# ENTER THE CROW 

An irritating pounding sound woke Daisy. She raised herself to a sitting position, stiff from her long night on the ground, and found the source of the noise in a tree twenty yards away. A redheaded woodpecker scoured the forest, testing the timber for rot, hunting for its breakfast.

The orange glow rising beyond the horizon slowly washed the gray from the sky. The morning air was chilly and crisp, but she could still feel some heat from the ashes of the fire. Sometime in the night, Bourbon had stoked the dead flames with a small bundle of wood, and the hot ashes turned the fuel to flame. Now, hot coals produced a radiant heat that she could feel from three feet away. She was glad for his effort, as the heat soothed her stiff hands.

Hetzen had hardly moved all night since he'd stolen a portion of her sleeping bag. Once Daisy sat up, he stared at her with one eye while his tail wagged twice in anticipation of breakfast. He kept his eye on his new female companion as she stood and stretched. She drowned the sand in her throat with the last of her water.

She retrieved a six-pack cooler that contained dry goods. She had packed in such haste yesterday that she couldn't even remember what was inside. Her fingers landed on a protein bar, but she opted to wait until she had fresh water to wash the gritty texture down. She came up with a banana, perfect for a quick burst of natural energy. Hetzen sat up and sniffed at the fruit in her hand, hoping she was generous with her meal.

"Sorry, buddy, this is my breakfast. Go catch a squirrel."

Bourbon woke and joined her by the smoldering ashes that were once their fire. He quickly collected a handful of small dry wood, then topped it off with a short piece of a dead beech log.

"We'll get a little heat going and make us some coffee."

Daisy nearly dropped her banana. "Coffee? We can have coffee?"

"Sure can, kiddo, as soon as I'm done making it." He reached into his bag, and like a magician pulling a rabbit from a hat, he presented her with a small metal percolator and two matching cups. "I don't normally bring this thing out here, but I thought, what the hell, it's a short trip." He hoped anyway.

"Bourbon, I could kiss you. Any cream or sugar?"

"Yup. Got both, but the creamer is that powdered shit. It was easier to pack. And I raided Tabitha's Diner during lunch and filled my pockets with sugar packs." He tossed a couple to her while he filled the percolator with water from his jug. He then scooped four heaping teaspoons of fresh ground coffee into the percolator's basket. He gave Daisy the task of finding three grapefruit-sized rocks while he worked on prepping the coffee.

She wasn't long with her job. Not far from their campsite was a small rock pile where two boulders had smashed together centuries ago. She collected three equally sized stones, carried them to their campsite, and placed them level in the hot coals. Bourbon delicately balanced the percolator and let the water begin to boil.

The knob on the percolator's lid was made of glass. As the liquid inside began to boil, it bubbled into view through the glass knob. Daisy watched the knob, fascinated by the simple process. Once the water began to change color as it percolated to the top, Bourbon checked the time—eight minutes to go.

Daisy sat on a log holding her empty coffee mug. Her mouth watered as time seemed to stand still. Waiting for coffee for eight minutes seemed like an eternity in the forest. She closed her eyes gently, trying not to forget about time.

The cool morning air woke her senses. The humidity carried a million different scents through the woods; leaves, dirt, moss, wildflowers, the nylon canvas, and possibly honey.

She scratched behind Hetzen's fuzzy ear as he lay by her feet. She watched the woodpecker search a dead tree for insects. Shards of wood dropped in a messy pile as the bird's tough bill chipped away. When the bird finally flew away, she turned her attention back to the percolator and waited anxiously. She became impatient once the aroma of brewing coffee beans and the smoky fire reached her nose. She breathed it in and wished she had a maple cream donut to savor with her fresh beverage.

Once the eight minutes expired, they enjoyed the best cup of coffee Daisy had ever had, even with the shitty powdered creamer. She relished every sip and listened to the forest come alive. There were so many unique sounds, and the sunrise cast a beautiful orange glow across the tree tops, reminding her of the desert.

They sat silently, indulging in a small second cup, neither feeling the urge to start packing and begin the day's hike.

Hetzen had become bored while waiting for the campers to start moving. He passed the time by lying on Daisy's sleeping bag, relishing the rare comfort of a soft bed. Daisy was almost finished with her coffee when Hetzen's head popped up. A whistle from the forest brought the dog to his feet, but all Daisy and Bourbon heard were the natural sounds—squirrels chattering, birds singing, frogs croaking, and a turkey gobbling from atop the hill. Hetzen stood motionless, ears perked, searching the woods to the south.

"What is it, boy?" Bourbon asked the canine.

"Think Flesti finally found us?"

"No, I don't think she'd come from that direction." Bourbon had just finished the sentence when a rumble approached, like a train with no brakes. "Another quake!"

Daisy could see the dry leaves and forest debris bounce off the ground, and then she felt the log she was sitting on violently shake her. She jumped to her feet, spilling the last few swallows of her beverage.

*Dammit!*

The shaking didn't last more than six seconds as the shock wave moved past them and toward Cain Lake.

They heard a loud crack from the top of the hill as their world shook. A 300-pound boulder rolled and bounced down the slope until it smashed into the rotting tree where the woodpecker had been working.

Rocks of all sizes followed the big one. They bounced and rolled, stirring up the leaves and dirt and creating a wave of dust.

Daisy slid behind a tall maple tree, using it as a shield to protect her ankles from the rolling rocks. She coughed and choked as the dirty air assaulted her lungs. A few more loose stones rolled into the flat campsite and settled once they lost momentum. She turned to ensure Bourbon was safe, surprised that the former sheriff hadn't moved a muscle. He stared up the hill, watching the falling debris, intrepid in the moment, as Hetzen took refuge behind him.

When the earth settled and the last stone came to rest, Daisy came out from behind the tree.

"You okay, kid?" Bourbon asked. A sly smile was on his face as if the earthquake had awakened something primitive in the fifty-three-year-old. His eyes were wide from a splurge of adrenaline coursing through his veins.

"Jesus, that was scary as hell. That's two quakes in the last ten hours," Daisy said.

"When there's one, there are usually a few more to follow. Mother Earth must be settling in her old age." He took the last sip of his coffee and spat some grounds out. "We'd better pack up camp in case there are any more loose boulders up that hill. We're sitting ducks here." He began taking down the tarp that had provided temporary shelter. His calloused fingers worked a stubborn knot tied in the front. He worked his way toward the back, working the rope free and pulling stakes.

"Can't we just sit and wait for Flesti in another area, Bourbon? She's got to be looking for her dog, right? We'll just keep him with us, maybe holler her name every few minutes until she hears us."

"We'll run out of supplies by tomorrow night. We've got one chance to find Flesti. The odds are against us. We'll hike as far as Shiner's Brook, then we'll need to turn back. The only way we'll find her is if we get lucky. There's a lot of land around this lake. Flesti could be six miles from here."

"I'd prefer to just camp by the lake and wait. She'll be looking for Hetzen."

"Where's the adventure in that?"

"I'm not looking for adventure. I'm looking for a story."

"Well, princess, when you want something, you gotta go after it. You gotta chase the story because the story isn't going to chase you."

She knew he was right, so she brushed the dirt off her arms and legs and rolled up her sleeping bag. Her legs felt heavy, and her pessimism weighed her down. But she needed to endure. "Which way do we need to go?"

"If we're lucky, we can follow our new guide," Bourbon nodded toward Hetzen, who was staring at him with wide eyes and perked ears. "What do you think, boy? Can you take us to your master?" Hetzen went to his side, rubbed his face against Bourbon's thigh, and sat down. He then stared into the trees, tilting his head in curiosity.

"What is it, boy?" Bourbon turned around and saw nothing. He squinted, scanning the tree line, then saw movement higher up. A black shape perched on a tree limb, still and stealthy. When it finally moved, it dropped to a lower limb and then took flight. It disappeared into the trees for a moment. It flew twenty feet over their heads when it reappeared, traveling northeast.

Bourbon watched the bird carefully. *There you are, you little fucker.*

Bourbon and Hetzen watched Poe disappear through the forest, knowing that was the direction they needed to travel. Bourbon didn't mention the bird to Daisy, and she hadn't noticed its presence.

When she finished packing, Daisy threw her backpack over her shoulders—Greenie the Meanie dangled from the side—and she gave Hetzen a pat on the head. "So, which way should we go?"

Bourbon pointed in the direction Poe flew, "That way. I'm sure Flesti is close."

They began their hike, traversing along the base of a short cliff made of eons-old granite rock. They scuffled over logs and around boulders.

Daisy followed Bourbon.

Bourbon followed Hetzen.

Hetzen followed Poe.

But none of them noticed the scruffy man atop the cliff, with two hatchets, who followed them all.

# 20

# DONUTS AT THE PARK

Cody woke at 5:30 am, just like most mornings. He was pissed to find Daisy had gone with Bourbon to interview Flesti. An apple-shaped magnet from the grocery store held her note on the fridge door. She said she'd return the following evening, but he knew better.

Her laptop and office supplies were still on the kitchen table, half-packed in her ragged book bag. She never went anywhere without her laptop, unless, of course, the destination was devoid of Internet access or electricity. She was headed for the south side of Cain Lake to find her interviewee.

*This fucking story is going to get you killed.*

There wasn't anything he could do about it, so he sat with his usual morning coffee on the front porch and watched the neighborhood come to life. Mr. Whitney, the neighbor across and down the street, walked by, holding a leash tethered to his spunky Shih Tzu, Barney. They seemed to disagree about the preferred cadence of their exercise, but the man with the leash seemed to have the upper hand. Mr. Whitney gave Cody a half-hearted wave out of awareness rather than geniality and kept moving without speaking.

*Good morning to you, too, miserable ass.*

Cody watched Mr. Whitney and Barney until they stopped at the next road, where Barney decided to relieve his bowels. As Mr. Whitney bent over to bag Barney's progress, a rumble echoed from the distance, followed by the ground vibrating and shaking everywhere. Cody lifted his coffee mug and relaxed his arm to absorb the earthquake's shock waves and avoid spilling his morning brew.

*Two quakes in twelve hours? Gotta be a record around here.*

Barney turned back to the house and strained against his leash, nearly dragging Mr. Whitney down the road. The old man tripped several times in his slippers but stayed on his feet. With a red face, Mr. Whitney cursed Barney out loud as he fought the little dog's determination.

Cody slipped back into the house to hide his laughter and check for any damage. At first glance, everything appeared intact. The only casualty of the tremor was a picture frame that had fallen off an uneven bookcase. He picked the eight-by-ten frame up, dropping a couple of small glass shards onto the floor. He smiled before he flipped it over, but his eyes became slightly watery when he did. He blinked away a single tear and stared at Willa's face. His former wife, murdered in cold blood, smiled back at him.

"I miss you," he whispered to the frame. She just stared back. Thanks to Jeff Bourbon, he'd received the framed print from Annabel Thompson's collection after she died. This was her favorite picture of her daughter and her husband. It was a close-up shot of them both, taken during their honeymoon to Portland, Maine. He stood behind her with his arms wrapped around her, the beach and a lighthouse behind them.

They looked like kids in the printed memory.

Cody ran his thumb over the cracked glass. He could still smell her Coppertone-tanned skin and the taste of her margarita kiss.

He placed the picture frame back on the shelf, a little further back, just in case there were any aftershocks from the earthquake. He decided to move all the pictures back as a precaution. There was a group picture of AJ, Alyse, Daisy, and him at Allison Park. Another picture leaned against the wall of him and AJ from years ago— Halloween night—they were dressed as Pirates. Another picture showed Daisy and Sammy playing in the sand at Cain Lake. The last picture on the shelf was a blurry candid photo that had been enlarged from a five-by-seven. Taken nearly twenty years ago, it was a shot of Michael and Cody on Christmas day, sitting on their new bikes in the basement, right where Santa had left them.

Everyone he loved was slowly vacating his life, whether by death or choice. He couldn't stand to lose anyone else, especially Daisy. He needed to get answers, find River Kelly, and stop the bloodshed. Hopefully, that would restore his friendship with AJ.

Alyse was gone, and there was nothing he could do about it. She made up her mind to leave. He was glad for that because he worried about her sanity. She wasn't happy in Stoneville. She needed to move on and forget this place. Start a new life and find happiness with someone else. Their love for each other could never bloom without causing a world of heartache. They'd eventually hurt each other or go their separate ways anyway, so why start a fire if it would only explode?

Daisy and Sammy were his life now. When River Kelly was found and stopped, he'd help Daisy find Flesti Thaed and get the answers she sought.

He worried he was too late to save River—the Red Devil. He shook his head at the stupid name the press had given her.

*Sounds like the goddam title of a supernatural thriller.*

*****

Cody expected Deputy Simpson to pick him up at 8 am. He was twenty-three minutes late when he pulled into the driveway.

"Sorry, buddy," Simpson apologized as his window disappeared into the truck door. "Mrs. McClesky's dog ran away after the earthquake this morning. Turns out he was sleeping in the bathroom, where it was cooler."

Cody climbed inside the truck. Simpson backed the vehicle out of the driveway and drove off toward town.

"Well, I've got good news and bad news," Simpson said. "The good news is no one died last night—that we know of. The bad news is that we have witnesses who saw you and Timmons get into a fight Saturday night. Those same witnesses also said you left on foot, walking down Redmill Road." He grimaced, knowing the information made would make his passenger feel uneasy.

"Yeah," Cody admitted, "But Daisy picked me up long before Chavez was attacked."

"I believe you, but Hassett isn't necessarily buying your alibi. She wants me to keep an eye on you."

"She's got it in for me. Not sure why, but she does."

"It's simple. Because you're an ex-con," Simpson admitted. "An ex-con with a knack for showing up whenever the shitter explodes. I think you're just cursed, and hope that shit doesn't rub off on me. Anyway, you might ask Daisy to call the sheriff on your behalf."

Cody wasn't sure if Simpson's remark was a compliment or an insult, but he pondered that it might be true. They rode in silence for a few minutes, contemplating their strategy to find River Kelly and stop the killings.

"So," Simpson spoke again, "What's our strategy for today? Or do we have one?" The seasoned cop was at a loss for ideas.

"Actually, I have an idea. Take a right up here and head toward Allison Park."

*****

After a quick detour to Mountain Mart and for two coffees and a box of donuts, Cody and Deputy Simpson pulled into Allison Park. It was still early and the park was empty. The park's lifeguards wouldn't arrive for another ninety minutes to begin doing whatever lifeguards do. The beach would open for summer swim lessons in a couple of hours.

Simpson chewed on a glazed donut as he shifted the Tahoe's transmission into park. He spoke with a full cheek, uncertain of Cody's plan, "You sure you want to do this? What am I supposed to do if something bad happens?" He peeked at his phone, "I don't have any phone service when I'm this close to the lake."

"I'll be fine." Cody pushed the door open and escaped the vehicle carrying nothing but a beach towel Simpson kept in the back of his Tahoe.

They marched from the little gravel parking lot through a row of sparse cedars and onto the gritty beach. The water was calm, not a single boat disturbed the peace. Cody untied his boots and carried them to the water. The cool sand felt good on his tired feet.

Apprehension kept Simpson off the beach. He stayed in the safety and shade of the cedar trees. He held the donut box and a pastry in one hand.

The gentle waves, barely discernible, tickled Cody's toes. He dug them into the sand and stared into the shallows where two dozen minnows schooled together for safety. The little fish darted out and then back again, unsure if the danger on shore was worse than the perils of swimming into the deep. The three-inch fish opted to travel parallel to the shoreline, huddled together for safety, waiting for the human to leave. Cody looked for signs of the blue micropods but saw nothing. The little blue lights had been scarce lately.

He pulled his shirt over his head and dropped it onto the spread out towel. Within seconds, all his clothes were in a messy pile on the beach. His muscles rippled in the morning sun as he hesitated to plunge into the cool lake water. He took small steps, building his courage with each. He was uncertain whether his hesitation had manifested from the water temperature or if he was just nervous about having a psychic vision.

*Oh, this is stupid. This is stupid. Fuck it's cold.*

Deputy Simpson, armed with his donuts, watched the naked man wade into the water up to his knees. He was about to bite into an éclair when he stopped himself, put the six-inch pastry back in the box, and selected a donut with a hole.

Cody kept working his body deeper until he was up to his hips, then dove under the surface. The cold water took his breath momentarily, and he could feel every muscle tense from the stimulation. He popped his head above water and exhaled with force, and sucked fresh air in. His breaths were short and fast, and his body was rigid. He kept his arms close to his ribs to trap heat.

It took mental focus to slow his breathing. He forced himself to relax, kept his body submerged, and accepted the cold. After a few minutes, he felt a sense of refreshment and began to acclimate to the lake's temperature, which was somewhere in the mid-sixties, he guessed. He moved toward the beach and stood in water just above his crotch.

Five micropods appeared before him. They were sluggish and dim compared to their previous state. Cody put his left hand just over the surface of the water. His hand hovered there, and the micropods grouped under his palm. He moved his hand to the left—they followed. He moved his hand to the right. Again, the micropods seemed to obey or mimic his movement.

He felt like a composer, conducting a little symphony of light.

The light of one of the micropods flickered and then went completely out. There was no body or evidence that the little creature ever existed. Then, the remaining four flickered and began moving toward the center of Cain Lake.

Simpson yelled from the cedars, "Everything okay?"

Cody gave him a thumbs-up, plugged his nose, and fell backward into the water. He was only in three feet of water but sank until his ass hit the sandy bottom. His eyes were closed, and his mind was calm. And then he was somewhere else.

He was standing in a dark room with no walls. He'd been here before.

"The shadow in the woods is the woman from the lake," a small voice informed Cody.

Cody turned around to see Roshan Kapoor standing with a smile on his young face.

"Ro! Roshan, I need your help. I'm trying to find the lady who's been hurting people."

"River. Yes, I heard you tell my mother. You're looking for the Red Devil."

"I prefer not to call her that, but yes. Yes, I need to find her before anyone else gets hurt." Cody was talking fast, unsure how much time he would have with the young clairvoyant. "Can you help me?"

"I have only seen quick flashes of River. My sight is hazy. The lake is weak. If it isn't restored soon, I will not be able to help you."

"I know," Cody acknowledged. "My...powers," he hated to use that word when he felt so powerless, "My powers are weak too."

"I do know this: the Red Devil is only the puppet. Flesti is the puppeteer pulling the strings."

"That's what I suspected."

"Flesti is using her weapon as a means of control."

"The knife?"

Roshan nodded. "They call it the Azure Blade."

"They?"

"The Cain family. Whoever yields the blade will be her most powerful sin eater. Possessing the blade will bring out your darkest fears and drive you mad with revenge or hate. Since Flesti can control the Azure Blade and people, she can have them kill for her and collect the sins of the victims. Even you could not resist her."

Cody's mind flashed backward, to the day he closed the garage door on his parents. It had been Flesti who made him do it. He wanted revenge on her. And he would like nothing more than to gut Levi Thompson with the blade for killing his brother Michael.

"You have two options," Roshan warned. "You can take the knife from River and risk being the next sin eater, or you can kill the puppeteer.

"Is that the only way to stop her? To kill her?" Cody asked. His voice was almost a whisper as he contemplated the notion.

"Someone needs to," Roshan said coldly. "It's the only way to end this. She grows weaker, too. But she'll be unstoppable once she has the knife with all the sins it has collected. She'll be able to control everyone who's been poisoned by Cain Lake."

"Thank you, Roshan."

Roshan smiled with pride. His image became translucent, as if he were made of thin paper.

"Wait!" Cody panicked. "Ro, the last time we spoke, you tore the picture of Daisy and me. You tore me out of her life. Why?"

Roshan put both hands together. When he pulled them apart, he was holding half of the picture. "You misunderstood, Mr. Cody. I did not rip you from the picture—I ripped her away."

Cody looked at the half picture. It was only the side of him, alone.

"What happens to Daisy?"

Roshan became a colorless cloud.

"What happens to Daisy, Roshan? Is she in danger? Roshan!"

The boy was out of time and disappeared.

Cody burst to the surface of Cain Lake—back to the real world. He gasped for oxygen and turned toward the beach.

Simpson stood just feet away, his boots nearly in the water. "Are you okay, Savage? Jesus Christ, I was getting a little scared there, buddy."

Cody's breathing was heavy as he crawled through the water. His knees hit the sand. "Yeah, yeah, I'm okay, Simpson." He wiped a watery streak of blood from his top lip.

"What the hell happened? Did you see something?"

Cody pushed himself to his knees, "Yeah, I saw something, and I know exactly what I need to do. If we don't stop River Kelly and find Flesti, something horrible will happen to Daisy."

# 21
# WATCH YOUR STEP

Daisy struggled to pull herself up a short hill littered with dead leaves and small rocks. Her tennis shoes were slipping with each step on the steep incline. The lack of traction doubled her effort to ascend the terrain. She huffed in frustration as she watched Bourbon climb like a goat. Aggressive boot treads provided him sure footing, and his ankles stayed straight under his weight.

"Should have worn boots," Bourbon gently admonished. "We're almost to flat ground. Use the trees to pull yourself up the hill, then step behind the tree. It will hold you in place."

"I didn't know I'd be climbing Mt. Everest this weekend."

Bourbon hid a smirk. "You can do this."

She stepped up, pulled, slid, and cursed until she finally reached Bourbon. The burning in her calves and thighs subsided a few degrees as she rested. Sweat on her forehead and nose glistened in the morning light, and her breathing was shallow.

She was glad to see the ground was flat for the next quarter-mile. "Can we rest for a bit? I need a snack and some water." She pulled off a shoe, shook it, and dumped the dead leaves and sticks that had infiltrated her footwear.

"We can, but Hetzen and Poe will probably go on without us. Up to you."

Daisy nodded, "Okay, let's go a little further. I can endure a little longer." She cleaned out her other shoe. "I'm out of water anyway."

"There's a natural spring somewhere in this area. I'm sure we'll find it. If not, I can spare some." Bourbon took a sip of his water and passed it to her. She wanted to gulp the entire container, but remembered her manners.

"Thanks," She took a timid gulp and returned the container to him.

Their guide, Poe, cawed in a tree above them. He seemed to be waiting, but Bourbon knew his patience would soon wane. Hetzen was nowhere in sight, but they heard him from time to time, nose to the ground, searching ahead for Flesti's scent.

While Daisy fixed the hair tie that kept her black locks from falling in her face, Bourbon scoured a bush and came out with a handful of blackberries. He presented them to Daisy with a smile.

"Oh, my God, those look delicious." She held her hand flat as Bourbon dumped them into her palm. Her mouth salivated at the anticipated taste of the ripe berries. She popped all ten of them into her mouth and enjoyed the sweet juice they produced. "Where did you find these?" She asked with purple-stained teeth.

Bourbon was already moving back to the area of the treasure. "Over here. You've got to look low for the good ones." He picked the wild berries and dropped them into a gallon-sized plastic bag with a zipper.

Daisy began picking from the bottom for the biggest and juiciest berries. She put several in the bag and several in her mouth. She could feel the fructose restore her energy.

"Ow! Fuck." She stuck a bleeding thumb in her mouth. "Why do they have so many friggin thorns?" The sharp, curved thorns of the berry bush grabbed and tore the skin on her forearms. She kept pulling her snack off the bush and received a scratch every time she reached low. She popped a couple more in her mouth. Her salivary glands tingled with pleasure. The pain was worth the reward, and in some way, she started to enjoy it. Nature was kind enough to nourish her, but she would have to trade a little blood for the gift. It was a small price to pay, but it seemed fair.

They worked their way around the thorny green bushes, picking and snacking, laughing and joking, playfully throwing the occasional rotten berry at each other. Once they'd filled their bellies,

Daisy felt renewed. She was charged and ready to take on the day, even though she knew the energy from the sweet fruit would be short-lived. But now they had a half-gallon of food to carry when their bodies needed the nourishment.

Bourbon stopped picking and zipped the bag. He put one finger to his lips and tilted his head so his ear could pick up any sound from the woods. He held his breath and listened intently.

"What is it?" Daisy whispered.

"Water."

Daisy listened. Her ears picked up the noise that had caught Bourbon's attention. It was the slight babbling sound created by a freshwater spring. They moved ten yards, listened, and adjusted their direction. Another ten yards, they turned uphill. Daisy could clearly hear the water flowing just below the ground's surface. They came upon a hole in the ground the size of a dining room table with six inches of cool, clear liquid seeping from the exposed granite bedrock. Smooth, clean sand lined the bottom.

The water trickled off a small lip of stone, just fast enough to make a sound and form a tiny cascade. The waterhole was draining and refilling at the same rate—three gallons per hour.

Bourbon smiled in delight.

"Can we drink it?" Daisy asked.

"Sure," he replied. "This water's been filtered by the land for years. You'll probably never drink anything this pure again. Let's refill our water bottles."

He removed the top of his clear plastic water bottle, placed a cloth handkerchief over the end, and let the water slowly fill the thirty-two-ounce container. The handkerchief filtered any debris— leaves, bugs, and pollen. Daisy imitated his actions, utilizing a spare sports bra as her filter.

"It's cold," she said.

Once they finished filling the bottles, they splashed their bodies, enjoying the cool sensation and feeling refreshed.

Bourbon popped the top off his water bottle, tipped his head back, and took a big drink.

"Holy shit!" Daisy exclaimed.

"What?"

"Your water bottle; look at it."

Bourbon inspected the bottle and its contents. "What are you talking about? I don't see anything."

She held out her hand to request the bottle. He placed it in her berry-stained fingers. She stepped forward. She was close enough to Bourbon that nothing bigger than his water bottle could fit between them. She blocked as much sunlight as possible from hitting the liquid. When she turned the clear plastic bottle upside down, they both saw it. Several little micropods glowed blue from within the container's contents.

Daisy moved closer to the bottle until her nose nearly touched its side. "Where the hell did you guys come from?"

"They must be coming from uphill," he said, pointing to a cliff in the distance with an altitude nearly one hundred feet greater than theirs, "From somewhere in the cliff."

"Should we go check it out?"

"Hell yes, we should go check it out."

They stashed the water bottle in Bourbon's backpack and began climbing the hill. Daisy's legs burned with each step, but now her curiosity carried her up the incline like an escalator. She was sure they would find more water and more micropods. What a story this would make for the Stoneville View. She thought about the headline, "Local Reporter Discovers Ancient Species in the Mountains." Her breathing was fast as she passed Bourbon on the slope. "Local Reporter Discovers Mountain's Secret." She slipped in her sneakers and nearly tumbled backward—"Local Reporter Falls to Her Death."

Bourbon passed Daisy back as she regained her footing. They came upon a boulder as long as a yacht and nearly as tall. It looked like it had broken from the cliff long before Stoneville had a name and rolled downhill until it settled in its position. The top was smooth from erosion, and the obstacle was split in half. The two halves were three feet apart—just enough room for a man to walk through. From the sky, it would have looked like a broken ship.

A tiny spring water moat formed along the broken ship's side. The water was trapped until the moat overflowed, and gravity pulled it toward Cain Lake. Bourbon studied the liquid and followed its path through the crack. The ground was muddy here, saturated by spring water that never stopped flowing, so Daisy opted to navigate around the rock.

Bourbon stepped slowly through the opening in the rock, staring at the ground and studying the water as he moved. He looked around at the mossy surface of the boulder and felt as though the rock was closing in on him. He could feel his chest tighten, his breathing grew shallow, and his skin became clammy. Claustrophobia had set in. It was the same sensation he experienced in crowded elevators and public buses. He hated tight spaces and wanted out of the situation.

He covered the last ten feet of the opening in three significant strides. A fallen tree blocked the end of the alley—nothing he couldn't manage to step over. He turned and sat on the waist-high log, spun on his left buttock, and threw his left leg to the ground on the opposite side.

The ground appeared to leap at him, leaves shooting upward, and Bourbon was sure a timber rattlesnake had struck him with its sharp fangs. Extreme pressure clamped down on his foot with a cracking sound. "Mother—" He began to curse, but winced in pain instead. Something held his foot, and he was sure it was bigger than a snake.

He brought his right foot over the log and discovered the truth. The source of his pain and agony was a rusty bear trap, its jaws biting onto his foot like a pit bull. The trap's teeth had punctured his Timberland boots, but no blood was escaping.

Daisy heard Bourbon's yell and scurried along the upper side of the boulder until she reached her trapped guide. "What the hell happened?"

"Argh," Bourbon yelled as he stood. "Goddammit. Someone left a fucking bear trap at the end of this opening." He seethed through clenched teeth, breathing hard from the agony he was in.

Daisy fell to her knees and tried to yank the thick steel jaws apart, but they wouldn't budge. "What can I do? It won't come off."

The bear trap had a strong spring on each side, like wings folded back on themselves. Both springs needed to be compressed simultaneously to open the trap and release his foot.

"Stand on each side—the springs—you gotta—argh—you gotta stand on the springs."

Daisy put her right foot on one spring, balanced while she held Bourbon's shoulder, and stepped on the opposite spring with her left foot. The jaws released slightly, but not enough for Bourbon to escape.

"It's not working," she panicked. She stepped off, and the trap's springs regained their tight grip.

"Dammit," Bourbon cursed through gritted teeth, "You're not heavy enough. Try again. I'll add my weight." He placed his hands on her shoulders as she stepped back onto the springs. Then he put his weight on her.

The jaws opened an inch wider. It was just enough for Bourbon to slide his foot free. He leaned to the right and fell to his knees, leaving Daisy balancing on the steel trap.

She stared at the menacing device, which reminded her of the gaping mouth of a jack-o-lantern. She was trying not to lose her balance and get chomped by the ominous contraption. She hopped up and backward with both feet, and the jaws slammed shut with a loud metallic snap.

Bourbon removed his boot and sock, checking the damage. The top of his foot was already swelling, pushing a black-and-blue color scheme to the skin's surface. Some skin was missing, a thin red abrasion contoured around the top of his foot. Blood rose to the surface, but did not run down his foot. "Got lucky, I think."

"You call this lucky. It broke your damn foot."

"Just one bone, I think. My boots saved my ass. Another inch higher, and I'd be dealing with a broken ankle. I think its rusty condition weakened its power—a little, anyway."

"Why the hell is there a bear trap here? Who would do that?" Daisy was talking fast, "Is this thing even legal?"

"Yes, but not this time of year," he said, slipping his boot back on. "Come on, let's keep moving before it swells too much. And, Daisy..."

She helped Bourbon to his feet.

"Watch your step."

# 22
# GETAWAY ESTATES 

T he what blade?" Deputy Simpson asked.

"The Azure Blade," Cody answered. He explained what Roshan had told him in his vision. Simpson found the information hard to swallow, but nothing in Stoneville was making sense lately.

Simpson's phone sang a custom ringtone. He accepted the call and hit the device's speaker button. "Yeah, boss?"

"Simpson, how far are you from Mayfield Court?" Sheriff Hassett inquired.

"Fifteen minutes. Maybe twenty."

"We've got an eyewitness who saw a suspicious female crossing the bridge on Woodruff. Black hoodie and blue jeans. Said she was heading east. I'm not sure what's out there. Looking at the map, I can only identify Mayfield Court."

Simpson scratched the top of his thin hair. "Sounds like she might be heading to Getaway Estates. That'd be my guess."

There was brief silence on the other end of the line as Hassett studied her map. "Well, get your ass over there and find her. It might be our girl."

Simpson disconnected the call and dropped his phone in the center console of his SUV.

"Mayfield Court?" Cody asked. "Where's that?"

"The trailer park on the east side of town. Popular residency for meth-heads, ex-cons, drug dealers, and, of course, little old ladies with no retirement."

"Sounds like an interesting mix."

"If River Kelly is going after sinners...that's a good place to find them."

Simpson turned the steering wheel of the Tahoe and made a U-turn. The truck lights flashed, but he kept the sirens off to approach in silence. They zig-zagged across town, past the businesses, suburbs, and one farm. They took a shortcut through Doug Bentley's freshly mowed hayfield and stayed on the private road on the edge of the field. Bentley used the road to access his fields with his tractors to mow hay and haul cut wood. Simpson was friends with the farmer and hunted the land on occasion, so he knew he wouldn't mind.

When they exited the field, they turned left and drove along a barbed wire fence that seemed to hold nothing back but hundreds of acres of tall grass. Four enormous oak trees—probably in their fourth century—were the only tall flora growing on the property.

Simpson killed the emergency lights and slowed the vehicle to a crawl. The grass in the field, five feet tall, hadn't been mowed all season and easily concealed the SUV's approach.

The highway department had recently mowed the roadsides in both directions, leaving a clean swath on both shoulders of the pavement. From the passenger-side window, Cody watched the wooden fence posts zip past.

Deputy Simpson brought the SUV to a gentle stop at the edge of the property, sixty yards from the entrance of Getaway Estates. The rectangular homes appeared ahead, little manufactured boxes in various colors and styles. It was difficult to see through the meadow's wild grass and brush, but it was evident that some of the residents had been there for decades. Automobiles were parked on the edge of the field, tires flat, windows broken, and rust and mildew rotting them from within. Outdoor furniture was turned on its side, with broken plastic and bent metal, showing no intention of repair. Clotheslines did their duty, holding damp baby clothes and work overalls in the wind, hoping for a steady summer breeze. Various toys were scattered throughout the yards, alongside plastic pools, slides, and bicycles.

"I'm not sure how we're supposed to find a suspicious female here," Simpson admitted. "There's probably more than one."

"Yeah, but how many of them are beautiful redheads?" Simpson agreed.

They approached a green street sign that read "Mayfield CT" mounted to a metal post. The post was tipped fifteen degrees from straight. Ten feet beyond the road sign was a stop sign perforated with bullet holes. Hidden in the tall grass, another monument sign of faux brick and carved letters read, "GETAWAY ESTATES."

The rubber tires took on a new sound as they rolled from the pavement to the gravel path. The rough texture of the gravel road vibrated the SUV, and the vehicle rocked from side to side as it dropped into and out of potholes.

Mayfield Court was a narrow street, barely two lanes wide. Cody's attention was instantly drawn to the second trailer on the left, burned black with a caved-in roof and all the windows gone. Yellow tape with a "CAUTION" pattern lined the perimeter.

"We'll never find her in here," Simpson said. There are about fifty trailers in this lot. If she went inside any of them, she'd see us before we saw her."

"Can we find out if any Road Barons are living here? Or any ex-cons? Someone who might qualify as a sinner in River's eyes."

"Hmm, not sure. Let me make a phone call to Marissa at the office. Maybe she can give us an idea." Simpson dialed his office and spoke to Marissa, the clerk, who said she'd do some digging and call back.

They waited. Simpson parked the SUV in the shade near lot three.

Cody watched as the blinds in the windows of some homes separated, curious residents watching the police vehicle. He looked to the trailer on his right, where a tan and white boxer challenged him to a staring contest. The dog won.

Ten minutes later, Simpson's phone rang. Simpson spoke and nodded at the same time, then hung up. "Lots 33, 42, and 51. Three homes with ex-cons and an accused pedophile out on bail awaiting his trial date. I guess we'll just work our way up."

The police cruiser crawled down the gravel road, weaved around parked cars, and dodged potholes. They made it to their first trailer of interest—lot thirty-three. Both men stepped out and approached the home. It appeared vacant, with tall grass and dirty windows, but a sweet old face appeared in the doorway before Simpson could knock on the door.

A woman in her seventies greeted her guests with a hearty smile. She wore a flower apron over a yellow sundress. Her hair, still dark despite her age, was pulled back and knotted in a bun while a pair of reading glasses rested on her head.

A black cat scooted between her feet, escaping through the half-open door, and ran through a hole in the trailer's skirting.

Cody could smell the aroma of cinnamon and nutmeg escaping the house. He imagined homemade cinnamon rolls on a cookie sheet with icing melting down the sides. It reminded him of his mother and brother. Michael and he used to fight for the first fresh roll when they arrived home from school. Ms. Savage always made cinnamon rolls on the first day of school.

The woman invited them inside, but they declined her offer graciously. Simpson told her he was merely checking the area to be sure everyone was safe. She seemed disappointed, upset that they wouldn't stay and visit for a while.

They moved on to the next trailer on their list. Lot 42 looked like a new home, with fresh dirt marks where the utilities had been connected and a sheet of paper taped to the window. Cody could only see the word "PERMIT" printed in a large font. A single vehicle was parked in the short driveway under a metal carport. The car was a silver Mercedes that should have stuck out like a Rolex on a homeless person. Still, many of the driveways on Mayfield Court were occupied with luxury vehicles and expensive trucks—low rent, large vehicle payments.

Deputy Simpson climbed the wooden steps that led to a covered, screened porch. The porch's door was wide open and propped with a gallon water jug.

Drops of blood formed a trail from the home's door, across the porch, and down the stairs. Simpson snapped his fingers to grab

Cody's attention and pointed to the blood. He drew his 10mm pistol and let it lead the way to the door. He knocked on the wall.

"Stoneville Sheriff's Department. Anybody home?"

No answer.

Simpson tried again. Still, there was no response. He followed the gun through the doorway and announced his entry. He swept the pistol from side to side, watching for danger over the front gun sight. He didn't have to go far before he found what he feared. A man in his mid-thirties was propped on the couch, wearing a white tank top and blue jeans. His dark skin had turned gray. A pistol—a Colt .45 with a nickel finish—lay in his lap. Even Death couldn't release the grip he had on the weapon. His head was slumped down, his chin resting on his collarbone. The victim must have known he was about to die, so he sat on the couch and waited for the darkness to take him.

The dead man's white tank top had turned dark red in a streak down the front. An oblong vertical hole existed just under his sternum. The weapon that caused the damage must have punctured his liver, stomach, and possibly his diaphragm. A second hole was evident about four inches below his belt line. Similar stains ran down his pant legs.

Another man lay face down in the hallway that led to the back bedroom. The officer knelt to assess the damage. This victim was unarmed, and his wounds were nearly identical to the first. Simpson stepped over the body, kept his arms forward, and steered his Sig Sauer 10mm down the hall. The bathroom and bedroom were clear of people. He stopped beside the bed. It was stripped of all bedding—no sheets, blankets, or pillows. Two ropes were tied to the headboard. They had been freshly cut with a sharp blade, which left red-stained ends.

"River, what did you find here?" Simpson asked quietly.

The trailer's back door was wide open, leading to the yard. Whoever River had freed from captivity must have exited in haste.

Simpson stepped through the open door and down a set of wooden steps. He was glad to exit the home, ripe with the stench of death, and welcomed the fresh air with a robust inhale. He crossed the backyard, staying along the side of the trailer, and ducked under an empty clothesline. The overgrown grass in the adjacent field caught his attention. His breaths were deep as his heart rate began to spike. And then he saw the tall grass move, pushed by some force he could not see.

"Stoneville Sheriff's Department. Come out of there with your hands up!"

The grass wavered, moving to the left and back to the right. He was sure it was the person freed from the trailer, hiding in the thick curtain of green.

Simpson stepped closer. Three crows burst from the grass, swooped toward the deputy, and landed on a low power line. They stayed perched, watching the man with the pistol.

Simpson breathed a sigh of relief, believing the birds had caused the movement until the grass moved once more. This time, he heard several footfalls. He took one more step and repeated his last command. He saw glimpses of black—too big to be a crow—moving through the bright, contrasting color of the grass. He moved side to side, keeping the gun's front sight lined up with the shadow.

Simpson barely had time to react. The Azure Blade was hurled toward him like an arrow shot from a bow. The blade, thrown from the cover of the field, sliced his thigh just above the knee. He felt the sting, but adrenaline forced him to stand his ground. Police training forced him to fire.

He shot once, twice, three times. By the time he fired his last shot, something zipped past his ear from behind. He spun around, expecting to see a second assailant, but no one was there. Then he felt the burning sensation at the top of his ear and knew he was cut.

He turned back to the grass. Again, the Azure Blade spun toward him, missed his neck, stopped in mid-flight just past his head, and retraced its path back to the grass.

Simpson was prepared to fire in the same direction. His assault was stopped when Cody pushed the pistol straight up.

"Simpson! Don't shoot! Don't kill her."

Simpson elbowed Cody out of his way. "Step aside, Savage, she's trying to kill us."

Cody stumbled backward. His feet hit the edge of a sandbox full of plastic cars and trucks. He spun to regain his balance. The edge of the sandbox blocked his feet. He went down, landing with a splash of gritty white sand on his face. The grit entered his eyes and mouth.

The blade flew from the grass ten feet from where it had entered. It spun toward Simpson, put a small cut in his left forearm, and returned to its owner.

"How the fu—" Simpson fired two more shots. He felt warm blood running down to his elbow. He side-stepped to the right and dropped to one knee, trying to focus on the subtle movements in the grass. He shouted at his attacker: "River Kelly, this is your last warning. Come out with your hands where I can see them, or I will continue to fire upon you."

He had ten rounds left in the pistol's magazine and was prepared to fire every single one. He didn't want to shoot. He'd never shot anyone in the line of duty. But, he'd seen what River Kelly had done inside the trailer. He knew what she was capable of. Dale Kelly was his friend and colleague, who'd never forgive him for killing his daughter, even in self-defense. He pointed the pistol low, hoping to hit an ankle or knee.

Cody struggled to his knees and attempted to rub the dirt from his vision.

The Azure Blade blew through the grass at high speed, spinning like a boomerang. Simpson fired simultaneously in the direction of the grass. His focus was so intense that he never realized that the Azure Blade flew just below his pistol and headed straight toward his chest.

Simpson's gun fell silent. He realized his mistake too late. He closed his eyes—arms still outstretched in a shooting position—and waited to feel his heart explode from the six-inch blade that had already killed twice today.

The pain never came. The impact didn't happen. He opened one eye. The Azure Blade hovered in place, one inch from his chest. The blade vibrated and glowed with an intense blue light. It moved closer, half an inch away. Then closer, until Simpson could feel it pressing against his skin. Scared to make a sudden move, he looked to Cody for an answer.

Cody was leaning forward in the sandbox, his left arm outstretched toward the hapless deputy. His hand resembled the color and brightness of the Azure Blade. His fingers were tense and shook from immense effort as they reached for the knife eight feet away.

Simpson realized that the only thing keeping the knife from piercing his heart was his temporary sidekick. Cody let out a guttural yell, defying the will of the blade and its master, determined to keep Deputy Simpson from certain death.

The knife yielded, forfeiting its aggression. The light emitting from within the stone weapon diminished, and the vibration stopped. It spun back to the grassy field, disappeared in the overgrown stalks of grass and weeds, and never returned.

Cody collapsed, half in the sandbox and half in the green grass of the lawn. A small drop of blood ran from his nose and down his top lip as he crawled out of the sand trap. He gently rubbed his eyes and spat sand from his teeth.

Simpson was sitting on the ground with his knees up, "How...how, the fuck did you do that?"

Cody held a hand toward Simpson, "I don't know. I just...I just reacted."

"Good fuckin' thing. Holy shit," Simpson was breathing hard from the excitement. "She was going to kill me."

"Not at first. She was toying with you. Her aim was perfect. She wanted to scare you away, but you became a threat. She's only killing sinners. Or, should I say, Flesti's only making her kill sinners?"

"Yeah, well, she damn near did. She's out of control now."

Across the field and down the road, they heard a motorcycle start and race away.

"Sounds like she just stole a motorcycle. Gonna be hard to catch her now." Simpson stared at Cody's left hand, noticing the skin had returned to normal. "Well, at least we know we have a secret weapon to stop her. Think you can do that again?"

Cody flexed his fingers, "I don't know. It took all my strength and energy. But if it will stop her from collecting sins for Flesti and save Daisy, I'll die trying if I have to."

# 23

# THE WALL

Daisy reached forward with the five-foot-long walking stick. Bourbon had cut a small ash tree and made her carry it to probe in front of her for more bear traps. She led the way, poking the ground in front, keeping a keen eye toward the forest floor to spot unnatural mounds in the leaves. Every time her stick hit the ground, he flinched with nervous anticipation.

Every step was slow and deliberate, but they were determined to get to the cliff. She put her hand back toward Bourbon in a gesture to stop. He heeded her command, then watched her stick the thick ash stick into the leaves like she was spearing a fish. Rusty teeth sprang from underneath the thick leaf carpet and clamped onto the wooden probe. Her heart jumped from the steel trap's attack. She turned and gave Bourbon a concerning look.

"Somebody's gone through a lot of trouble to protect what ever's up here."

The twosome had been following a trickle of water that originated from the cliff ahead. They were almost to their destination now. A chill ran up Daisy's spine, knowing the ground was littered with steel deterrents.

The dry leaves were noisy under the hikers' steps, and the high sun created strong shadows in the forest. The woods at this elevation were eerily calm and silent, in contrast to the natural sounds that filled the air that morning.

She broke the silence with small talk, gasping for oxygen between sentences. "How's the foot?"

"Fine."

"I haven't seen that stupid bird in a while, have you?" She stopped to rest.

"Nope."

"The dog, either. What was his name again? Hudson?"

"Hetzen. I think it's German for dog."

"Hetzen," she repeated, trying to brand the name to her brain. "He's a good dog. I hope he stays away from these traps. Reminds me of a dog that used to live on the streets in Arizona. His name…Well, I don't know what his name was, really…but we called him *Ocho*."

"*Ocho*?"

"Yeah. He'd appear every morning at 8 am and every night at 8 pm, begging for breakfast and dinner. She giggled at the memory.

Bourbon winced in pain.

"Should we turn back?"

"No," he sighed, "I'll be fine. I'm curious about why these traps are here. What's so important about this hill? They have this whole area booby-trapped. The cliff creates a natural funnel, forcing any bush-whacking hiker through here. Hard to avoid the traps."

Daisy pointed to a mound of leaves as they resumed their ascent. They could recognize the traps now without having to set them off, but they did anyway to avoid anyone else getting injured and to make their retreat safer.

They continued climbing for another twenty yards and stopped just feet from the cliff.

"Well, end of the line, I guess," she said.

"Yeah, I guess, but something—"

"Wait!" Daisy set her backpack on the ground and leaned it against a small boulder to keep it from rolling back down the hill. "There's a little opening. Over there"

Fifteen feet from where they stood, a large stone slab had broken away from the cliff's side. It was the size and shape of a car door. Looking at the cliff straight on, it would have been impossible to tell there was an opening behind it—a cave. The leaves on the ground were packed and crushed, forming a narrow trail that led to the cave's entrance.

Bourbon hobbled to the monument, "Might have broken off during the earthquakes."

"It looks like it was there on purpose—hiding that hole. What do you think it is?"

Bourbon shrugged, "Maybe a bear cave."

"What do you think is inside?"

"Uh, bears."

"If a bear lived in there, wouldn't it have been caught in one of these traps?"

Bourbon scratched his beard, examining all the little pieces of rock that had broken off and rolled down the hill. "Well, the cliff must have an intricate system of caves that collect rainwater. That's where this little stream is coming from. Now we know."

She asked for his flashlight.

"You're not going in there, are you?"

"I need the details, Bourbon. I need to take a peek at least. Are you coming?"

"Oh, hell no. If there's one thing I hate in this world, it's small spaces."

"Are you claustrophobic?"

"Nope. I just get nervous in confined spaces."

Daisy rolled her eyes. "I'll check it out." She squatted at the cave entrance, retrieved her phone from her pocket, and took pictures. She checked her phone service, not surprised by what she saw. She slid the phone into her back pocket and shined the powerful flashlight into the cave, illuminating stone walls that had been dark for centuries.

The cave was narrow, and the walls came together at the top to form an inverted V-shape. Daisy guessed the opening was naturally made. There was no evidence that the tunnel had been created by human hands or mechanical means. She popped her head outside, "It's much bigger than it looks. Are you coming?"

"Nope. And neither should you. Why don't we mark our trail and come back with someone who knows how to explore caves?"

"And get all the credit for discovering it? No way."

"Daisy, please, don't go in there. What if there's another quake while you're inside, and the ceiling collapses? It's not safe."

They argued for a few minutes, contemplating everything that could go wrong, but Daisy was adamant about exploring where the water and micropods originated. She assured Bourbon that the cave was safe and promised to turn back if anything looked too dangerous to traverse. She ducked inside once more and followed her curiosity.

Bourbon watched her during the first eight feet of exploration. The cave seemed to decline as Daisy made her way further from the entrance. She turned ninety degrees to the left and vanished. Bourbon could still see his flashlight reflecting back. He sat on the ground, removed his left boot to check his injury, and waited for his companion to return.

*****

Daisy explored at a snail's pace, checking every wall, studying the loose rocks, and scouting with her eyes before moving deeper. Water seeped through an occasional crack, ran across her path, and disappeared between the rocks, but the cave was mostly dry. The terrain beneath her feet was flat but sloped at a ten-degree angle, and she guessed that water had eroded and smoothed the floor eons ago.

The air was stagnant and cool. A musty odor brought back memories of her high school locker room—green scum growing on the grout between the tiles, sweaty uniforms left in lockers, and a floor that never seemed fully dry.

Bourbon shouted from the entrance to check on her.

"I'm fine," she yelled back.

She knew she was walking parallel to the face of the cliff until the tunnel turned right. The opening grew wider, although the height seemed constant. She turned back to the left and nearly dropped her flashlight in surprise. A blue glow illuminated a chamber before her, and the distinct sound of running water filled her with enthusiasm.

Her pace quickened, and she nearly fell into a twenty-inch-wide fissure. The flashlight illuminated the crack, which was twelve feet deep. The bottom of the fissure was less than the width of her foot. She would have been wedged in the space if she had fallen until Bourbon came looking for her. She easily hopped the gap, but when she landed on the other side, the distinct sound of plastic hitting rock echoed off the cave walls. She spun around just in time to watch her cell phone bouncing from one side of the crack to the other as it fell into the narrow bottom.

"Dammit!" She cursed through her teeth. She didn't want to yell too loudly and alert Bourbon. She knelt beside the opening and pointed the flashlight downward, holding it tight to ensure she didn't lose that, too. The flashlight illuminated the phone's plastic edge. It was too deep to retrieve without the proper tools and some help. She stood, brushed the dust from her knees, and accepted the phone's fate. There was nothing she could do but keep going.

The glowing chamber ahead beckoned her. She recognized that glow—that color—and was drawn to it like an insect to a porch light. The micropods in Cain Lake produced the same hue and intensity as the night they gave Cody back his hand and saved his life. She had to descend a little more, and the chamber was to the right.

When she entered the hollow space, she couldn't believe her eyes. The ceiling was higher—nearly twelve feet—and the walls were adorned with centuries-old drawings. The chamber was divided into two lower and higher levels, with a difference of six feet. Two sets of stairs carved by ancient tools ascended from the lower chamber to the upper. One staircase was to the left, the other on the opposite side. The design was reminiscent of an auditorium stage. The left steps were broken and crumbled from a chunky stone slab that had fallen at some time in history, but they were still functional with a bit of caution.

She could hear water trickling into the upper chamber like someone hadn't entirely shut off a bathtub faucet. The water, filled with blue micropods, cascaded gently over the edge that divided the chambers and flowed through a channel that cut through the middle of the lower chamber. The energized blue water entered a small pool, no larger than a kiddie pool like the one she bought for Sammy, and then formed a gentle whirlpool before disappearing through a crack.

Daisy pointed the flashlight upward, where the walls revealed a world of ancient drawings that reminded her of the petroglyphs in Arizona's parks. These renderings had a different feel from the ones she remembered as a teen. Swirls of blue and black were reminiscent of Cain Lake itself. There were depictions of trees and animals, many drawn with black or brown stains but highlighted with blue. Flocks of birds flew in the sky, and three large crows—almost as tall as she—were sketched on a far wall.

She felt herself tearing up, overcome with emotion, as she realized she was in the presence of something ancient and historic. She crumbled inside, thinking about what would happen to this sacred place if it were exposed to the rest of the world. Would it be exploited or commercialized? Would it be exposed for financial gain? Could she and Bourbon keep this a secret from the rest of the world? Was that a selfish notion?

"Bourbon!" She yelled back through the cave. "You need to see this."

She moved along the wall, focused on the art, and then stopped in the middle of the room. The center petroglyph's subject seemed to hit her in the heart. It depicted a pool of dark water with two people inside. The only red ink used in the masterpiece was drawn on their chests. The red ink swirled into the dark water and overspilled into a second pool, which was bright blue.

A female figure stood over both characters in the scene. She held a blue dagger, the tip dripping with the scarce red ink.

At that moment, everything Daisy loved about these chambers shook like the earthquake that rumbled earlier, the epicenter inside her. A revelation erupted. This was not a natural wonder admired by native residents, but a sacrificial chamber used to give Cain Lake what it desired—sins and blood. The story was right there on the wall.

She checked the hall. Bourbon was still outside. "Bourbon, can you hear me? Are you coming?"

*Fucking chicken-shit.*

She hadn't seen the pool in the upper chamber yet. Her curiosity overpowered her fear. She climbed the unbroken stairs to investigate, hoping Bourbon would work up the courage to enter the cave. Ahead, to one side, a small opening in the ceiling allowed natural light to find its way inside—the top of the cliff. The light reflected off the granite surface of the chamber, producing strong shadows that hindered her ability to see beyond the well.

The water she had heard earlier trickled through the upper cave wall and ran directly into the eight-foot-wide well. The well itself had short walls made of adobe and stone, which were obviously created by humans after its discovery. She shined her light into the abyss. Her flashlight was incapable of penetrating the depth of the water.

She circled the well, inspecting it from different angles, curious about its formation. It appeared the original well was created by water eroding the rock for millions of years. A leak in the wall allowed water to run down the side and form a small puddle. She stepped over the puddle and noticed reflective little water spots on the dry floor. She checked above her—there were no leaks. And then she realized what the puddles were.

Footprints.

Her breath escaped her. Her throat held a scream that she tried to conjure for Bourbon. She frantically spun and checked the shadows along the wall. As the light washed away the dark, a gruff-looking man stared back at her.

# 24

# TRAILER 42

Getaway Estates was living up to its name. Not only did River Kelly elude Deputy Simpson, but the owner of the maroon trailer, Kyle Jackson, had been getting away with several crimes. Seventeen-year-old Vanessa Scott had been Jackson's captive for two days—until River Kelly showed up to eliminate the sinner.

Since she was known to disappear occasionally, no one had reported Vanessa missing. Once River freed her, Vanessa ran to a neighbor's empty house and hid until Simpson and Cody arrived.

Now, Vanessa sat in a lawn chair, covered with a light blanket, as several women comforted her and waited for an ambulance to arrive. They brought her water and lent her a cell phone to call whomever she needed. No one was answering her calls.

Vanessa explained her ordeal to Simpson with a strong Dominican accent. She reminded Cody of Daisy. He wanted to leave—run to her—and find her safe at home. But he knew she wasn't there. She was following Flesti through the southern forest of Stoneville, hoping for a story, chasing a dream. His only relief was knowing that she probably wouldn't find Flesti on the south side of the lake. Flesti had to be close, somewhere in the shadows, so that she could control her new sin eater.

A kind-hearted neighbor—an elderly black woman with yellow eyes and jack-o-lantern teeth—tended to Simpson's cuts. She bored Simpson with talk about being a nurse during the Korean War and working nights at a Veterans Hospital for the thirty years that followed. She wrapped Simpson's calf and joked about how she sometimes missed the war: "Soldiers complained a lot less than civilians."

By the time Simpson was bandaged, Sheriff Hassett was kicking up dust in her Jeep Gladiator, making her way down Mayfield Court. She was followed by the ambulance that was coming to Vanessa's aid. The quiet neighborhood had become a circus as residents filed out of their homes. They stared from their lawns, paced the street, and snapped pictures and videos. Dogs barked at the commotion. Simpson and Cody could already hear the malicious gossip—how the police raided trailer 42 and shot the tenant.

"What the hell kind of mess did you two make?" Hassett barked at Cody and Simpson as she threw a pair of Ray-Ban sunglasses over her eyes. She stood over Simpson, still sitting with the resident nurse, as she finished wrapping his leg in gauze. Cody watched as she admonished the humble deputy. She appeared taller than he remembered.

They explained everything that happened: how they found the two male victims, the knife attack, and River Kelly's escape. They conveniently left out Cody's telekinetic moment when he stopped River's weapon from piercing Simpson's heart. She wouldn't know how to process that detail.

"You let a 120-pound gym teacher with a knife best the two of you—a trained deputy with a gun and Stoneville's most fearsome fighter?" She shook her head in disbelief. "Show me what we're dealing with, Simpson. Savage, wait here. Let's try to keep crime scene contamination limited."

Deputy Simpson vacated the chair, thanked his nurse, and walked Sheriff Hassett to trailer 42. They entered through the back door.

The trailer had become hot and stuffy since both doors had remained open. The small window unit air conditioner rattled and hummed annoyingly, struggling to cool the manufactured home. Hassett walked to the bedroom and pulled the electrical plug from the outlet, putting the dying appliance out of its misery.

Even the open doors couldn't allow the smell of the two corpses to escape. Hassett figured the smell of cat piss and pot existed long before the stench of death.

The man on the couch was identified as Kyle Jackson, an ex-con arrested for child pornography, who spent his time now selling fake vape devices and crystal meth. He was only a few years into his twenties and throwing his life away with his addiction to young girls and money. He'd never had a day job in his life. He was a drug dealer and a liar, convinced the only way to thrive was to cheat the system, take shortcuts. But shortcuts had only given him a life cut short.

"Jesus," Hassett whispered to herself. She stared at the wrecked bed with four cut ropes. "What the fuck was going on here?"

"Well," Deputy Simpson said, "I believe Mr. Jackson had our young victim tied—"

"That was a rhetorical question, Simpson. I have eyes. I can see what this was. Little sonovabitch got what he deserved."

"Maybe we should pin a medal on River rather than hunt her like a criminal," Simpson remarked. He scratched the crest of his skull.

"She's dangerous. She's no vigilante, Simpson. She attacked Larry Larson without any provocation, stuck her knife in Anthony Chavez's chest, and now this. What's next?" She pointed to the man lying in the hallway, "Who's the other asshole?"

"No ID, but a neighbor said he was just a visitor—pulled in about an hour ago. Found $300 in his pocket—cash—so he was probably here to buy something."

Sheriff Hassett hated these predators and thought she'd left these heinous crimes in Chicago. Stoneville was supposed to be quiet—a sleepy hick town with fat deputies who were bored with their job—a place where she could relax and not take her career so seriously. She was wrong. She was intense, callous, and angry. She hated this version of herself, and so far, she could only feel normal when in the presence of Jeff Bourbon. He understood how the job hardened her heart, but it softened in his presence.

Hassett realized the risk Deputy Simpson had taken. He wasn't used to this kind of confrontation. She placed a hand on his shoulder. "How are you doing?" Her tone was sincere, almost apologetic.

"Little hungry. Could use a drink, but—"

"Your wounds, Simpson. How are your wounds?"

"Superficial mostly," he felt her genuine concern. "I'll be alright."

She didn't entirely believe him. "Okay, I'm going to have you stay here. Take some statements and wait for the coroner to arrive. Then get yourself to the hospital and have those cuts properly cleaned and dressed. I'll take Savage home. I think we've utilized him enough."

"The DA wants him to stay on this and find River."

"Yeah, well, he can kiss my ass," she responded with irritation in her voice.

"He has abilities, boss—Savage. I saw it with my own two eyes. He saved—"

She raised a hand to indicate that he should stop speaking. "Not now, Simpson. I don't want to hear how Cody Savage can magically see whatever the hell it is he sees. I'm not in the mood. I want facts, evidence, and leads. That's what will put River behind bars. And if Dale Kelly thinks he can save his daughter after this massacre, he needs to wake the hell up."

She walked out the front door, down the porch steps, and stopped to catch her breath. She stared at the poor girl curled in a lawn chair, hugging her knees as two paramedics interrogated her. A neighbor woman stood behind the chair and stroked Vanessa's hair.

Sheriff Hassett's anger returned. She paced up the gravel road and pretended to fiddle with something inside her Jeep while she dried her eyes.

*Where are you, Bourbon? I wish you were here to help.* She'd come to admire Bourbon's way with people and his calm demeanor. The saint of Stoneville would have found River Kelly by now. He probably would have talked her into turning herself in and putting handcuffs on, too. He had a way with people she couldn't help but admire—a skill she didn't possess.

Bourbon had called her two days ago and mentioned returning to the woods for a few days. He needed to get away and clear his head.

She thought that was odd. The man lived alone on the outskirts of town with nothing but the Cascade River to keep him company.

"Retirement too stressful for you?" She quipped over the phone. He didn't laugh. He said he'd call her in a few days, and they'd grab lunch.

Lunch. She was sick of lunch. She wanted dinner, wine, and dessert. She had to keep reminding herself that the man was still mourning the loss of Annabel Thompson. He'd been crushed by Annabel's death, even though he hid his grief.

She composed herself, placed her Ray-Bans over her puffy eyes, and marched back to the crime scene.

*****

Shari Kapoor's van found its way down Mayfield Court. Shari was barely visible inside the silver van. She turned into the second driveway, the word "CORONER" in gold vinyl letters set on a thick black stripe reflected the midday sun. The van reversed down the congested gravel road. An annoying backup alarm beeped in everyone's ear until the Ford stopped beside Sheriff Hassett's Jeep.

Shari exited the vehicle, gathered her gray medical kit, and greeted the sheriff. Hassett went over everything she knew about the case and the two corpses inside. They walked together, entered the trailer, and stopped to capture the scene visually.

"It's a bloodbath," Hassett warned Shari.

As Shari pulled blue latex gloves over her hands, the memory of a pontoon boat painted with red liquid flashed in her mind. "I've seen worse." She knelt beside the second victim—the man on the floor and began a visual inspection. She wanted to bag and tag the dead bodies as fast as possible so she could take her time collecting evidence in the bedroom, in case Kyle Jackson wasn't working alone. She didn't have to say what everyone else was thinking; Vanessa Scott was the actual victim here.

Shari knelt beside the body on the floor as Cody walked through the back door. She turned to Simpson, who was leaning against the kitchen counter. "What's he doing here? He's no use to this investigation."

"Cody saved my life," Simpson said in a validating tone. He crossed his arms and looked down at Shari. "And he's here at the request of Dale Kelly."

Cody approached the coroner with caution and took one knee across from the body. "Shari, I'm sorry about yesterday. I didn't mean—"

"I don't want to hear your apology, Savage. I'm busy here. And before you say anything more, let me tell you this: Roshan is not what you think he is."

"But he's so much more than what you think, Shari. He's special."

"I know he's special. He has always been special. But not in the way you believe. He's just a normal kid who doesn't, or can't speak, who likes to draw pictures."

"His pictures are his way of speaking. He sees things no one else can. He speaks—" Cody cut himself off this time. He knew it would break Shari's heart if she knew that Cody could hear Roshan's voice while she suffered in silence. He decided not to push the subject further.

"You're contaminating my crime scene," Shari hissed. "Sheriff, please remove this man from the room so I can continue my work."

"Let's go, Savage," Sheriff Hassett ordered. She led him out the door and to her Jeep. "I'll take you home; we'll handle this from here. If you want to help, go see if your friend AJ Timmons can lead us to River. It seems the two of them were well acquainted before all of this shit went down." They walked to the sheriff's vehicle in silence. She climbed behind the wheel and started the V-8 engine.

Cody took the passenger seat and buckled his seatbelt. "What if she attacks again?"

"Let's not worry about that until it happens. I've got enough shit to deal with right now: the attack on Larry Larson, Anthony Chavez stabbed while riding his motorcycle, these two dead perps in the trailer, and we still don't know who killed the Bristol cousins."

Cody spun in his seat. This was the first time he'd heard about the Bristols. "Duke and Aaron Bristol? The cousins that everyone mistakes as brothers?"

Hassett nodded, "Mm, hmm." They pulled off Mayfield Court, leaving the grizzly crime scene behind. "Duke and Aaron were the two men shot at Full Throttle the same night River Kelly attacked Larry Larson."

"Jesus, I know those two were assholes, but who would want them dead?"

"A lot of people, actually. They were involved in numerous shady deals. I've got a witness who will testify that the Bristols helped Cricket Morrison kill Andrew Mills. I can't wait to tell Bourbon. They were Levi Thompson's right-hand men. So, who knows what else they've done? I'm guessing it had something to do with drugs. Aaron was found with a bag of crystal, and Duke was carrying a large sum of cash."

"So, River either had an accomplice at Full Throttle, or you have another murderer walking the streets?"

"My money's on Anthony Chavez."

"The guy killed on the Triumph?" Cody questioned.

"He was at Full Throttle that night, and he's not exactly citizen of the year. If your theory is correct, and River is going after sinners, that might explain why she killed him. But she was outside. How would she know who was shooting inside?"

Cody explained his theory. "If she's killing sinners, she can see with more than just her eyes. How did she know that girl, Vanessa Scott, was tied up in the trailer? You see the world in black and white, but to stop River Kelly, you need to accept the gray areas. Eventually, you'll have to realize that some of Stoneville's residents are unique."

"Like you, right?"

"Yeah, like me. And Flesti Thaed, Jesse Lewis, Roshan Kapoor, and River Kelly."

Hassett drove in silence for a moment, contemplating Cody's words and thinking about all the strange things she'd seen lately. She glanced side-eye at her passenger, "What really happened back there? And don't bullshit me. I want the truth."

"I'll tell you over a slice of pizza if you have time."

"I'll make time." She clicked on her left turn signal and turned down a side road that would shorten their route to Pizza Primo.

# 25

# THE CHAMBER

Daisy lay on the stone floor in an uncomfortable side position. Her right arm tingled as it lost circulation, a result of her body weight pressing down against the hard surface. She wasn't sure if she had been knocked out or if she had blacked out until she felt the welt on the side of her skull. She remembered now—the face in the shadows, followed by a very short struggle, and then the blow to the head—the blunt side of a hatchet.

A dirty and frayed rope bound her wrist in front of her. The skin underneath prickled and burned from the rough fibers.

Near the well, a pair of torn-up leather boots faced her. They were very old boots—the left missing its laces—and Daisy guessed they had put thousands of miles on their soles. They stepped toward her, and she could see the legs of the man who was responsible for her captivity. His blue cloth pants were just as ragged as his footwear, with deep stains that were as impervious to washing as a tattoo.

The man approached and stepped over her. She held her breath, too scared to talk, terrified to breathe.

*At least Bourbon's safe. He'll come looking for me.*

"What shall we do with this one?" A gruff voice above her asked.

'This one?'

"The big man? Hm, we'll wait and see," a raspy voice responded.

*Aww, fuck, there's two of them.*

The deeper voice spoke again, "Leave him be for now. He's not going anywhere, brother. He'll serve his purpose."

Daisy crunched her abdomen and pulled herself into a sitting position on the floor. She felt blood return to her arm, bringing a shot of pain with it. She spun on her butt just enough to see the second man in the dim light of the cave and Bourbon lying unconscious on his side, ten feet from the well. His head was bleeding, but she could see the rise and fall of his chest as he took long, slow breaths. Her throat burned from the lack of water, and she only wanted to quench her thirst. Water trickled through the cracks in the cave wall, filling the well below. It teased her dry tongue as it dripped clean and clear, and she couldn't have a single drop.

Her voice squeaked, "Bourbon? Bourbon, can you hear me? What did you do to him?"

The man who cracked her aside the head turned on his heels. He inadvertently kicked up a little cloud of rock dust, causing Daisy to cough. The reaction made her throat burn even more. The man squatted with an empty expression to admire his prize. Daisy kept her head turned away. She didn't dare face her captor and was even more frightened to face this reality.

The man gently lifted a lock of her hair and slid the strands between his thumb and two fingers. She yanked her head sideways, freeing the soft lock from his light grip. He smelled the sweet scent that had transferred to his skin.

Daisy finally mustered the courage to turn and face him. He appeared to be the same age as Bourbon, with rugged features and gray hair. Long whiskers on his face were chaotically groomed by a dull blade—perhaps by the two hatchets he carried on his waist. Thick, greasy hair dropped past his shoulders. Flaky gray skin with patches of discoloration formed what nearly looked like a mask over his face. His teeth were surprisingly white, although they barely showed.

But his eyes—it was his eyes that shocked and mesmerized Daisy. The whites of the spheres were faint blue and glowed similarly to the luminescent water in the well. The irises of each eye had the tiniest little sparkles, like minuscule diamonds floating in black melted wax. The little diamonds made subtle movements, picking up the slightest light in the room and aiming it back at the bound journalist.

"The lawman will be fine. Mr. Bourbon's a rather durable fellow, don't you think?"

"I think you'd better untie us both, asshole."

"Your spirit is feisty, Ms. Torrez," he responded as Daisy watched a beetle-like insect crawl out of his beard and burrow back into his thick hair. "We will discuss your fate soon. Please relax while you wait."

"How do you know our names? Who are you?"

The big man ignored her question and stood. "Martin, give our guest something to drink."

Daisy spun on her ass to face the opposite direction to get a look at Martin. He was a portly man with the same rough characteristics as the first. He smiled in her direction, but his lazy eye made her unsure where his focus landed. He had the same diamond eyes as the man with two hatchets. Martin's face was almost clean-shaven, although nearly as filthy as his boots. His receding hairline made him look almost entirely bald. He wore a tight green T-shirt that reminded Daisy of the ones she'd seen soldiers wear in commercials for the Army—olive green fabric stretched over tight muscles. The young soldiers wore it much better than Martin. His bulbous stomach stretched the fabric to its limits. The shirt's lack of length exposed the pale skin of his underbelly.

Martin held a large blade with a deer antler hilt. The ten-inch blade of intimidating steel was scratched and chipped, proof of its age and daily use. It had a single edge, and the backside of the steel was dented and hammered from years of abuse.

Martin sheathed the knife and stepped toward Daisy. He held an empty canteen up to the dripping water that escaped the chamber wall and let it fill partway. Cold shimmering eyes were fixed on Daisy as the canteen filled.

Daisy struggled against her restraints while the first man checked on Bourbon. He pulled the rope wrapped around Bourbon's wrist. Satisfied with the knots, he returned to his conscious captive.

The canteen was half full when Martin took a long drink and held it to Daisy's lips. She turned her head in protest, refusing to drink after the haggard stranger. Martin shrugged, took another swallow, and capped the container. He stretched his arm, canteen in hand, to the first man, who was paying no attention, "Cecil?" He nudged his brother with the canteen.

Cecil took the container and gulped. Water dripped down his beard, and he wiped it away with the back of his wrist. The beetle wiggled to the surface in quick-lived protest. Cecil screwed the canteen's cap tight and handed it back to Martin. Martin sat on the edge of the large well, crossed his arms, and watched Cecil's interaction with their hostage.

"We've been waiting for someone like you for a long time," Cecil told Daisy.

"Forget it, creep; I have a boyfriend."

Cecil nearly smiled at the insinuation but returned to his stoic state. "I'm terribly sorry, Miss Torrez, but we cannot allow you to leave."

"Please, I have to get home to my son." Her voice shook from fear.

Cecil took a seat on a loose boulder, a stone that appeared to have fallen from the wall or ceiling, no doubt a result of the recent earthquakes. He stared at Bourbon for a moment. "The sheriff will never leave this cave. He's a witness to what we must do. It's unfortunate, but no one must know of this place's existence. As for you, we require your pure heart. You will become our salvation—poison to the well."

"To stop the blue water," Martin clarified. He sat straight as if proud of their plan.

Cecil smiled for the first time. It was a creepy, wide smile full of malice, like he simultaneously had a terrible but fun idea. "This will be the last time we feed the well. But, instead of giving the well a sinner, we'll feed it someone completely innocent. Then, we will finally be free to leave this chamber prison."

"You can't leave until you feed me to the well?" Daisy tried to understand. The thought of it all sounded so bizarre that she considered she might have been drugged during her captivity and was experiencing hallucinations. "Why can't you leave this cave?"

Before Cecil or Martin could answer, a shadow dropped from the tiny hole in the chamber's ceiling. The two brothers jumped but lost sight of the movement.

"She's here," Martin clamored as he jumped off the sidewall of the well.

"Calm yourself, brother. It's only her little spy—the pestering crow." Cecil gripped one of the hatchets hanging around his waist. "I'll split that feathered-fucker in two if he flies through here again."

"Poe?" Daisy asked. "You're scared of Poe." She began to understand. "You're afraid of Flesti Thaed, aren't you? She's the reason you're hiding in this cave."

Cecil and Martin were silent, scanning the cave—their prison—looking for the dark bird lost in the shadows.

"How long have you been here?"

Martin looked at Cecil for an answer. Cecil lowered his weapon and looked at the ceiling, trying to calculate the number. "What year is this?" He asked Daisy. She told him, and he began counting on his fingers. He stopped when he counted them twice, then shrugged, "I don't remember the numbers after twenty-nine," he admitted in disappointment.

The journalist pushed her fear aside as curiosity bloomed like a timid spring flower. There was a story in this cave, in these two men. Perhaps it was more interesting than the story of Marion Cain. Maybe it was the same story, interwoven like the tree roots under the forest floor. She sat higher and attempted to keep the dialogue open. "Maybe it was just a bat."

"I think he left," Martin said, ignoring Daisy's suggestion.

"He'll be back," Cecil responded. "And she'll see what we're doing. She'll know we're going to put an end to her reign."

They watched for another half-minute and decided to give up the hunt. Finding Poe in the dimly lit cavern was like trying to see an ice cube in a hailstorm. The colorless bird was lost in the dark or had left the chamber without notice. The two men, realizing their search was futile, returned to the well.

Daisy wasn't sure how much time she had. Cecil and Martin could pick her up and make good on their intent anytime. She needed to distract them—take their minds off their agenda and hope to survive long enough to tell this story. "I can help you. If you let me go, I can bring back help. You don't need to be scared of Flesti."

"She would kill you all." Cecil barked. "You are all infected by the lake now. Anyone who's swum in our lake is hers to control. She'll do anything to keep the lake's power to herself. Haven't you discovered that yet?"

"The blue lights?" Daisy realized. "They provide a supernatural energy to Marion—to the two of you." And also Cody. "Cain Lake has kept you alive for all these years, hasn't it?"

"No!" Cecil barked. "We are stuck here, in this cave, most of the time, like prisoners. If we go to the lake, our presence will be discovered, as you have discovered us. If the town knew what the well can do—what the lake can do—then we'd be exposed. So, we've been banished to this dark hole, living in isolation, never able to swim freely in our father's water."

"You're siblings."

Cecil nodded slowly, reluctantly.

"There are two of you. Can't you overcome her?"

"The well has provided us," Cecil nodded toward Martin, "with life eternal, but that is all. Marion has developed the ability to control others and the water itself. The power that feeds Cain Lake originates at this well. It leeches into the ground, follows the underground veins, and eventually ends up in the lake."

"Can't you just dam the water? Stop it from going into the lake?"

"We've tried, Miss Torrez. We've tried. But stopping the water is like trying to catch smoke with a fishing net. It just keeps flowing around and through the tiniest holes and cracks. It keeps finding its way to the lake. So, our last hope is to kill the well's power."

"So, if I'm following you correctly, you need to throw an innocent person into the well to counteract the sinners the lake feeds on?"

The brothers dropped their heads as if ashamed of their intentions. Cecil spoke to the floor, "It is not a moral decision but one of self-preservation."

"We can stop her," Daisy protested. "Together. Cody, my boyfriend, can help. We can defeat Flesti. I can come back with him."

"It's too late," Martin said and drew his knife. "She has our mother's stone blade. She'll cut us all down, just like she did our sisters and brother Theodore."

"A stone blade?" Daisy asked.

Cecil stood and looked at Martin's crude weapon, "She calls it the Azure Blade. A weapon she can control that feeds on the sinners. It becomes more powerful with every kill. The blade collects sins— feeds them to the lake when she purges. She gets her power from the lake, and we get our power from the well. Absorbing the blue light keeps us alive, but it also makes us vulnerable to Marion's psychic control. She can control anyone affected by the light."

Cecil continued his explanation, "Once she grows weak, we hope to take the Azure Blade from her, and she will no longer be a threat to us."

"I've never seen Flesti with a blade," Daisy admitted. "She carries a walking stick and a backpack, but I've never seen any kind of blade in her possession."

Cecil and Martin stared at each other in disbelief. "What do you mean she doesn't have a blade? She used it to kill our siblings."

"She doesn't have it anymore," Daisy stated. "She's using others to do her dirty work. She had the church pastor killing for her. He collected the sins and purged them in the lake. His name was Jesse Lewis."

"Perhaps this pastor has the blade," Martin speculated.

"He doesn't," Daisy assured them. "He used an ax to kill his victims. Plus, he's dead now. Someone shot him after he was captured."

"She's lost the blade, Cecil," Martin said. "The bitch has been defenseless all this time."

Cecil squeezed the handle of his hatchet. "That doesn't make her defenseless. She can still squeeze our brains with her mind, make us do whatever she wills. She could have me kill you with a thought."

Daisy could see the betrayal on their faces. These two men had lived in fear of their sister, Marion Cain, for what must have been decades, even centuries. She thought about the images she found of Flesti Thaed, born Marion Cain. Based on her research, she was certain that Flesti was born in the 1700s, and the lake had sustained her all this time. These two men were proof of her theory. Now, she was more fascinated than frightened.

She wanted to know more about their story—about the entire Cain family. "What happened to your family?"

The two men glanced at each other, considering whether they should answer.

Daisy leaned toward Cecil. "Tell me everything."

# 26
# TWO LOONS

"Tell me everything," Sheriff Hassett instructed Cody as she lifted a slice of pepperoni and black olive pizza from a circular tray. "Every goddam detail." She bit down on the triangle of cheese and dough and waited for his description of the day's events.

Cody described the events that had occurred at the trailer park, even including the detail about the black cat that ran from the first trailer, as if it should have been an omen. He fiddled with a straw as he gave his rendition of the day. When he finished, he plunged the straw into his Styrofoam cup of Mountain Dew and drank like he was trying to rinse a bad taste from his palate.

"And what about Simpson's version of the story?" Hassett responded.

"What version is that?" He set the cup down.

"The version where you used your 'abilities' at the scene. What the hell was that supposed to mean?"

"Oh...that," he answered casually, like it was something he did on a daily basis. "Well, if you really want to know, I was able to stop the Azure Blade from killing your deputy. You're welcome."

"The Azure Blade? It has a name?"

"Mm, hmm." Cody tore the crust off his pizza slice and dipped it in butter garlic sauce.

"How the hell did you do that?"

He took a bite of the buttery dough, "I just sensed the knife...it was a reaction, not a skill. I think my abilities allow me to connect with the knife, just like Flesti."

Hassett shook her head in disbelief, but what other choice did she have but to hope it was true? "Think you can do it again?"

"Maybe. But I don't know if we can rely on it—someone could get killed."

Sheriff Hassett sucked Diet Coke from her cup, washing the pizza dough down. She gazed out the window, hoping the answers were outside, but saw nothing but vehicles cruising the street. She thought about River's next move. "She'll kill again." She turned back to her company sitting across the table. "Who would be her next target? If we can figure that out, we might be able to stop her before she acts." She set the drink on the table. Her expression softened a little as she watched Cody eat his pizza crust before the rest of the slice. "Let's say I believe you. Okay. So, you have this magical ability—"

"It's not magic."

"Okay, it's some kinda 'connection,' as you call it, with Cain Lake and the micropods. Flesti Thaed has this same connection. The knife has this same connection. Now, River Kelly has this connection. So, if you're all connected, why the hell can't you track her? Or the knife?"

Cody thought about Hassett's theory for a moment. "You want me to try tracking the knife?"

"Hell, yes. Flesti seems capable of knowing who has it. She wouldn't be controlling River Kelly otherwise. Whoever has the knife is her puppet. So, why can't you sense the knife?"

Cody shrugged, "Maybe I can. I haven't tried."

"Would you try?"

Cody looked around the restaurant. "Here?"

"Wherever you can. If you can track this bitch down, I don't care where or how you do it. Hell, you can sit in my bathtub with a margarita if that's what you need. We need to be proactive before we have another victim. I need to stop this chick today."

"The lake—Cain Lake might be the only place I can connect with River and see her. The energy that connects all of this is strongest there. Maybe I can find her using the lake's energy. I don't know.

Worth a shot. But the energy in the lake seems to be waning as if the micropods are dying off."

"Then we'd better hurry while we still have a chance."

******

After Hassett added a generous tip to their bill and paid the waitress with her debit card, they left the restaurant and drove south until they reached the white church at the lake. It was a twelve-minute drive across town and out to Cain Lake.  She parked the Jeep Gladiator in the center of the parking lot. Her phone rang, "I'd better take this."

Cody stepped out, giving Hassett a moment of privacy.

He felt his stomach dancing in his abdomen, unsure if it was from the garlic butter or the sight of the church. Whenever he saw the old structure with its stout belfry and stained-glass windows, he was conflicted between good and bad memories. His mind was like a video game of Pong, bouncing back and forth with thoughts of his beautiful wife and the ugly aftermath of Jesse Lewis's actions.

His eyes fixed on the heavy wooden doors that were closed but always open to the lost, the broken, and the damned. He was tempted to step inside, take a pew, and ask for the help of divine power, but asking anyone for help wasn't in his DNA. Besides, he always felt alone in a church, even when the congregation surrounded him. Perhaps that's how he was supposed to feel—one-on-one with God— but no one else had ever described a similar experience.

His thoughts were interrupted when the church's big door opened, and Willa stepped out. She glided down the front steps and smiled at him. His knees buckled, but he managed to stay on his feet. He knew she wasn't real. He knew it was his imagination wishing she'd come through that door, but he wanted to run to her and lift her in his arms. He wanted to feel her one more time.

She waved timidly.

He closed his eyes, shook his head to regain focus, and then resumed his gaze. The church door was closed. The woman had

173

vanished. That brief moment of seeing his dead wife would have to be enough right now.

He thought about their wedding day and the morning Jesse Lewis found him drunk in the cemetery. He thought about the night he found Annabel Thompson running for her life, hands tied, lost in the woods as she escaped the Sin Eater. All the victims of Cain Lake resulted from what was happening under the water's surface. All the problems he'd faced since his return to Stoneville were connected by a supernatural energy that flowed through this town. Maybe this church had something to do with it.

And then he thought about Daisy and their unborn child. He loved Stoneville but wondered if this was where he'd want to raise a child. That would be a conversation they'd need to have when she returned from her trip in the woods.

He hoped Daisy was enjoying herself with Bourbon, surrounded by nature, enjoying the views from the hilltops, and listening to the sounds of the forest while a crazy woman with a deadly weapon terrorized the town. He was jealous. He should have taken Daisy to find Flesti Thaed himself instead of forcing her to go behind his back and recruit Bourbon as a guide.

Sheriff Hassett disconnected her call and stepped out of the patrol vehicle. She followed Cody to the edge of the parking lot, where gravel gave way to grass. They stared for a moment in silence, relishing the picturesque view of the town's aquatic treasure.

Two loons, paired for life, graced the water and then dove under the surface in unison.

"Should we be worried about them?" Hassett asked, staring at the mountains that supplied Cain Lake with abundant water.

Cody knew she wasn't referring to the loons. "Bourbon and Daisy? No. No, I don't think so. Bourbon knows his way around the lake. And he'll do anything to keep Daisy safe. She's not the outdoor type, but Bourbon will keep her out of harm's way. They'll be okay. She's probably already driven him crazy with questions, and they're on their way back," he hoped. Cody started into the grassy field that led down to the lake. He stopped himself. "Wait, are you and

Bourbon a thing?"

"No. Not that it's any of your business, but no, we are not seeing each other." Her eyes dropped, revealing her emotions, and Cody could tell that the truth disappointed her, as if she were admitting it for the first time.

"Maybe you should if you like each other. Take it from a guy who lost his soulmate; these opportunities don't come often, and they can pass in an instant."

She felt her face turn hot. "Get your ass in the water, Savage."

Cody chuckled and started descending the overgrown field. "What will you do?"

"I'm going back to the trailer park. State boys are taking over the investigation. I'll swing back here if I can. But if you see something—" she shook her head, not believing she was letting him attempt this, nor the fact that she was hoping it worked. "You get your ass to a phone and call me immediately."

Sheriff Hassett climbed back into the SUV and drove away, leaving Cody to figure out if he could harness the power of Cain Lake and track a killer. She was skeptical of his psychic abilities. She'd never believed anyone could or should be able to see beyond the limits of our vision. But she was desperate now. Another murder on her watch would be a black mark on her department. She was severely understaffed, outnumbered, and tired as hell.

# 27
# SWARM OF MEMORIES

Cody meandered down the hill behind the church. The lawn around the church had been adequately maintained—probably the strenuous effort of a good Samaritan—but the field behind the building was overgrown with knee-high grass and weeds. The church kept a walking path to the dock with a few strategically placed stones. Now, the path was overgrown and difficult to distinguish from the surrounding vegetation.

Wildflowers added dots of color everywhere amidst the greens and browns. Bees, slow and fat with pollen, hovered from orange to yellow to purple. They moved away from Cody while pollinating the field, exhausting themselves from the intense effort it took to collect nutrients for the day. Cody moved slowly, cautious not to disturb their labor. He gently pushed through the tall grass, weeds, and flowers, without disturbing the helpful insects.

At the dock, Cody removed his boots and socks and rolled his pant legs over his knees. There would be no stripping naked or exposing himself entirely to the world, even though the lake appeared to be mostly void of human activity. He saw only a few swimmers on the north shore and a jet ski off to the southwest.

He stepped into the water. Cool liquid soothed his hot feet, and tiny stones along the lake's bottom massaged his soles. He'd been walking so much lately in old work boots that he'd become accustomed to the discomfort. The pain was only noticeable once he freed his feet from the leather grip of the Timberlands. He wanted to stay on the beach and let the sand and water continue to soothe his feet and ankles, but his task was too crucial for self-indulgence. He didn't enjoy having psychic visions. They confused his mind and emotions. They made his nose bleed and his head hurt. But if he didn't find River Kelly soon, more lives could be lost—including hers.

His T-shirt was removed and tossed onto the wooden deck boards of the old dock. The sun, hot on his chest and shoulders, felt like fire on his white skin, and the water beckoned him to extinguish the heat.

He walked further until the gentle movement of the water's surface splashed softly against his knees, wetting his pant legs. The bottom of the lake had turned to clay at this depth, thick and sticky, and he sank until it appeared he no longer had feet. He stared through the amber-colored water, looking at his footless legs, which reminded him of what his left arm looked like weeks ago. His missing hand—a result of his actions to escape a burning barn—left him with nothing but a stump wrist. The power of Cain Lake, the micropods, and Flesti Thaed had brought it back.

He swirled the water with his new hand, appreciating his ability to grip a smooth rock on the bottom. He plunged his right hand downward until he was elbow-deep and pressed his palms to the rich clay bottom. Bent over, he swirled the water and splashed it against his upper arms, chest, and face. The lake's cool temperature invigorated him.

Cody waited for the micropods to appear.

He waited.

He waited some more.

After thirty minutes, his heart sank into the clay. The lake had denied him a vision—some insight to locate River Kelly. She had stolen a motorcycle at Getaway Estates and could be anywhere now. But where? Did she leave town? Disappointed, he went to the dock, stepped up, and followed the creaking boards to the end. There, he sat with his feet dangling in the water.

He tried to swallow, but his dry throat refused to obey.

He was heartbroken that the lake was dying. Not for himself. He didn't want the ability of foresight any more than a drowning man wanted a glass of water. However, Cain Lake's mystic power could have its benefits. After Levi Thompson and Cricket Morrison nearly beat him to death, he was healed in the very water that now wet his feet. It had kept Flesti Thaed from growing old, even reducing her age like the legendary Fountain of Youth. Jeff Bourbon had felt its effects, too, making him feel like a 'young buck' again.

There were benefits to the lake's supernatural effects, but also perils.

Cain Lake was amazing and terrifying.

*****

It seemed like hours had passed. Despite his patience, Cody's connection to Cain Lake was lost. The deadly blade, somewhere in River's grip, could not be detected. Tracking her was going to be impossible. If he were going to find her, he'd need a lucky break.

Instead of leaving, he took a moment for himself. The lake was like a magnet to a heart as heavy as iron. It refused to relinquish its pull on him, so he stayed a moment longer. He'd never felt so at peace as in this place. Part of him was glad, hoping the madness in Stoneville was over. Maybe Sheriff Hassett had caught River Kelly while he was wasting time at Cain Lake.

His mind wandered, thinking about his future with Daisy. He even picked out a few baby names while he reflected on being a father. A couple made him smile, and a few made him laugh to himself.

Resisting the magnet's pull, he stood.

He walked the dock back to shore. On the beach, he slipped his socks and boots back over the wrinkled skin of his feet. His T-shirt scratched against his sun-burnt shoulders. Once dressed, he began his march up the hill.

The white church atop the hill looked down at him with stained-glass eyes. The bees were still hard at work, detecting the nectar scent of the wildflowers, chasing the source, and scouring the flower petals.

A honeybee buzzed Cody's head. With a gentle wave of his hand, the bee moved away and returned with another. A third and fourth bee flew around his waist. His heartbeat escalated, and he wondered if he'd disturbed a nest. A half-dozen bumblebees joined the honeybees. Cody kept moving slowly, trying not to push his luck or become the victim of a stinging swarm.

The sound of the bees grew with every step, humming and buzzing that filled his brain. The sound vibrated through his brain and clung to his skin like sweat on a humid day. He turned back to the lake and nearly collapsed from the sight. Thousands of bees followed, forming a shape that Cody thought looked remarkably like a black crow. As the swarm approached, Cody froze, cloaked in darkness by the crow. The buzzing grew deafening despite his effort to block the noise by covering his ears with his palms.

Not a single bee touched or stung him.

He wasn't sure what was happening then, but knew running would be a grave mistake. The vibration from the bee's wings created energy that Cody could feel all around him like a coat of paint. The energy permeated his skin and synced with his brain waves. The sensation was similar to his experience with the micro-pods in the water.

The world around him went silent, and someone flicked the lights off. He wasn't sure if he had gone blind and deaf at once, or if the density of the bee swarm had blocked out the sun. There was no up or down, no north, east, south, or west. He wondered if this was what death felt like, just floating in a void of emptiness.

Little streaks of light formed horizontally and wrapped around him, swirling like the little eddies he'd been watching at the lake. The lights formed images as if he had a hundred moving TV screens wrapped around him on all sides. The effect made him dizzy, and he could taste butter garlic in the back of his throat. One screen locked in place and became crystal clear. He set his attention to it and regained his balance while fighting the urge to vomit.

After a moment, the world and his stomach both settled. The

monitors were no longer moving. The largest image floated right before him, a waving rectangle of light.

In the light, he could see Flesti Thaed sitting on a log. He recognized the timber from his trip around Cain Lake. It was the last place he saw Jesse Lewis alive before someone shot him dead. Flesti stood, using her tall walking stick to brace herself. She looked weaker than she had when they last met, and he wondered if she might be sick.

"She's not sick," a timid voice said. "The lake's energy is draining, and as a result, Flesti is losing her powers."

Cody turned from the view of Flesti, "Roshan?"

"Hi, Mr. Cody," Roshan smiled.

"Are you doing this? How?"

Roshan Kapoor waved his hands gently, and the screens shuffled. "This is my gift from Cain Lake. I can access memories—just pieces sometimes, like a jigsaw puzzle—of anyone affected by Cain Lake's energy. Right now, I'm transferring those memories to your brain so you can see them, too."

"How are you able to do that?"

"It's quite easy—and complicated—but everything we experience is an interpretation from our brains. Light hits your eyes, is converted to electrical signals, and is carried to your mind via the optic nerve. Your brain interprets the signal and forms an image. The same is true with all of your senses. I can take a shortcut and send signals straight to your brain."

An image of Willa sitting on the back of his motorcycle flickered on a screen.

"You've hijacked my mind," Cody said in amazement. "So the bees—"

"Not real. Well, not all of them."

"You could have used butterflies, ya know?"

Roshan almost smiled. "Butterflies don't have a hive mind. The bees think alike, move alike, and will swarm. It's the power of the swarm that has the same energy as the micropods. The two species are very similar."

Cody shook his head in bewilderment. "You're a scary little bastard. Can Flesti do this?"

"No," Ro answered. "I can only send signals via your senses and interfere with the real stimuli you receive from the tangible world you occupy. But Flesti Thaed can intercept your outgoing signals, like when your mind tells your hand to make a fist. She can block the signal or change the command."

"Or when your brain is telling your heart to beat. That's how she's controlling people. That's how she can manipulate River Kelly into killing."

"Correct."

"Can she change a person's emotions—make them angry or vengeful?"

"No, but the Azure Blade can. Together, Flesti and the blade are extremely powerful. That is why she cannot possess the knife."

Cody returned to the screens, "And she gets this power from Cain Lake. So, the only way to stop her is to let the lake die—or kill it ourselves."

"I'm afraid so. But you'll have to hurry. Once she gets the Azure Blade, she'll purge it into Cain Lake. All those sins she's collecting—"

"Will power the lake like nothing before." Cody finished. He stepped closer to the screen and watched as if he could learn something new. "Ro, if we let the lake's power dwindle completely, will I lose my psychic ability?"

"We'll all lose our gifts. Anyone affected by Cain Lake will become normal again, and there are many more than you know."

Cody scanned the scenes in front of him. Most of the little acts playing out like muted TV commercials made no sense. He didn't recognize the people or places. He finally realized these were Flesti's memories. If Daisy's theory was correct and Flesti were Marion Cain, then she'd have three lifetimes of memories. "Ro, what's so important about this knife—the Azure Blade?"

"The Azure Blade." Roshan pulled his hands back with open fingers, then slid his right hand to the left and his left hand up. The screens obeyed his commands. A new memory presented itself to

Cody. Amazed as he watched, Cody turned and gave the boy a grin, "Now, you're just showing off."

Roshan was silently focused on his performance. He opened his right hand wide and gestured by pulling his palm behind his head. Invisible wires snapped an image forward and centered with Cody's eyes. Cody reached forward with caution and placed his hand inside the light. He felt a tingle, bees crawling over his skin. He retracted the hand, fearing being stung, even though he knew they weren't real.

"Here!" Roshan exclaimed. "This is the first memory you need to see."

The image, like a hologram, depicted a serene body of water. Cody knew it was Cain Lake without needing further reference. A dock four planks wide and sixteen feet long was crookedly stretched over the water. The middle of the deck bowed downward until it was two inches underwater. At the end of the dock stood a girl, perhaps twelve years old. She had dirty blond hair and wore a gray dress that looked like it had been made of cheap fabric that refused to sway or wrinkle—an uncomfortable cover for a girl whose family couldn't afford something more suitable. Cody could not see her face, but he could see the object she held and the red liquid dripping onto the dock's planks.

"Mother fu—. Is that Flesti?"

"No," Roshan answered. "That's Marion Cain. The little girl who will someday become Flesti Thaed." Roshan gestured again with both hands as if turning an invisible globe. The image rotated until the girl's face showed.

Cody pointed at her right hand, "She had the Azure Blade when she was just a girl. But where did the blood come from?"

"Her sisters," Roshan's voice was a meek whisper as if talking about the sin physically hurt him.

Cody felt an intense heat choking his neck. He knew it wasn't the sunburn. "She killed her fucking sisters? What the hell? Why?"

"She only murdered two of them. She had two more. After finding the bodies, Marion's father, Laramie Cain, blamed his hired helper for the murders. He tied the man, rowed him to the lake's center, and dropped him overboard with the Azure Blade."

"So, she's been looking for that knife the whole time. Bourbon mentioned she was searching for something. Now I know what. She wants her goddam knife, and somehow, it's ended up in River Kelly's possession." Cody stepped forward and stared with squinting eyes at the image. He pointed to two faces hiding in a barn window.

"Ro, who are those boys?"

Ro, exhausted from his efforts, killed the image. Although he wasn't there in physical form, he breathed heavily from his efforts. "Those are her two brothers who witnessed her wrath, Cecil and Martin."

# 28

# THE CAIN FAMILY 

Daisy's heart beat so loudly in her chest that she was sure the two Cain brothers could hear it, too. Little echoes reverberating off the floor, walls, and ceiling, enhanced every sound in the cave. She could hear every drop of water that trickled through the stone, a chirping cricket hidden in a crack, and Bourbon's soft breathing. She could even hear her eyelids when she blinked. Somewhere in the chamber, a scuffling and pecking sound caught her ears, but she couldn't locate the source. The Martin brothers were either accustomed to all these noises or their hearing had diminished over the years.

When Cecil and Martin spoke simultaneously, it was impossible to understand what either of them was saying. But she was fascinated with the story they weaved. She tried to focus on their words, blocking out the static of the natural echo chamber.

The brothers argued about irrelevant dates and names in their story and occasionally trailed off on a different subject. But for two hours, they divulged, sitting in near darkness, trying to recount everything pertinent in their lives.

Cecil did most of the talking while Martin listened nearly as intently as Daisy. They'd never told anyone their story—no one seemed to care. Between chapters, Martin would stare at Daisy, mesmerized by her elegant lines and smooth facial features. It had been a couple of lifetimes since his wife died during the war, "The one between the North and South," he explained. He referred to her as "Tilly."

While Cecil described their life story, Martin built a small fire on the left side of the well to add warmth and illuminate the stone chamber. He fed the fire with a small stack of wood they kept in a concave wall—the start of their winter supply.

Cecil sat on his rock while he repaired the braids of an old rope. The rope was frayed and dirty, but Cecil knew it was too important a tool to discard. Everything they possessed showed mileage and age, and the rope was no exception. He pulled about six feet of the line through his hands until he found the point where things began to fall apart. Line over line, hand over hand, he weaved the five braids back together. He stopped working every twelve inches to test his efforts by pulling the rope with both hands like a mini-game of tug-of-war.

Cecil spoke of the lake and his parents. His father's name was Laramie Cain, and he'd come to forget his mother's real name, referring to her only as "Ma" or "Mother." He recalled that she belonged to the Abenaki Indian tribe.

The family's patriarch was a French commandant during the War of Conquest. After the French had lost their territories to Great Britain, Laramie Cain became a hunter and trapper along the St. Lawrence Valley. He met his bride while trading with her father, and the two fled to the northern foothills of the Adirondack Mountains to escape the likelihood of another war.

They settled on the lake and began a family. "Mother loved the water," he added. After the fighting ceased between the Redcoats and the Minutemen, other families found their way north or west and settled in the region. The small lake would come to be known as Cain Lake after the original settlers. Cain Falls was the first unofficial name of the town.

Cecil's story became more interesting as Daisy listened. His recollection of Cain Lake's history was surprisingly clear, even if he couldn't remember his mother's name. The events surrounding his sister's sins, however, were muddled by the years. Martin chimed in, trying to fill the gaps, although his accounts seemed more fantastical than accurate.

Daisy struggled to produce enough saliva to moisten her tongue and ask a question. She found herself wishing she had a pen or tablet to write notes, but her memory would have to be enough for now. She spoke with a dusty voice, "So, what was Flesti's—sorry, Marion's sin?"

Cecil continued braiding the hemp rope, paused to check the shadows for Poe, and continued with his anecdotal story.

Martin retrieved an old bucket he'd stolen from a sap line during maple season years ago. He bent over the well's wall and reached deep with the metal pail to fill it with water. He placed the pail on the ground beside Cecil, who dipped the freshly braided rope into the water and pulled hard against its fibers to tighten the braid. He continued:

"Mother owned a simple stone blade. Where it came from, nobody knows. She kept it hidden somewhere in the barn that Father had built. We'd never seen or found it," he nodded to Martin to indicate his brother. "Had no idea it even existed. We later learned that the blade was used during spiritual ceremonies and funerals, shit like that. It was even rumored that it was the instrument used by my mother's people during sacrifices to the earth. Of course, none of this can be substantiated now."

Cecil paused in his story and stood, stretched his back and legs, and twisted his neck with a cracking sound. His muscles and joints took on the attributes of the hard rock. Daisy noticed the man's fingers on his right hand. The knuckles of each digit were swollen and bent in multiple directions, affected by the tight, tense labor of working the rope back to form. He held his right wrist with his left hand and tried to flex the cramped hand. Stiff fingers resisted. He stepped over to the well and plunged his fist into the water until he was elbow-deep.

The water glowed with its notorious blue light. Little micropods danced along the surface and dove toward the depths. Daisy couldn't see the little performance by the water creatures, but she recognized the blue glow reflecting off his skin and clothes.

Cecil was silent, even closed his eyes for a moment, and when he finished and extracted his hand from the well, every finger was as straight as a pencil. He flexed and wiggled his digits, sighing in relief. He sat at the edge of the well's wall and stared deep into the water, reluctant to continue.

Daisy remembered how Cody was gifted a new left hand from the lake. The well seemed to be a condensed version of Cain Lake, and possibly more potent.

"Cecil, what happened to the blade?" Daisy asked. "What did Marion do?"

Cecil was blank.

"Cecil? Cecil, tell me what she did?" Daisy's voice was hungry and persistent. She needed to know more, but Cecil just stared into the water.

Martin stepped forward, "She killed our sisters." His voice was high and fast as if the crime was still fresh in his mind, the blood still wet. The words echoed off the chamber walls as if he'd spoken them twice. "She found the Azure Blade in the barn and killed Bethany and Camille."

The mention of the two names produced a guttural sigh from Cecil. He felt forced to complete what he'd started. "Bethany and Camille were our eldest sisters. Marion was jealous of them, but they all loved each other."

"Jealous of what?" Daisy interrupted.

"I'm not sure. Maybe their intelligence or their beauty. They were a few years older, and the local boys began to take notice of them. I think Marion accidentally found that knife while doing chores. She couldn't stop herself. We didn't see it happen. They found them in the hayloft—Elizabeth had been stabbed in the back, Camille in the stomach." Cecil held his abdomen with his hand as he remembered seeing the wound.

"Martin and I saw Marion on the dock with the blade. She dropped it there—right there. That's where a hired helper found it minutes later. And then our Pa found him. Martin ran away, and I followed. We didn't want Pa to kill Marion. He was crazy with rage after finding the girls. So we just ran like cowards. Like we didn't see anything."

"You were children. You reacted like any kid would in such a horrible situation."

"Shortly after we ran," Cecil recalled, "Pa beat the farmhand unconscious. He tied him up and rowed our boat to the middle of the lake. It was a foggy morning, so we couldn't see very well. But we could hear the man awake and plead for his life as he and the Azure Blade were dropped into the water."

"Didn't you tell your father the truth?"

"We didn't come back until dark," Martin added. "By then, it was too late. Pa blamed the hired man. The knife was gone. So we stayed quiet. We never trusted Marion again, but we lived with her secret."

"Until she killed Theodore," Martin added.

"Theodore?" Daisy asked.

"He was our youngest sibling," Martin continued. "Penelope died of a disease. Dorothy ran away, and we never saw her again."

Cecil circled the well, one lazy step at a time. He dragged his left hand along the top of the wall as he went around. "We grew up knowing what Marion had done. Keeping it from our father was difficult, but it was Mother who knew something was wrong."

"But your mother never discovered the truth?"

"She died while giving birth to Theodore. I think Marion hated him for it."

"And how many of you—how many children were in your family?"

Cecil was counting on his fingers again. Martin beat him to the answer, which was nine. He grinned with pride for out-counting his brother.

"It wasn't until we were teens that we discovered our lake's secret. It affected every one of us in different ways, but Marion was the strongest. She's dangerous, Ms. Torrez. She'll kill everyone you love if you cross her."

Daisy swallowed the warning hard. "I'm not interested in crossing her; I just wanted to know her story—your story. And now I have it. Now, all I want is to go home to my son."

"I'm sorry, Ms. Torrez, but you can't leave this cave. To stop Marion's madness, we need you. We need to kill the lake's power. If we neutralize the lake, she'll be too weak to stop us, and we can finally avenge our sisters. But we have to do it before she gets the Azure Blade."

"What do you mean I can't leave? What the hell are you going to do with us?"

"The well, my dear. The well feeds on the sins of the guilty, just like the lake. We've been satisfying its hunger for centuries with the souls of the guilty, the sinners, and the criminals."

"You're fucking insane," Daisy yelled, realizing her dilemma. She fought the tight rope around her wrist, but her struggle only tightened the knots. "You throw people in the well, you sick fucks?"

Cecil dropped to one knee beside her. There was a callous expression on his face, like a mask from a horror movie.

Daisy tried kicking him, but even her legs were no match for Cecil's strength. He dropped his elbow on her, suppressing her fight with his body weight. She fell to her side and began to weep, realizing she was hapless to escape her peril. She choked on terror, but managed to speak with broken breath as Cecil crushed her with his weight. Her words were barely audible, but Cecil was close enough to understand, "But, I'm not a sinner. I'm not a sinner."

When Cecil replied, there was almost a hint of regret in his tone, "The well is charged by the guilty. To taint it, we need an innocent soul. We need you."

# 29
# ROAD SIGNS

Roshan's voice faded, leaving Cody alone in an illusion of bees buzzing noisily around him. Invisible wings vibrated the air. The little pollinators began to fly away; first one, then ten, fifty, a couple hundred, and the world was silent again. The bees returned to the beautiful field of colorful flowers, but the only thing Cody could see was the ugly image of Flesti Thaed standing on the dock holding a blood-dripping weapon. It was branded on his brain, burned into his memory like a scar.

He couldn't begin to understand why a little girl would commit such a heinous crime. He guessed she was about ten years old in Roshan's projected memory. But then again, he couldn't understand why River Kelly acted the way she did. During the summer months, as a rescue diver, her job was to save people. Now, she was cutting them down in bar parking lots and trailer parks.

So why was she acting this way?

The Azure Blade was the answer to his question. It was the common denominator between Flesti and River. It was driving them.

Flesti's malicious agenda had no bounds. When Cody was fourteen, she had made him close the garage doors, and his parents died from the outcome. Jesse Lewis had committed numerous crimes under her influence. And now, River was under her spell.

Cody's objective was clear, and he hoped Roshan would guide him to the Azure Blade. No matter who possessed it, he had to find and destroy it.

The sound of car tires rolling over gravel derailed his train of thought. Someone was pulling into the church parking lot.

He climbed back up the hill until he reached the building. He expected to see Sheriff Hassett returning, but he didn't recognize the vehicle. He held his position and waited to see who had arrived at the church.

The vehicle, a green Ford Mustang Mach I, backed up slowly. Then, the front tires turned toward him. The car crept forward until it was only three feet away, and he was staring at the driver's windows. The window began to drop, receding into the metal door as Deputy Simpson worked the crank inside. When the glass pane was halfway down, Simpson flashed a toothy smile under his thick mustache.

"Need a lift?"

"Damn right," Cody answered. "But I'm not sure where to. Shouldn't you be at the hospital?"

"Nah, I left the trailer park as soon as the state boys showed up, and I briefed them. Paperwork can wait until tomorrow. We've got a killer to catch."

"We?"

"Can't find the Red Devil without you, Savage."

"I'd rather not refer to her by that name."

"Well, you're not the one she nearly killed...But, yeah, I get it. That's a bit callous of me. I know she's your friend."

Cody just nodded.

"Well, you're not going to find her without a ride, and it just so happens that I have one of the fastest cars in town." Simpson patted the car's steering wheel. "Now, are you going to get in, or do you need an engraved invitation?"

Cody jogged around the car and entered the passenger side. The Mach I was careful not to spin the church's gravel driveway as it left, but the engine was ready to prowl. They pulled out of the parking lot and headed toward town, where they thought they'd have the best chance of finding River Kelly. They talked about the car, the incident at the trailer park, and River Kelly's weapon of choice.

"So, if you can track the blade..." Simpson started, "What's it called again? The Blue Blade?"

"The Azure Blade."

"Yeah, so if you can track the Azure Blade, then you can find her, right?"

"Right. But I'm not sure I can. I've lost my connection to the lake. I've been here for a couple of hours and saw nothing." He didn't want to tell Simpson about his encounter with the bees, thinking it would sound crazy to the deputy. It was difficult enough trying to explain how he had psychic visions that were powered by water. Now he had to describe seeing old memories in a swarm of bees?

"So," Simpson scratched his bald spot. "We just drive around and hope to see her?"

"I'm not sure. But there's a chance Roshan might be able to help us."

"Shari's son? Do we need to go pick him up?"

"No. No, he'll come to us," Cody hoped.

Simpson just shook his head in confusion.

"I know it sounds crazy."

"It sounds as crazy as a fucking house of monkeys if I'm being honest. Like a bunch of monkeys whacked out on crack, crazy. But, hey, right now, we have nothing. No leads. No sightings. No idea where she went or what her motive is."

Cody rolled his window up to cut some of the wind noise that caused them to nearly shout. "Actually, I think her motive is simple."

Simpson side-eyed his passenger, waiting for the semi-psychic's explanation.

"I think she's killing the sinners in town to give the knife power. Every kill energizes the blade. Can't figure out how all that works, but when Flesti gets that knife from River, she's going to feed the sins—the energy—to the lake to regain her power."

"So, Flesti's manipulating River. River kills the sinners. The blade's energy increases, and Flesti revives the lake's power, plus she becomes unstoppable with her new toy. Have I got that correct?"

"Pretty much."

Dave Simpson slowed the car at an intersection and stopped five feet from the octagon sign. "Yeah, a house of cracked-up monkeys has nothing on this town." The car began to roll forward.

"Wait!" Cody shouted.

Simpson threw his foot back on the brake.

Cody opened his door. "Do you see that?" He pointed to a paper poster hanging from the stop sign's post with a laminated finish.

"It's a missing dog poster," Simpson acknowledged.

Cody exited the vehicle and approached the letter-size plea to help find Sisko, a four-year-old Siberian husky. But he didn't see a dog. He couldn't see the letters or a phone number written in sloppy handwriting. Instead, he saw what appeared to be a drawing of a woman on a motorcycle. It was a rough sketch created with fast strokes and loose lines. The bike in the picture was parked at a gas pump with a green starburst in the sky. Cody immediately recognized the clue. "Roshan, you're a genius." Cody ran back to the Mustang. "See that?" He was pointing to the poster for the lost husky.

"Yeah," Simpson replied. "Think the dog has the Azure Blade?"

"No. No, of course, you don't see it. When I look at that poster, I see River on a motorcycle. She's at the BP gas station. Pump number eight. Let's go!"

This time, Simpson let the wheels play on the blacktop, squealing with delight as they turned left. They zipped across town, only slowing when they crossed the railroad tracks, then headed northeast until they reached their destination.

The BP gas station was busy, but there was no sign of River Kelly. Two motorcycles were parked beside the building, but a pair of male riders soon exited the store and mounted the bikes.

"We're too late," Simpson said. "She could have gone anywhere."

Cody had Simpson pull the car forward until they were parked at pump number eight. Cody jumped out again and visually searched the ground while Simpson waited in the car with the engine idling.

Cody walked around the pump, looked in the garbage, and stepped back for a better view.

A truck behind Simpson's car honked twice, which Cody and

Simpson ignored.

Simpson lowered his window to speak to his new partner. "Anything?"

"No. Everything looks ordinary. There's nothing—" Cody stopped mid-sentence and walked back to the pump.

The truck honked again.

"Just a fucking minute!" Cody yelled.

Simpson stuck his left hand out the window and displayed his police badge for the man to consider. The truck backed up and drove around them while identifying them as "Assholes" as he passed the parked Mustang.

"There," Cody said, pointing at the pump-topper sign that, seconds ago, was a promotion for a cheap roller-grilled hot dog. It still looked like a hot dog sign to Simpson, but to Cody, it was another drawing. This one depicted the same woman on the motorcycle. She was cruising down a road with no distinguishable characteristics. "Well, that could be anywhere." Cody stepped closer and realized the double horizon lines of the drawing were train tracks.

From the BP station, the closest railroad track crossing was behind them. River had somehow circled back toward town as if she had no particular destination.

"I think she must have turned up the road and circled back," Cody surmised as he climbed back into the Mustang.

"You got that from a hot dog sign?"

Cody laughed, "Trust me, it doesn't look like a hot dog sign to me."

Simpson bent, lowered, and looked again. He side-eyed Cody, "Looks like a greasy wiener."

"It is, to you. But Roshan has the ability to hack my mind, forcing me to see what he wants me to see. He sends a different signal to my brain from what my eyes do. He can follow River Kelly—or the Azure Blade. I'm not sure which. He draws what he sees at home and then projects that image into my mind. The fucking kid is remarkable."

Simpson put the car in gear and let out the clutch. "I'm going to need a serious vacation when this shit is over."

*****

They sped up the road, turned left at the next intersection, and left again. They made their way southeast until they crossed the railroad tracks.

"Now, where?" Simpson asked.

Cody just shook his head. "I'm not sure. Just keep driving until we see more signs."

Simpson did as advised. They made it back to town, circled the hospital, went past the library, and scoured the park. Roshan's directions had ceased, and Cody sensed all hope draining from his chest. It appeared River Kelly would not be caught tonight. The sun struggled to illuminate the sky any longer as its last light diminished fast.

Simpson flicked the Mach I's headlights on. They drove for forty-five minutes without a single clue or notion of which direction to go.

They parked by the community baseball field. A chain-link fence ran a lap around the green diamond field, adorned with banners from local sponsors. In his rear view mirror, Cody watched one of the banners turn blurry, and a new image replaced the advertisement. Cody jumped out of Simpson's car. What was formerly a Pizza Primo advertisement was now an illustration of the woman he sought.

He described Roshan's drawing to Deputy Simpson, "She's walking through a metal gate with a chain link fence. Like every other drawing, her back's to me, and I can't see her face. There's a dog staring at her—maybe a Great Dane. She's holding the knife. Inside the fence, there's a yellow truck with big tires."

He stepped closer to the banner as the vision faded, and Pizza Primo reoccupied the space.

"Fuck!" Cody cursed and climbed back in the car. "I have no idea where that is. We'll have to wait until another image appears. If another image appears."

Simpson fired up the Mach I's engine. "We don't have to wait,

196

buddy, 'cause I know exactly where that is. And it's not too far." He refrained from spinning the tires on public property, but once the wheels were on the street, he gunned the engine, and they sped away.

# 30

# THE SAINT & SINNER

he two of you are fucking crazy!" Daisy shouted at Cecil and Martin Cain as fascination turned to fear. She struggled against the ropes binding her wrists, but her effort only seemed to tighten the knots. "You bastards won't get away with this. If you throw us in that well, the sheriff, state troopers, and my boyfriend will come looking for us. They will find you. They will arrest you if Cody lets you live."

"There is no leaving this cave until we've tried to fix the well, Ms. Torrez." Cecil retorted with a calm voice. "If you survive the experience, then you may leave. And so shall we. We will no longer have to stay here. We can live anywhere in Cain Falls."

"At least let Bourbon go!"

"Sorry. Once our sister is dead, we'll need to use the old sheriff's sins to revitalize the well. Only a sinner can bring the well back to its original power."

Daisy began to chuckle. "Ain't going to work, asshole. Bourbon doesn't have any sins."

It was Cecil's turn to chuckle. "Is that what you believe?"

"That's what I know. The whole town of Stoneville has nothing but respect for Jeff Bourbon. He's the best damn thing that's ever happened to this community."

Cecil nodded, partially agreeing with Daisy's argument. Then he corrected her. "Do you know the two men who were killed at that rancid bar the other night? Duke Bristol and his cousin Aaron."

She was silent for a moment, thinking about the news report and Bethany Smart's report from WKED. Bethany had never mentioned the victim's names. How were Cecil and Martin privy to this information? They seemed to know more than she did about her town. "So fucking what?" Daisy finally responded. "Those scumbags probably got what they deserved."

"Oh, they did. They did. But do you know who pulled the trigger?"

Daisy looked over at her subdued guide. He was still unconscious on the floor. She was worried about him now. He'd been still too long, yet she could see his lungs expand and contract. He was lying on his side, his hands tied in front. His back was to her. She wanted to see his face before she died. She wanted to see a friendly face that would give her that "It's going to be okay" look. But he didn't turn.

She began crying as the gravity of her situation became clear. That same gravity pulled her back to the floor, limp, tired, and ready to give up. She thought about the nameless baby that grew in its womb, never getting a chance to see daylight, never getting a chance to experience anything wonderful in this world.

Cecil knelt beside her; the little beetle in his beard peeked out. His liquid eyes seemed to cast a light upon her face as the cave grew darker. "It wasn't him. No, Bourbon didn't pull the trigger. He was too much of a coward to do the job himself. So, he hired someone to do it for him. It was some out-of-town ex-con on a motorcycle who did Bourbon's dirty work."

"Then throw him in the well."

"We can't. The young man is dead, killed by the Azure Blade. We thought Flesti had the knife and attacked him herself to protect the sheriff. They have some sort of relationship, you know? That is why we were sure Flesti had the blade. Either she or her pawn killed the only witness who could testify against Mr. Bourbon."

"How the hell do you know all of this if you've been living in a cave?"

Cecil looked into the well, swirled the water once with his fingertips, "You're boyfriend is not the only one gifted with the power of clairvoyance, Ms. Torrez." His creepy smile made chills run down Daisy's spine. She shuddered, thinking about these men watching the rest of the town, like some creepers stalking children.

"There's also the matter of his secret," Cecil continued. "Mr. Bourbon has a secret he keeps from his lady friend, the new sheriff."

Daisy shook her head in disbelief. She didn't know what Bourbon's secret was, didn't want to know. She wouldn't let them bait her, and she wasn't going to ask. She distracted herself from the accusations by focusing on the problem at hand.

River Kelly. She must have the blade. It must be why she attacked Larry Larson.

Daisy sat up again, realizing how this whole story tied together. She unraveled the tangled ball of thoughts and facts in her mind like any good journalist. She contemplated the facts.

*Bourbon had the Bristol cousins killed. Simultaneously, River Kelly attacked Larry Larson. The timing was just a coincidence. The chaos allowed the hit man to get away unidentified. The hit man was later killed for his sin, presumably by River Kelly. Now, Flesti is controlling River with that goddam knife. Flesti's going to restore the lake's power and kill her brothers. The brothers are trying to temporarily eliminate the lake's power so they can kill Flesti.*

She looked to the ceiling, praying no one else had been hurt since the tragedy at Full Throttle.

*Please, Cody, stay out of this one. Please, be home watching a movie, eating popcorn, and waiting for me to come home.*

The cave had cooled, as the shadows began to swallow the light, and Daisy felt goosebumps rise and fall on her skin. She felt as hollow as the room that had become her prison, and just wanted it all to end. She had no more words to plead her case. The Cain brothers were determined to fulfill their sick agenda, and there was nothing she could do about it.

Martin disappeared in the shadows and came out with an armload of wood. He began placing each split piece on the fire. The flames were initially smothered, but once the air reached the hot coals, the dry wood smoldered and burst into bright orange flames. The heat was uncomfortable against Daisy's skin. She turned away to shield her face from the fire's radiance. Her goosebumps refused to vanish as white smoke rose and escaped through a small hole in the cave's ceiling.

She stared through the hole, wishing she could turn to vapor and escape this hell as easily as the wood smoke. Through the opening, the night sky revealed two bright stars set against a blue-black canopy. They were extremely close to each other, like two lovers dancing cheek to cheek for eternity. She watched them dance and twinkle until the smoke became too thick and blocked them from view. She knew they'd be the last stars she ever saw. She named them Cody and Daisy.

"It's time," Cecil said.

"Don't you think we should wait—"

"It's time," Cecil demanded. "We've waited long enough."

"Waited for what?" Daisy asked with a shy tone.

Cecil ignored her question. He grabbed Daisy by the left arm, thick fingers bruising her silky skin, and lifted her to her feet. She struggled against his pull, but the big man was like fighting a gorilla. She was dragged to the well. In a desperate effort, she put her foot against the well's three-foot wall. It was constructed of cement and stone, probably to keep anyone from inadvertently falling into the eight-foot-wide hole.

Martin reached for Daisy's other arm. When he lifted his arm, he exposed his heavy belly and his crude knife with a ten-inch-long blade.

Daisy broke Cecil's grip and snagged Martin's knife with both hands. She spun back around, intent on killing the alpha male. She thrust the blade into Cecil's soft stomach, then pulled it straight out with a satisfying grin. She forced the knife back inside, creating a new hole, and waited for the light in Cecil's brilliant eyes to fade to black.

Martin pulled her back, holding both elbows to thwart a third attack.

Daisy continued watching Cecil's eyes, eagerly waiting to see the diamonds lose their light.

They just sparkled back at her. Cecil grabbed Daisy's wrist and squeezed until the pain was too much for her. The knife clanged as it hit the stone floor. She looked at it. The blood was dark—nearly black—and little specs of light seemed to emit from the surface. Cecil's wounds refused to bleed. Instead, the little micropods within his body formed a seal over the cuts, refusing to let their symbiotic relationship die. It was the same phenomenon that had saved Cody's life twice.

Cecil grunted with amusement rather than pain. "That hurts. Hurts a lot." He kept his grasp on Daisy's wrist, and Martin kept his grip on her elbows. They pulled her back to the well.

Daisy closed her eyes. She considered jumping into the well on her own accord—save herself the humiliation of being flung like a rag doll. She wondered if she would reach the bottom if she dove headfirst. A million stupid questions when all hope is lost.

There was a shuffling sound to her right, and Martin disappeared. Her eyes were still closed, but she felt the younger brother's absence. His heavy breathing was gone. His musty body odor no longer offended her nose.

She sensed motion to her left, and Cecil released her. She opened her eyes, amazed to see Jeff Bourbon on his feet. He had a powerful grip of his own, cinched around Cecil's throat.

Daisy's spirit bursts like a firework. Hope was alive. Her baby would survive. And Jeff Bourbon would make the Cain brothers pay for what they'd done. She didn't know how he'd finally freed himself. Sinner or not, Bourbon was her savior—her baby's hero. All that mattered was that they had a chance to survive.

Bourbon pushed Cecil backwards. Red-hot rage boiled within his veins, and Cecil struggled to breathe. The pit bull-like grip Bourbon had on his throat only tightened as Cecil struggled to escape. Cecil's eyes were wide with surprise. He couldn't understand how Bourbon had escaped until he saw Poe. Poe was standing on the ground amidst a mess of short ropes. He hopped on bony legs and cawed frantically as if wishing to join the melee.

"I'm going to kill that fucking bird!" Cecil cried.

Bourbon turned to Daisy just as Martin regained his footing. The younger brother had been tossed to the ground but was back on his feet. Martin wrapped two thick arms around Daisy and lifted her feet off the ground. He was headed for the well.

Bourbon threw a thick fist of right-hand knuckles into Cecil's face and released his grip.

Cecil gasped for air as he fell to his knees.

Bourbon shot toward Daisy and Martin and tied them both up with his powerful arms. He reached with his right arm, wrapped it around Martin's head, and grabbed his face. He began twisting Martin's head sideways until his neck was ready to snap.

Martin let go of the girl. She landed hard on her left hip, then rolled right to move away from Cecil, who was trying to get off his knees.

Martin spun in the same direction to break Bourbon's grip. He was fast for a little fat man. His spin brought him around until he was facing Bourbon, and then he lunged forward, staying low like a linebacker to tackle his opponent. He hit Bourbon's ribs like a bus and pushed toward the well.

Bourbon threw his right leg back to brace himself, putting the brakes on the bus.

"Don't let him go in the well!" Cecil yelled to his brother.

Cecil recovered from Bourbon's blow. He joined Martin's assault by wrapping his bony arm around Bourbon's neck. Cecil pulled high. Martin pushed low. They tried to bring the big man to the ground beside the well.

Bourbon knew he wasn't going to out power the men. He shouted his final advice. "Daisy. Run!"

Instead of resisting further, Bourbon changed his momentum and pulled the two men. They all hit the short wall of the well and flipped over the edge, head first.

Daisy heard the loud splash. Cool water, displaced by the mass of the men, rose upward and overflowed into the cavern floor. She watched the water flow with gravity and cascade to the lower chamber. It poured from a three-inch hole in the front of the pit wall, which Daisy hadn't noticed before. The water glowed with lumi-nescence, like the lakes she'd seen in videos when people stirred a certain algae. The spilling water illuminated the cave, quickly extinguishing the dying fire.

Daisy ran to the well and yelled her friend's name. She peered over the side. The water inside the well was churning and bubbling, and she couldn't tell if it was from some supernatural effect or the three men still struggling under the surface. She waited several minutes until the water's surface had regained its calm. She tried to look deep into the void, but all she could see was her reflection at the surface.

"Bourbon!" She called his name over and over. But there was no answer.

A hand finally broke the surface. A smile broke across Daisy's face. She reached for him and took his grip. When she pulled, it was Martin's face that appeared. She tried to let go in a frantic scream, but Martin's wet grip stuck. He began to pull himself up, using Daisy as an anchor. His weight crushed her ribs against the wall, making it impossible to breathe.

Daisy searched for the ten-inch knife that had dropped to the floor. Her fingers stretched toward the handle, but it was far from her reach. She used her leg to reach the fire and hooked a half-burned piece of firewood with her toe. She was able to pull it close. It made for an effective club when she struck Martin twice in the head.

His grip relaxed. She twisted her arm free and watched with satisfaction as Martin sank below the surface.

*****

The following two minutes seemed like hours as she waited for Bourbon to surface. She gripped her makeshift club so tightly that splinters skewered her skin. With an overdose of adrenaline, she didn't even notice the pain. She finally dropped the log and conceded to Bourbon's fate. He was gone, but so were the two brothers. She turned to the cave entrance and ran as fast as she dared. At the crevasse where she'd dropped her phone, she stopped for a moment. It was impossible to retrieve the device, so she quickly gave up hope of its retrieval.

In the dark cave, she felt her way for the last twenty feet. The lack of light confused her senses. Her pounding heart was the only sound she could hear. Shaky fingers led the way, groping the wall's rough texture. The low ceiling gave her a gash on her forehead, which disoriented her further. Finally, the warm, fresh air of the mountain urged her through the small opening where she'd entered. She was free of the cliff's terror.

Somewhere to the left side of the cave's entrance, her backpack and Greenie the Meanie were waiting for her. Still reeling from the blow to the head, she made out her pink backpack in the darkness. She dropped to one knee, pulled the pack over her shoulders, and cinched the straps.

She jumped and turned simultaneously, hitting the wall again, and bounced backward.

*Not a wall. Softer.*

The wall moved backward, as surprised as she was. It was a man—tall and solid—who merely let out a grunt.

"Bourbon?" *No. Bourbon would be wet from the well. Who the hell?*

A pair of glowing blue eyes blinked back at her, like looking at the stars with binoculars. The diamond sparkle declared that this was not Bourbon.

*Definitely not Bourbon!*

The shadowy figure reached for her. He was six inches taller than Jeff Bourbon and nearly twice as wide. Daisy dodged his clumsy reach and jumped down the hill. After her feet hit the slick leaves, she slid on her thigh another ten feet. She heard metal snap and felt a bear trap clamp to her backpack, missing her arm by inches. The trap held tight, but she pulled with all her strength until the staked chain ripped from the wet ground. She jumped back into an upright position and moved as fast as she dared. She could see the huge rock split where Bourbon had stepped into the bear trap.

She had to risk it. Jumping like an Olympian, she made it through the field of traps, cleared the log, and darted down the center of the boulder, ruining her new Adidas sneakers in the wet black soil.

The third Cain brother followed behind; although his pace was slower, he seemed to know all the right places to step.

With her eyes adjusted to the darkness, she kept moving like a skier on a slalom course, weaving through the trees. The bear trap and its light chain jingled as she ran, and she considered dropping her backpack, but she didn't want to toss the crucial gear inside. If she could outrun the giant behind her for another ten minutes, then she'd take the time to pry the trap off her pack.

She looked to the sky and saw Star Cody and Star Daisy hovering in the northern sky over Stoneville. The were still together, shining bright, so that's the direction she and Greenie the Meanie ran.

# 31
# CATCH THE DEVIL 

Cody's palms sweated as Deputy Simpson steered the classic muscle car into a rough, paved parking lot. The lot was narrow, forty feet from side to side, and not much longer. The Mustang crept toward a chain-link fence and stopped. A single street light illuminated a rusty metal sign hanging on the fence. Cody read the business's name to himself: Big Sid's Towing and Hauling.

"Sid's is the only tow truck business in town," Simpson confirmed. "Three years ago, he hauled this car up from Sodus Point. This is where all the impounded vehicles go. Gate's not closed, but I don't think they're open."

"No, but somebody must be here," Cody responded. "Why else would River come here? She must have a target."

Simpson just nodded.

They left the car blocking the front gate, with the doors open, making it too wide for a motorcycle to escape. Cody went to the right, and Simpson stayed left, leading with his 10mm. Walking in a half squat, they entered the gate and stayed in the shadows.

"What about the dog?" Cody whispered. "The dog in the drawing was huge. I'm guessing it was Sid's watchdog."

"That's Magnum, Sid's security. I've never seen him be aggressive unless Sid gives the right command. I've walked right by Magnum plenty of times without incident, but if he thinks you're a problem, then you've got a problem."

"Maybe you should stay behind me," Simpson said with a firm grip on his gun.

"No, let's split up. Surround her if we find her."

"You gonna face her without a weapon?" Simpson asked. "She hates you the most, after what happened to your buddy."

"I'll be okay," Cody hoped.

A door closed somewhere in the distance. Their view was obstructed by dozens of damaged vehicles parked on the property. The cars and trucks were aligned in two neat rows down the center of the property. A driveway down the middle provided an access corridor for Sid's long tow truck to enter and turn around. The single streetlight reflected off the shiny, metallic fence that encircled the property. Cody guessed it was almost two acres of scrap cars, trucks, and SUVs. Three yellow tow trucks were parked on the right side, just beyond the row of wrecked vehicles.

"I'll go toward the office," Simpson said, pointing toward a building with corrugated steel siding and a low-pitch roof. "If she's looking for somebody, that's where she'll find them."

Cody nodded, "I'll circle around in case she tries to escape on the other side. Meet you at the office." He split to the left, creeping behind the collection of damaged vehicles.

Deputy Simpson went right, clearing the street light without being detected, and followed the line of bumpers toward the office. He hid between the cars, scanned ahead, slid to the next gap, and crouched behind the vehicle fenders when he paused. Thirty yards ahead, a dim light shone through the office window.

He kept moving, thinking about the way the Red Devil had nearly pierced his heart earlier. She had complete control of her weapon as it spun past him. He was lucky to leave the trailer park alive. Would he be so fortunate the second time? He wiped the sweat off his brow with his forearm and moved halfway to the office before ducking between cars.

"Looking for me?" A female voice whispered behind him. Simpson spun, pistol ready to fire, and aimed at nothing but air. He stood erect, braced his shooting hand to steady his sights, and called to River. "Come on out, River. We just want to talk." He backtracked ten steps and spun the gun barrel between a Ford Explorer and a

Volkswagen Atlas. There was no one there.

Simpson heard the chain link fence behind him rattle. He quickly turned toward the sound. She wasn't there either. He took six significant steps back toward the office when something whizzed by his nose. The sound of the Azure Blade was unmistakable as it returned from the direction it came. The blade was blazing with blue light that could have been mistaken for flames. The light momentarily blinded Simpson as his pupils contracted. It took a moment for his eyes to acclimate to the dark again.

Simpson's trigger finger grew anxious. This part of the lot was shrouded in darkness. His Sig Sauer pistol pointed like a hunting dog in the direction he believed River was located. The gun had found its target. River's athletic frame came into focus. She backed away slowly, making her way toward the office one step at a time. Simpson mimicked her stride, stepping forward with every step backward.

"River! River, drop the knife and stay where you are. I promise we're not going to hurt you."

The feminine shadow took one more step backward. A motion-activated security light lit up the yard, punching Deputy Simpson's eyes like pepper spray. He lost sight of his target and held his left hand to his brow to block the intense lumens of the floodlight. He dashed forward and stopped abruptly. The woman didn't move. Simpson kept his right arm outstretched, ready to fire if she tried to throw that damn knife again.

Then Simpson heard the rattle of a chain and felt something crush his forearm as Sid's second security system leaped upon him. Magnum, a 115-pound Cane Corso—head like a Great Dane, body like a Rottweiler—growled and snarled as it pulled on Simpson's arm.

The deputy fired a shot in the air to ward off the dog. It worked. Magnum jumped back, releasing his toothy grip on Simpson's arm. He disappeared into the shadows but lunged right back. Simpson spun on his ass, putting his feet toward the canine to block the next attack. In a desperate attempt, he dug his heels into the pavement and pushed himself away, hoping to move beyond the reach of the canine's chain. Magnum's jaws snapped just short of the deputy's leg but managed to get a grip on the cuff of his pants.

As Simpson fought against the immense power of the security dog, he lost his grip on the pistol. Without looking, he knew the woman with the knife was standing just feet away. Magnum straddled Simpson's pistol, and Simpson knew that he would be dead if Cody didn't show up again to save him.

Magnum let go of the pants. Instead of pulling on his prey, he lunged forward. His teeth, white in the night, snapped closed three feet from Simpson's face. The good deputy was backed against a stack of tires that formed a wall eight feet high and twenty feet long. He braced his legs against the dog's shoulders, pushing back in the fight for his life.

Magnum lunged again. His leather collar broke from the force of his attack. The massive beast jumped upward, hoping to land on his victim and pin him to the ground. Two-inch teeth flashed—a blue light zipped by Simpson's face. Magnum let out his last high-pitched wince as the Azure Blade ripped through his throat. Magnum dropped on Simpson's legs, pinning him as he intended. But he wheezed for air through his cut trachea and bled profusely out of severed arteries.

Simpson's emotions twisted and knotted as he watched the dog die on his lap. He was relieved that the dog's fury had come to an end, but did his life have to as well? Magnum was doing what he was trained to do, and now the beautiful creature was dead for it.

"What the fuck?" He yelled at the woman. The deputy wriggled out from under the dog and pushed himself to his hands and knees.

She stood motionless, her black hoodie cloaking her in the intense gleam of the security light. The Azure Blade glowed with excitement. She moved closer to Simpson, pointing the blade toward his face, and picked up his gun before he could scramble to grab it. As she picked up the Sig Sauer, she lowered her weapon. Simpson lunged at her, hoping to get a grip, so she couldn't escape until Cody arrived. But his injured forearm failed him, and as he grabbed the back of her hoodie, she dropped her head and threw her arms forward. She backed out of the hoodie, leaving Simpson with nothing but a handful of clothing.

She stood in a black T-shirt and stared at the confused officer for a moment.

Nobody moved when they heard footsteps approach from behind them. Cody had heard the commotion but had to navigate the maze of cars and piles of tires in the dark to reach the ruckus.

He stopped behind the woman with the knife. She didn't turn around to face him. The security light shone on her like a stage spotlight, illuminating her in its powerful light, casting her in a white and gray hue.

Cody felt his breath leave his lungs. She didn't have to turn around. She didn't have to speak. All she had to do was stand in plain view for Cody to know the truth.

The Red Devil was not River Kelly.

She wore jeans, tight as paint, with just a hint of a silver thong peeking from the top.

Cody's breath finally returned.

He forced a whisper, "Alyse?"

# 32

# FINDING RIVER 

Cody kicked and pushed a half-dozen tires as he freed himself from the pile that entrapped him. Stale, moldy water that had accumulated during rain showers splashed out of the tires and soaked his clothes. The pungent water urged him to work faster, so he pushed the tires off his abdomen and legs until he could finally get his feet under himself.  Climbing over the pile of rubber, he looked for Deputy Simpson, who was pulling the car tires from the fallen stack.

"You okay?" Simpson asked, reaching out with his good arm.

Cody grabbed Simpson's hand and stood, "Don't worry about me. How's the arm?"

Simpson held the bleeding dog bite on his forearm. "Doesn't hurt too bad, but it's bleeding pretty good."

Cody stepped over a tire, which stubbornly trapped his boot. He pulled his leg free and kicked the tire to the side. The used tires had been neatly formed into a wall minutes ago. Now, they lay strewn about the yard.

Magnum the Cane Corso lay dead in a pool of blood, and Alyse Burns was nowhere to be found.

His memory of the last minute was a blur, but it came into focus as he escaped the tumbled pile of Goodyears. Alyse had surprised him. First, it was her presence. Then, it was her attack. She'd thrown the Azure Blade at Cody, just missing his head. That was no mistake. It was a warning. The knife got stuck in a wall of rubber radials. That was a mistake. Cody grabbed the knife, felt the pain of a hundred blades stab his mind, and then a voice echoed in his skull.

"No. Let go!" Flesti Thaed had demanded in a telepathic assault. Cody had no choice. As long as he was touching the blade, Flesti could make him open his hand. Her control ceased the moment he broke contact, leaving him disoriented with a burning skull.

As the knife fell from Cody's hand, it returned dutifully to Alyse. As she caught the weapon, she threw her right heel into Cody's midsection. The kick knocked the wind from his sails. Knuckles from her left fist dropped down on his cheek. Her punch was stronger than it should have been, nearly breaking his cheekbone. A second kick came immediately after the punch, sending Cody over a small stack of tires and into the taller pile, which collapsed on top of him.

"I'm sorry," Alyse had said. "I can't stop it. I can't..." There was shame in her voice. Torment in her eyes, and Cody knew Flesti was controlling her actions. "Cody, don't follow me, you'll get yourself killed. Please!"

*She could have killed me. She chose not to.*

Cody snapped back to the present and turned to the injured deputy, "Did you see which way she went?"

A bloody finger pointed to the chain link fence beside the office. Simpson described how she had climbed a large tractor tire, hopped onto the dumpster, pulled herself onto the roof, and then jumped over the fence.

*Fuck.*

Cody and Simpson walked to the office. An elderly man with thick glasses sat in a ragged leather chair with stuffing falling out of its arms. The man's hair was white as snow and still thick for his age. Cody guessed he was close to seventy years old. A large belly rested in his lap, and he could have been asleep on the job. But the blood running down the back of the chair indicated the man had worked his last shift.

"Sid?" Cody asked.

Simpson stepped over to the  to the resting corpse and pulled the head forward. "Nah." There was a single wound in the back of his skull. "This is Ruben—Sid's employee. He works nights, answering calls and driving one of the trucks. He was a gruff, miserable old bastard. Still...”

Cody called the deputy's name for attention, then nodded to the wall behind him. A large map of the town hung on the wall. Across the region, from frame to frame, the word SINNER was written in large letters.

Simpson took a picture with his cell phone and sent the image to his boss. While Simpson sent the text message, Cody found a few clean rags and a roll of duct tape. He wrapped a rag around Simpson's arm and secured it with the tape.

“We best get you to the hospital. This might need a few stitches.”

“No, I'll go later. It'll be fine for now. Let's go after that bitch.”

“That bitch is one of my only friends, Simpson. We can't hurt her. Flesti Thaed is controlling her.”

“Well, then, let's go find that bitch.”

Cody agreed. To save Alyse, they had to find Flesti before she possessed the Azure Blade. They had to keep following Alyse, but it was late. Cody wasn't sure he'd receive another image from Roshan. The little artist was probably tucked into bed by now.

While Cody thought about their next move, Simpson called the district attorney, Dale Kelly, to let him know his daughter was not the killer they sought. Kelly was, of course, thrilled to hear this revelation. Simpson disconnected the call with the DA, and scratched at his balding head.

“Mr. Kelly must be elated to hear the news,” Cody said.

“He is, but now he's concerned about River's whereabouts. She's not answering her phone, and he hasn't seen her in days.”

“I think I know exactly where to find her.”

*****

Cody knocked on the front door of the blue house on the hill. The lights were off, but he knew AJ Timmons was home. He kept knocking and ringing the doorbell. “AJ. AJ, open up! Come on, man. I need to talk to you.”

A light upstairs finally turned on. Then, another in a hallway, and one more somewhere near the foyer. The heavy front door finally opened.

AJ Timmons was wearing long pajama pants and a Ghost Rider T-shirt. His thick brown hair was a mess. He squinted through tired eyelids at Cody and the off-duty deputy standing at his door.

"Jesus, Cody, you know I work early. What the hell's going on?" He stood in the doorway, with his body blocking the view of the interior of his home.

"Where is she, AJ? I know she's here." Cody said, reigning in his attitude.

AJ knew there was no denying what Cody was insinuating. He slowly opened the door and allowed the two visitors to enter. Someone descended the stairs to the left, her steps as light as a cat's. River Kelly appeared with glossy eyes. She was biting a thumbnail. Her eyes darted back and forth from AJ to Cody and Deputy Simpson.

"She's been here the whole time," AJ admitted. "She didn't mean to hurt Larry Larson."

Simpson nodded at River but spoke to AJ. "Son, have you been watching the news?"

"No, sir."

"There have been a lot more victims than just Larry Larson. Except," Simpson swallowed hard. "He was the lucky one. People are dying."

"Sinners," Cody added. "She's killing sinners."

"I didn't kill anyone," River broke out in tears and shame. "I didn't mean to hurt him. The knife...I know it sounds crazy, but that goddam knife made me do it."

Cody held up a hand. "We know all about the knife, River. And we're not talking about you."

AJ closed the front door. "Who? Who are you talking about?"

"It's Alyse, AJ. Alyse has the Azure Blade—"

"The what?"

"It's Flesti's knife—the one River attacked Larry Larson with. Her ability to control people is amplified if they possess that knife. She's killing sinners, just like Jesse Lewis used to, and she's going to use the knife to bring Cain Lake's power back."

AJ moved to River's side as they interlocked their fingers. "So, what's going to happen to River?"

Deputy Simpson took out his phone. "River hasn't killed anyone. And Larry Larson admitted that he's had a crush on her since high school. He might drop the assault charges. And with her father being the District Attorney, I'm sure we can reach a deal if she cooperates and tells us where the knife came from and how it came into Alyse Burn's possession."

*****

AJ moved to the kitchen and hit the start button on his coffee machine, which had been already been programmed to begin brewing at 4:30. As the carafe filled with freshly brewed Ethiopian coffee, River retreated upstairs to dress. The sweet, earthy aroma teased their noses. Once the coffee pot finished, it beeped a notification. The three men added cream and sugar to their beverages as River returned, dressed in jeans and a New York Giants T-shirt, prepared to be debriefed. AJ handed her a mug, made just the way she liked it. She kissed him without saying thanks.

They all sat at the dining room table.

Simpson's eyes lit up when he tasted the organic beverage for the first time. It was pleasingly smooth and bold, with notes of blackberry and blueberries and a hint of lemon. He held up his cup and gave AJ a satisfying smile.

"It's the volcanic soil," AJ confirmed. "Grows better beans."

Simpson dove back into his cup, forgetting about the pain in his arm.

Cody gulped down half of his hot beverage, wiped his mouth, and turned to River. She sat close to the table with her hands wrapped around the mug. She seemed to enjoy the heat and steam on her face more than the taste of the imported beans.

"River, how did the Azure Blade come into your possession?"

219

She was hesitant to speak, fearing that she would incriminate herself. AJ reached over and took her hand, and she sat straight, cleared her throat, and began her explanation.

"I didn't know what it was," she said. "At least, I didn't know it was dangerous. I knew it was a knife, but I hoped it was valuable."

"Okay," Cody said. "But, where did you find it?"

She rubbed her forehead. "Diving. I was diving in Cain Lake. It was the day I first met the two of you. I was with the search and rescue team, looking for that missing girl."

"Darcy Poole. That was the day Deputy Archer pushed AJ into the lake."

River nodded. "You yelled that he couldn't swim and went in after him."

"Actually, Archer kicked me in the head, and I fell in, half-conscious," Cody remembered. "I nearly drowned, but you saved us both. Now, we want to save you."

A tear dropped from River's cheek and nearly landed in her coffee. "Before that happened, we were searching the middle of the lake. I'd moved toward an area that was over thirty feet deep. I swam at about half that depth when I noticed something blue in the water."

"The Azure Blade?" Simpson asked.

"No," River continued. "It was a little blue light, like a jellyfish no larger than a tick. And then it became two. They swam right in front of my face mask. They continued to divide and multiply over and over. Soon, that single mini jellyfish became hundreds. They moved in unison, like a swarm. It was the most beautiful thing I'd ever seen. I lost focus, mesmerized by the lights. I was scared, but it was so peaceful."

She tested the temperature of her beverage with her lips and took a sip. As the coffee went down, her story came out.

"Then what happened?" Cody urged her to continue.

"The lights began to swirl around me. I became disoriented and couldn't tell which way was up. I finally calmed myself, trusted my training, and followed my bubbles. The bubbles always rise to the surface. But the water kept swirling, and soon, I could feel myself being pulled down to the bottom. The pressure was immense at that depth. I kicked so hard. I kicked and pulled, but nothing I did worked. I gave in, certain I was going to drown. As I was pulled to the bottom, I saw it—just lying there—a blue oblong stone like nothing I'd ever seen before. Once I grabbed it, the little jellyfish disappeared, and the water released me. The little blue jellyfish guided me to the Azure Blade."

Cody, Simpson, and AJ listened quietly, hanging on every word River spoke. She told them how she had the sheath made. She repeated Dr. Claxton's theory about the ancient knife and how it could be made of a rock called chert. And she admitted that a woman's voice urged her to seek revenge whenever she held it.

River admitted she wanted revenge on the Road Barons for putting AJ in a coma. She apologized to Cody for having malevolent thoughts about him and the Barons.

AJ interrupted her story, "I don't blame you, Cody. I did, at first, but River finally convinced me that it was my fault. I followed you to that old store. I put myself in that situation and would do it again."

"I hope you never have to, brother."

"Me too," AJ admitted.

"So," Cody pulled his chair closer to River. "How did Alyse get the knife away from you? Did you attack her, too?"

"No. No, I like Alyse. I never intended for it to end up in anyone else's hands. I thought I put it back in the sheath after the shooting at The Fuel Line. But I must have dropped it because it was gone when I got home. I panicked and came here. I knew I was in so much trouble."

"She's been here ever since the night of the shooting," AJ confirmed. "Even when I had the party for Alyse, River was hiding upstairs in the bedroom. That's why I couldn't let you into my house that night. I was afraid you'd sense her here with your abilities."

Cody leaned back in his chair. A sense of relief flooded his emotions. AJ didn't hate him as much as he'd thought. He stared at his coffee cup for a moment. "You should have told me then...trusted me. You know I would have had your back."

"I know. It was a moment of poor judgment. I'll never doubt you again."

"My abilities are gone. I can't find Alyse or anyone else in trouble. I'm just ordinary Cody again."

AJ stood, swallowed the last ounce of his coffee, and nearly broke the mug, slamming it down. "Well, now that we're all caffeinated, Alyse is out there with Flesti Thaed mind-fucking her with an ancient knife. We owe it to her to help. Let's go find our friend."

Cody and Simpson stood as well. Cody shook AJ's hand, "Are you sure you're up to this, buddy?"

AJ nodded, "Hell, yes. Alyse has been there for me every day since you returned to town. I'm not going to abandon her now."

Cody just nodded in agreement and swallowed the last of his drink.

River almost smiled seeing the two friends together again. "Cody, does Daisy know where you are? Do you want to call her first?"

"No, it's okay. She's probably out of cell phone range. She's hiking around Cain Lake with Bourbon, trying to find Flesti Thaed."

"Aren't you worried about what will happen if she finds her?"

"She won't. Flesti's powers are dwindling as the lake dies—just like mine have, so she must be close to the blade, on the north side of Cain Lake. Daisy's looking for her on the south side. Trust me, she's safer where she is."

# 33

# RUN LITTLE RABBIT 

Daisy stopped running toward the stars. She'd been jogging down-hill for a quarter-mile, but the distance seemed like a marathon as she dodged trees, climbed over logs, and descended cliffs. The direction was aimless, and she didn't care where she ended up, as long as she was putting the danger behind her. The terrain changed, heaving upward for thirty yards at a steep angle, so she climbed until her legs began to feel like they would fail. As she crested the hill, the land flattened in an area the size of a basketball court, clear of large trees, and lined with a stone wall on one side. It appeared to be an old farmer's meadow, perhaps from the 1800s. The scent of apples and grass pollen saturated the air.

An animal yipped ten yards ahead and dashed off, cutting through the tall grass in fear of the human. Dark shapes and shadows with silver highlights from the moon's dim glow filled her vision. Anything could be in front of her—a bear, coyotes, Bigfoot. She didn't care. Nothing could be worse than what was behind her: the third Cain brother chasing her with a double-edged ax. The weapon reminded her of the Sin-eater's deadly instrument of death that Cody had used to cut his hand off to escape a burning barn, before chasing down Charlie Archer. But this was no improvised tool. It had a forged steel head and a solid hardwood handle. It was not meant for slicing through flesh but rather splitting wood and perhaps animal bones.

Exhaustion took its toll, and she needed to rest before continu-ing her escape. As dew formed on the grass, the moisture wicked through her pant legs. She found a small rock, just large enough to sit on to keep her ass from getting wet.

A thick cloud pushed across the dotted sky, blocking the stars and moon. The silver highlights that gave the landscape shape and depth were snuffed out in an instant. The only light now was the bio luminescence of a few dozen fireflies, but that was no help to her.

She hated the dark.

She concentrated on her breathing, trying to slow her circulation and restore her energy. It took longer than she anticipated. While she breathed deep through her nose and exhaled slowly through her mouth, she watched the fireflies float amidst the tall grass. She counted them to occupy her mind.

*…Nineteen, twenty, twenty-one, twenty-two.*

Her breathing resumed its regular cadence. With her lungs and heart pumping silently now, she could close her eyes and listen. She held her breath in short intervals, trying to hear the heavy foot-steps of her pursuer. It was quiet. She held her breath, listened, exhaled slowly, and repeated the process. This went on cyclically for over ten minutes. The night was as silent as an empty church until a little cricket, hidden under her rock perch, performed a solo melody as it called for a mate.

*I feel ya, buddy.*

She was feeling optimistic that the third Cain Brother had given up his pursuit and returned to the cave, only to find it empty with a flooded fire and Martin's knife on the floor. He'd probably piece it together and know what had transpired in his stone home.

The bear trap was still biting onto her backpack, and she knew the rattling noise it made was making her audible for a hundred yards, maybe more. She used a couple of heavy sticks as leverage, combined with her body weight, to open the steel jaws. The chore made her sweat, and her heart rate spiked for a moment from the effort.

With the extra weight off her bag, she gingerly unzipped the backpack, fearing the sound was like a bugle in the still night. At the bottom, her fingers searched until they fell upon the berries she'd picked earlier. Savory morsels of energy. They hit her tongue like a flavor bomb. A dopamine spike convinced her she'd be alright, but her adrenaline reminded her not to drop her guard. She took a timid bite of a wild apple and chewed slowly so she could listen while she ate. The tart flesh of the fruit made her mouth water, and she welcomed the sensation.

An hour passed. She slipped a hoodie over her shoulders and kept a headlight in her pocket as a precaution. She knew it would be a mistake if she turned the light on. The powerful beam would slice through the dark and give away her location. She needed to endure the night until the sun arose and painted the forest with its warm light.

She finally felt safe enough to relax, but couldn't muster the nerve to start walking again. She wanted to stay still—silent, inconspicuous, like a newborn fawn hiding in the bushes. She closed her eyes and whispered something like a prayer, but not to God.

"Please, Cody. Please, see me right now. Please hear me. I'm lost. Bourbon's dead. I've never asked for your help, but if there has ever been a time in my life when I needed anyone, it's now. I need you to find me. I never should have left."

She cried into her shirt sleeve to muffle her weakness, careful not to reveal her location. Once her sobbing stopped, she listened to the forest. It was deathly quiet as if only darkness existed, and she feared this might be similar to actual death—no light in a tunnel, no pearly gates, no angels singing upon her arrival.

Unless the cricket was an angel.

The heavy cloud that tortured her finally moved to the east, revealing the quarter moon. Star Cody and Star Daisy revealed themselves, still floating in a lover's embrace.

As dim as the moonlight was, it was still light, filling her with a sense of security. Her pursuer might be visible now, even in this dismal light.

She hated this. She was tired of being the scared little fawn.

She was certain Cody couldn't hear her plea.

*He's not coming, dumbass. He's not going to save you. So, get off your ass and do something!*

She stood, wiped away her tears, then gripped a handful of hair at the back of her head and slipped a tie from her wrist around the locks to create a ponytail. She twisted the hair tie three times and began working on a plan. If Cody weren't to save her, she would have to save herself.

*****

An hour passed. Daisy sat on her rock, waiting in anticipation—waiting to confront the third Cain brother.

A small fire now glowed at her feet, announcing her presence to the world, and the big Cain brother that would surely see it. It provided unnecessary heat. More importantly, it eased her loneliness. She ate more berries and a protein bar and drank nearly all her water.

Somewhere on the edge of the meadow, a stick broke. She had covered her entrance with hundreds of dry, dead branches, which formed a natural proximity alarm. In her hand, she held a chunk of rock the size of a softball, but shaped like a slice of pizza and nearly two inches thick. It wasn't her only weapon, but it was the only weapon she held.

Another stick broke.

She stood and stepped slowly toward a wiry apple tree with twisting limbs that intertwined. The tree had a broken leader that had fallen to the side and leaned on the ground. The fractured end of the leader was stuck in the tree about chest high. The dead limb was bare, its leaves long dead and gone, although the rest of the tree thrived with leaves and small yellow apples. She kept the tree between her and the figure entering the meadow.

Jonathan Cain, Cecil's fraternal twin, who was much taller and muscular, watched Daisy move behind the tree. She kept the wiry tree between them. He came closer, parting the tall grass until he was near the fire and exposed his actual size.

Daisy swallowed hard, wondering if she was making a mistake. She was too tired to run anymore, too scared to question his intentions. She studied his weapon—a deadly double-headed weight on a three-foot handle against her slice of pizza.

Jonathan paused and felt the heat of the fire, expecting the little woman to run. But she stood her ground, frozen behind the apple tree. He didn't want to kill her. She was supposed to go into the well alive. He didn't want to scare her any more than he already had. He set his ax on the ground and rested the handle against the rock. The cricket fell silent as Jonathan began to creep toward her, his palms up in a nonthreatening gesture. He took six small steps toward her without anything to fight with besides his hands, but that was enough. He had the hands of a giant, capable of crushing her skull with a squeeze.

Daisy struggled to control her bladder when he was close enough to smell. The scent of body odor, wet moss, and dead leaves drifted downwind toward her. He was a head taller than Jeff Bourbon and twice as wide. Mainly in the shoulders and back. Despite his age, his hair and beard still had most of their black color, and streaks of gray adorned his chin and temples. He raised his hands, "Are you going to keep running, little rabbit? I'm not going to hurt you. I just need your help. Can you help me?"

Daisy mustered the courage to speak, "Help you? Like, go into the well of hell, where your brothers tried to throw me? Cecil and Martin Cain are your brothers, am I right?"

"Yes, I'm Cecil's twin, Jonathan."

"So, Jonathan, Marion Cain is your sister?"

"Also true. I assume my brothers have told you all you need to know—maybe more. But we just want to protect you from Marion. Once the lake is dead, we can kill her, and she won't hurt anyone ever again."

"I'm not afraid of her."

"You should be, rabbit. You haven't seen what she can do. She can control everyone who's been in the lake. The longer you spend in the water, the more it affects you. And you've spent quite some time in our lake. I can sense it in you."

"Is that how you found me?"

"Yes. That, and your fire. I can sense the lake in your body, and she will, too. Then, you're hers to command." Jonathan took short steps as he tried to convince Daisy to give up. He'd reached the outer limbs of the apple tree, his eyes locked on hers as he stared her down. He reached out with an open hand and spoke. His voice was deep and smooth, even hypnotic.

"Come, little rabbit. Don't make me chase you anymore."

"Stop!" Daisy demanded. "Don't come any closer to us."

"Us? You're all alone, little rabbit."

"Daisy held the headlight and pushed the power button on. "That's not exactly true." She shined the light to Jonathan's right. He turned to follow the beam and laughed at its target. Hanging from the tree limb, eye level with the giant, was Greenie the Meanie.

"That's Greenie the Meanie. His job is to protect me. I wouldn't piss him off if I were you."

Jonathan grinned with amusement. Did she seriously think this plastic monster was going to save her? He took a step to snatch the little creature from the tree for further inspection. The sound of metal snapped, and he felt a crushing pain around his ankle. Steel teeth bit into flesh and bone. Jonathan grimaced in pain and fell to the ground. His right hip landed hard on a stone, exacerbating the pain shooting through his nerves. Once he'd realized his mistake, he sat up and started prying a rusty bear trap off his foot.

He was impressed by the rabbit's resourcefulness. He knew the trap was his own, and how smart was she to have used it for defense?

He yelled in anger and pain and turned back toward the tree trunk. Daisy hit him with a bright beam of light from her headlight, blinding him momentarily. She ran around the tree and dropped to her knees. As she did, she brought all of her weight down with the pizza rock gripped tightly. The sharp rock smashed the top of Jonathan's trapped foot. She hadn't dared to go for his head—that would have put her within reach of his hands, which could grip her like the trap around his ankle. She leaped back, as fast as a rabbit, as he swiped at her with a large paw.

She ran past the trapped bear. He lunged for her, only to find the trap was tied to the tree trunk. The jolt nearly dislocated his knee. The teeth of the trap dug deeper into his flesh. He twisted on his ass to try working his foot free. Powerful hands grabbed the sides of the trap. He squeezed with enough force to open the jaws and free himself.

He cursed out loud. When he turned back to see where she was running, she hit his eyes again with the bright beam of the headlight. He lost sight of her again. Fighting to stand on his half-chewed ankle and injured knee, he sensed her presence beside him. Then he felt the weight of his ax drop on his good leg. It didn't break a bone—the ax was too heavy for her to swing with power—but it did leave a painful gash in his calf.

On the upswing, the blunt side of the ax head caught Jonathan in the chin, steel against bone. He reeled from the blow, and the stars that danced in his eyes were from a concussion.

The headlight fell from her hands as she wrestled with the heavy ax. It landed too close to Jonathan, so she didn't dare to pick it up.

Daisy snagged Greenie the Meanie from the tree, lifted her backpack as she ran, and only stopped for a moment to kick dirt over her fire, leaving Jonathan Cain in the dark.

Jonathan collapsed in defeat, chuckling to himself. Lying in the dark, unable to walk, he conceded that he'd been beaten by a hundred-and-twenty-pound girl and her plastic dinosaur. He chuckled at himself a little. "Run, little rabbit. Run." He rolled onto his back and gazed skyward toward the stars, as if they were his audience, and spoke to them as if they'd granted his last wish. "I love a good chase."

# 34

# THE DEFENDER 

Deputy Simpson's pain from Magnum's bite increased with every passing minute. He had to concede that the cracked bone in his arm and the multiple puncture wounds he'd suffered were winning against his desire to stay on the hunt for Alyse Burns. To make matters worse, his dominant hand—his shooting hand—was now useless as the swelling in his wrist and forearm tightened around tendons and ligaments.

"I can barely move my fingers," the deputy said as he tried to wiggle his digits.

So, he volunteered to take River Kelly to her father's house, promising Cody he'd go straight to the emergency room afterward.

River donned her shoes and kissed AJ as they held each other for a moment. There was a nervous tone in her voice as she thought about facing her father, and she was reluctant to even go to his house.

"He's the only person who can help you now," Simpson reassured her.

She climbed into the passenger side of Simpson's old Mustang without waving goodbye, and they drove down the long driveway and turned right onto Redmill Road.

Cody stood at the top of the driveway, watching them leave. Once the roar of the Mach I's engine was gone, the night was smothered in silence. Above, two bright stars he'd never noticed before twinkled in the dark sky. He wasn't sure why they drew his attention. Their proximity made them more intense than most other stars in the sky. He smiled, thinking about Daisy, and wondered if she had noticed the two heavenly bodies. He was sure that she was probably sitting around a little fire with Bourbon, complaining about the mosquitoes and planning their agenda for tomorrow. He hoped she was enjoying herself, even though he wished she hadn't gone into the woods without him.

As Cody star-gazed, AJ went back upstairs and dressed. He returned to the driveway wearing jeans and a black hoodie, which Cody thought must have been too warm but didn't comment on the choice of apparel.

AJ pulled a key fob from his jeans pocket and hit a button. The sixteen-foot-wide garage door lifted with a low growl as an electric motor smoothly raised the door. A harsh light from the garage flooded the driveway. Cody squinted against the intrusive light. His eyes had just adjusted to the shade of night, and now they were being assaulted. When he was finally able to see, he set his attention to the two vehicles gleaming in the fluorescent lights. They were washed, waxed, and polished to perfection. The Ram TRX had its back to Cody, parked facing inward, as if it were put to bed for the night. Cody hadn't seen it since the night he and AJ were attacked by Levi Thompson. Alyse had used the truck to drag two motorcycles up the road to distract Levi and his companions.

From the right side of the garage bay, an unfamiliar face stared back at Cody. AJ clicked the key fob again. A chirping sound emitted from the garage as the strange face lit up with anticipation.

"What the hell is that?" Cody asked, stepping toward the SUV.

"That's my new Land Rover Defender. Got it yesterday. Shall we break it in?"

Cody walked around the Defender to admire the modern design, careful not to touch the clean paint. He pulled the passenger side door open. "Hell yeah! Shit, I'd ride in your wheelbarrow if it gets us to Alyse."

"I don't own a wheelbarrow, so this'll have to do."

They took their seats inside the vehicle. Cody melted into the luxury fabric of the bucket seat. Red ambient light bathed the interior like a spaceship from a movie.

AJ started the engine with the push of a button. A twin-turbo V8 engine came to life with a unique roar that echoed off the garage's walls.

They left the brightly lit garage and entered the night. The Defender eased down the driveway, took the same direction as Simpson's Mustang, and accelerated like a horse out of the gates.

"So, how are we going to find her?" AJ asked.

"I'm not sure. It appears she's been making her way toward the lake. If I were a betting man, I'd say she's going to meet up with Flesti Thaed and give her the knife. Let's head toward the lake and hope luck is on our side."

"Since when has luck been on our side?"

"Well, we got two of the prettiest girls in town," Cody japed.

AJ smiled for the first time in days. "Hell yeah, we did."

*****

Across town, a small house sat in a quiet neighborhood. Within the house, not a single light was shining through the windows. It was bedtime in the Kapoor household. The county coroner was reading a spicy romance novel on her iPad while her husband snored in the bed beside her. Her day had been exhausting, but there was no sleeping until she had an opportunity to escape into her book. She slides the page to the left with her index finger and dives into the next. She's immersed in a fictional world of romantic pirates and beautiful castaways. Stoneville and the day's grim events are pushed to the deepest recesses of her mind. Her attention is lost in the Caribbean Sea, where she can tune out the world and forget about the blood and the carnage she witnessed at the trailer park. The e-book wraps her in a world she's never been to and won't leave until it's time to brush her teeth.

Downstairs, in one of the two children's bedrooms, Roshan Kapoor was lay in his bed. He was almost asleep until an image slapped him awake. He slid out of bed and eased a chair from under his desk. He was careful not to make a sound. Sitting at his desk in his pajamas, he turned a knob on his desk lamp. The bulb illuminated the work surface and a 9"x12" sketchbook. He flipped to a blank page and drew frantically with a marker.

Roshan's eyes were nearly closed, but his hands were a blur of speed and color. He dropped the blue marker, picked up green, and then black. For five minutes, he sketched and colored, transferring an image that burned in his brain to a two-dimensional work of art.

When the drawing was completed to his satisfaction, he dropped the markers and put both hands, palms down, on the paper. The difficult part came when he held his hands over the picture and concentrated on his creation.

*****

"Stop the car!"

AJ hit the brakes at Cody's request, bringing the SUV to a quick stop. "What the hell? What is it?"

Cody stared at the large screen console of AJ's new vehicle. A few seconds ago, a GPS mapping system displayed the roads they were traveling. Now, the map was a static image—a depiction created by Roshan Kapoor.

"Can you see that?" Cody pointed to the display.

"The map? Yes, of course I can see it. What about it?"

"Of course, you can't see it. Thank you, Roshan. I don't know how I'll ever repay you."

"What are you talking about? Who's Roshan?"

Cody pointed to the digital screen mounted vertically between them. "Your map looks like a map to you. But to me, it looks different. Roshan, the coroner's son, is projecting his drawing into my optic nerves. I see what he wants me to see. He's been doing it all day."

"Seriously? That's some creepy shit, but whatever. So, what does he want you to see? Can you see Alyse?"

"Yes. She's sitting on a bench. There's water in the background."

"A beach?"

"Has to be. She's probably waiting for Flesti to come for the Azure Blade. Giving up the blade is the only way she'll be free of Flesti's control."

"There's a shitload of beaches in town—the town beach, Allison Park, the fishing piers, and all of the private property along the lake. It could take us hours to check them all if we can't narrow it down, and Alyse doesn't have that kind of time, especially if she's meeting Flesti."

Cody studied the image for a moment. There weren't many details to help him determine the exact beach. But then he noticed a chain in the foreground that only appeared diagonally in the bottom corners. "The marina! She's at the marina. I can see chains in the bottom corners?"

"Yup. Makes sense. The marina is the only beach that has chains along the water."

They steered the vehicle back onto the road, and the 648-horse-power engine pushed them to 60 mph within four seconds. They had to drive through town and head east to the public marina.

They rode in silence for a moment. As glad as he was to have AJ riding with him again, Cody's heart beat rapidly. He hoped it was an effect of AJ's Ethiopian coffee, but he was afraid that his best friend might not be ready for this, and he was scared that bringing him might be a mistake.

# 35
# LOST IN THE NIGHT 

The little noises of the forest seemed louder in the dark. Squeaks, snapping twigs, hoots, growls, chirps, and whistles filled the air and Daisy's imagination. She leaned against a black cherry tree that was twice her width. The rough bark grabbed at her shirt. She fetched a water bottle from her backpack and swallowed the last drop. A gentle breeze dried the sweat on her forehead, providing some relief from the sultry night air. She pinched her shirt collar and fluffed it forward and back to fan her neck and chest. All she wanted was a shower in the safety of her apartment and a hug from Sammy.

Without her headlight, she was lost more than ever. The thick canopy of leaves above made it difficult to keep track of the moon and stars. The terrain looked the same at night, no matter which direction she traveled. If she waited long enough, the sun would join her and illuminate her escape from the massive state forest, but that would give Jonathan time to catch her if he could walk. And she didn't want to be caught. She didn't want to be thrown in that well.

*That fucking well.*

She gripped Jonathan Cain's ax, holding it across her body. The ax was a heavy burden, and she thought about dropping it. It took all her effort to carry the weight, but she lacked the courage to leave it behind. If her assailant was following her, she didn't want him to be armed with the deadly weapon. She was too tired and weak to run through the dark woods anymore.

Shadows and silhouettes surrounded her. Because of the thick canopy of leaves, the forest floor didn't receive adequate light for new growth, so the woods were vast and open. Had it been daylight, she could have seen for a hundred yards. But in the dark, hazards lurked everywhere, and a broken ankle or sprained knee would make her easy prey.

She was grateful for the little bit of light the moon provided.

Her mind turned to Bourbon, and tears streamed down her cheeks. How was she going to tell everyone what happened to the former sheriff? Would they send a search party to find the well and recover his body? Would she be sending someone else to their demise, confronting the deadly Cain brothers? Finding the well again seemed impossible. The woods were so much bigger than they appeared on any map she had ever studied.

Amidst the sheet of black above, she located the two stars she'd been following. Star Daisy seemed so small now, dim when compared to its earlier glow. Funny how she felt the same.

A noise behind her brought her attention back from the heavens. Soft steps in the leaves approached, muffled only by the dew on the ground. Once again, she felt like prey. She'd seen rabbits freeze in fear, hiding from a human or hunting dog, so she emulated the behavior and held her breath. Her grip tightened on the thick wooden handle of her weapon as she slowly turned ninety degrees to see her coming doom.

A dark figure emerged through a row of twisted alders and tall grass. She could see the movement, but not the shape. It closed in. The black shadow breathed heavily as it studied her, and then the shadow took a familiar form, and Hetzen appeared before her. Her shoulders dropped, and she relaxed as she exhaled. Her sense of loneliness dissipated. She placed the ax on the ground and stayed in a crouching position to welcome her new friend.

The black dog shoved his head into her lap. His tail whipped from side to side as she hugged his neck and scratched his ear.

"Oh, Hetzen," Daisy whispered. "You good boy. Oh my God, I'm so glad to see you."

Hetzen pulled away, trotted ten steps and came back. When Daisy went to scratch him, he pulled away and repeated the action.

Daisy realized he was trying to lead her. He wanted her to follow him. But to where?

She stood, hoisted Jonathan Cain's brutish ax until the weight rested on her right shoulder.

"Okay, boy, I'm going to trust you. You've lived in these woods your whole life."

Hetzen spun in a little circle, knowing Daisy understood his wishes.

"Let's go."

They marched back uphill for less than fifty feet, and for a moment, Daisy thought she had misjudged the dog's intentions. With his nose to the ground, Hetzen turned right and descended a short gully. He stopped every few minutes so his two-legged companion could catch up.

As they neared the bottom of the gully, they turned back to the left and meandered through the woods. Daisy thought the dog might be confused, but she noticed they always turned back so that star Cody and star Daisy were at her two o'clock. The zigzag pattern of their path seemed consistent.

Hetzen turned again and switch-backed up a steep hill. Daisy struggled to follow while the black mutt waited patiently at the top. The ascent was arduous, with jagged granite cliffs and loose leaves concealing the hazards of her path. A single misstep would end her journey sooner than she desired.

She froze in place as a rumble came over the horizon. At first, she assumed a low-flying jet was off course, but soon recognized the sound. It was the same roar she'd heard earlier when the earthquake rattled her campsite. This time, it was more significant than a light tremor. It was violent and threatening. The ground moved under her weight. She shifted right and clasped her arms around a dead ash tree with rough bark that scraped her cheek and eyelid. She gripped the bucking tree, praying that the roots stayed grounded. Three rocks, the size of soccer balls, rolled down the hillside, bouncing under gravity's pull. One slammed against her ash tree, splintered the surface, rolled over her foot, and tumbled past.

The soft ground cushioned the weight of the stone, preventing her bones from being crushed by the weight, but not sparing her pain. The tree held its position despite the damage from the impact.

She buried her face and belly against the tree for protection, fighting the urge to cry out in pain and frustration. Hetzen whimpered at the top of the cliff, but Daisy couldn't hear him. The world shook around her, and she was blind to the violence. In less than half a minute, the shaking stopped, and the world settled back to its calm state.

She waited two minutes to be sure it was over before leaving the safety of the tree.

"Hetz? Hetzen?"

The dog's square head peeked over the ledge at her. He gave a sharp bark to confirm his loyalty.

"Good boy. I'm coming, buddy. I'm coming." She touched her cheek, feeling the abrasion from the jagged tree bark. The wound stung from sweat and pressure, and she imagined it looked much worse than it was.

She followed the cracks of the ledge and summited after what seemed a very long time. She looked back, unsure how far she'd climbed. The faint moonlight lit the forest floor below her, but the height was impossible to determine. She guessed it was an elevation gain of about thirty feet. Hetzen gave a happy whimper that Daisy interpreted as his way of saying, "Good job."

Ahead of her, beyond the trees and shadows, an eerie blue light snaked along the ground. It wasn't easy to judge the distance, but she knew exactly what she was looking at. She gave Hetzen a happy little scratch and patted his head before hiking toward the stream of light.

## 36

# THE MARINA

Cody and AJ parked the vehicle on the side of the road at the marina's entrance. There was no way to drive onto the marina property because of two yellow gates, closed and chained together, that blocked the entrance. The steel gates prevented trucks from entering the marina and driving away with a stolen boat. Driving around the gates was impossible due to the deep ditch along the road. Cody and AJ exited the Land Rover, jumped the ditch on foot, and walked into the marina property. AJ acknowledged the security camera mounted on a nearby power pole.

"Think anybody's watching?"

Cody shrugged, "I doubt it. Thing looks like it's from the 70s." It didn't matter if they were being watched or not. They were going in.

Above the camera, a street light flickered on and off, the big bulb inside fighting to stay alive.

The ground rumbled from the south, and then the two men started to feel the vibrations of the earth rattle their bones.

"Another quake!" AJ shouted.

They rode out the twenty-second tremor with ease without having to worry about structural damage or falling debris. The private park had only one building, a bathroom, that was stout and durable enough to survive the earthquake with ease, although the dying lightbulb above them succumbed to the shaking.

They walked the long driveway in the dark until they were within reach of the second streetlight. They didn't bother trying to conceal their approach. They didn't care if they were arrested for

241

trespassing or recognized by Flesti. They were here to find Alyse and determined to stop her from hurting herself or anyone else.

The marina's driveway ran down the middle of the property until forking left and right. A white sign with a red arrow read "ALL TRAFFIC," with an arrow pointing to the right. They instinctively followed the sign and walked thirty more yards down the pavement road that guided them along the park's right side.

Forty yards ahead, at the water's edge, Cody could see the light from another streetlight reflecting off shiny boat rails, waxed paint, and white canopies. There were fewer than ten boats moored to the marina's docks. The water was so still that the boats floated motionless on Cain Lake's surface.

A chorus of frogs sang from the shoreline, the first proof that the park contained life. Their high-pitch twills, mid-tone tweets, and baritone croaks covered the sound of Cody and AJ's approach, although anyone at the beach would have heard their voices at the gate. Three little brown bats scoured the surface of the lake, devouring mosquitoes. Their silhouettes banked, swirled, and ascended as they hunted their tiny prey with fantastic speed and accuracy.

A row of metal posts separated the lawn from a twelve-foot-wide concrete walkway that formed a seawall. Each post was spaced ten feet. AJ couldn't help but count them—twelve in total. A single metal chain was suspended from post to post, the entire length of the concrete. They stepped over the black chain.

A female figure sat alone under a dim street lamp. A frenzy of flying insects swarmed the inviting light. They spiraled upward, then dropped down, and made the climb again. Their delicate wings glistened in the artificial light like a slow-spinning tornado of bugs. Every ten to twenty seconds, one of the bats would cut through the storm and sink its teeth into a fat moth.

Alyse Burns sat on a park bench, seemingly unaware of the storm above her head. Her legs were criss-crossed under her, and she never looked at Cody or AJ as they stepped beside her. She fiddled with a fingernail, digging into the chipped paint to remove the acrylic coating. Looking at her, no one would possibly suspect she had murdered several men that day. Or that she was being controlled by a woman who wanted to feed on sinners. She just looked like a person in pain—empty on the inside, broken on the outside.

"Alyse?" Cody said, his voice as soft as a nurse in a maternity ward.

She didn't move. A fleck of fingernail paint fell on her lap as she dug harder.

Cody was cautious. His steps were small and slow. The last time he'd confronted her, she kicked his ass into a pile of tires. Somehow, the Azure Blade had made her faster and stronger. He sat on the bench with her. AJ stood behind but close enough to hear them talk, ready to react if Alyse attacked. He wanted to run to her, hug her tight, but knew that if she lashed out with the blade, Cody was more apt to disarm her. He gave them space, reading the situation and trying to predict what might happen. The scene could play out in a dozen ways, all of them ending with someone hurt. This situation, he thought, might go better if she didn't feel outnumbered.

Alyse tucked her bloody hands into the kangaroo pocket of her hoodie. Cody assumed that's where the Azure Blade was hiding. She finally looked up, but not at her friend. She stared toward the vast emptiness of the dark lake. Her eyes were transfixed on the ghosts of her memory that only she could see. She was thin and dehydrated, and in the artificial light of the streetlight, Cody could not recall ever seeing her so pale. Surely, she had been foregoing food or water during her time under Flesti's control. She wore the same clothes he'd seen her in two nights prior. She'd been neglecting her own needs for the Azure Blade's desire for blood, for Flesti's agenda to feed sins to Cain Lake.

"Alyse, are you alright?" Cody tried again to gain her attention. He squatted beside the bench, staying low seemed like less of a threat.

She finally turned toward him. Dark skin under her eyes contrasted against her white cheeks. She shook her head. Tears tried to form, but her body refused to relinquish the vital fluid.

"Wh...What did I do?" She asked. Her voice was like a rasp on wood.

"Stop. Don't do that to yourself, Alyse. You know it wasn't you."

"I was holding the knife, Cody. I saw the news on my phone. They called me The Red Devil."

"You're an angel...always have been." He slid onto the bench and sat beside her, but maintained some space.

Alyse's head dropped. "They thought I was River. They were after poor River. My God, she's probably going through hell."

"She's okay. She's been at AJ's house the whole time. Deputy Simpson took her to her father. She'll be alright. I promise."

"AJ must hate me right now. Everyone must hate me."

"No, no, AJ doesn't hate you. He's here, waiting for you. He knows that Flesti is responsible for the blood and carnage. She's been controlling you this whole time."

He hugged her without fear, even though he wasn't sure what she'd do with the blade. If she stabbed him in the back, then so be it. His friend was hurting, and mercy and understanding were the only ways for her to heal.

AJ stepped silently away from the pair sitting on the bench. He took out his cell phone, covering the harsh light of its screen, and called an ambulance. He was sure Alyse needed medical attention, and if this were a trap, then the paramedics would be here soon for Cody and him.

Even in her state of shock and haggard appearance, she was still beautiful. She smelled like sweat, blood, and lavender. He remembered their fiery relationship that seemed like decades ago, but it was still fresh in his mind. They'd made promises to each other that were broken before he went to prison. They vowed that not even steel bars would keep them apart. That was a lie they both believed. Since his return, there were times when he wondered if he was meant to be with Alyse. As incredible as Daisy was, the fire between him and the woman he was holding now still burned within his chest. But Daisy was like water: constant and fluid, safe and necessary, and she had extinguished what little flame flickered between Cody and Alyse when he returned to Stoneville.

The thought of Daisy made Cody reflect for a moment. What if she had been the one holding the Azure Blade? She was too weak to handle this kind of situation. She would have died if she were in the same position as River Kelly or Alyse Burns. Daisy wasn't as strong as the other women in his life. She was like a timid flower, blooming for the sake of beauty. If she ever had to face Flesti Thaed, she would likely wither and die.

But Alyse was a fighter, and Cody loved that about her.

Cody's mind dug deeper, thinking about the child growing in Daisy's belly. He'd do anything to protect his unborn child. That included smothering his feelings for Alyse or killing Flesti Thaed if he must. Hell, he would even go back to prison if he had to.

Cody broke their embrace and knelt on one leg while holding her hands. She stared back into his perfect gray eyes. Guilt and shame reflected back at her.

"Alyse? Alyse, where's the blade?"

She considered his question for a moment, then resumed her stare toward the darkened shoreline of Cain Lake. "She has it." She lifted her arm and extended an index finger toward the water.

Cody looked over his shoulder. A shadow took form as faint moonlight reflected off the tiny ripples on the lake's surface, like a million silver snakes slithering along the top of the water. He knew the shadow all too well. She stood as silent and still as the boats moored along the dock. She was alone—no annoying crow at her shoulder. No black dog standing watch. Just Flesti Thaed standing in wait for Cody Savage to make a move against her.

In her hand, a light was born in the shape of a dagger.

Cody stood and could feel the slight tingle of his left hand as it tried to mimic the Azure Blade's power. For a moment, it felt powerful, capable of shattering anything he threw a punch at. But the glow flickered, and the fist became as dim as an exhausted matchstick until the light died. Cain Lake's power was nearly dead now. His power was almost depleted.

Flesti now drew her strength from the weapon in her hand, and Cody knew he was at a serious disadvantage.

# 37
# THE SNAKE

Hetzen led Daisy to a stream of water no wider than the length of her arm. It flowed down the gentle grade of the hill, persuaded by gravity and directed by the contours of the land. It was the usual path for all the water that had escaped the Cain brothers' well within the cavern. She regarded how the water glowed. It reminded her of pictures she'd seen in travel magazines—tropical cenotes in Mexico. She'd always dreamed of swimming in the underground reservoirs. Now, here she was, thousands of miles from the closest one and scared to death of what the glowing blue water meant for the fate of Cain Lake.

Her heart was pounding fast and hard. Sweat had dampened her shirt, and her breathing was shallow. She stood still to rest, her hands on her knees, watching the stream go by.

There was no stopping the flow. There was no way to prevent the micropods from spilling into Cain Lake and giving Flesti Thaed a surge of power. But what Flesti would do with the power was anyone's guess. She used it to stay young and strong. She used it to control people. But keeping the lake at full power meant feeding it the sins of the townspeople. And in a town full of sinners, that could be catastrophic.

She thought about the people who'd acquired that label in the last few months. What did it mean to be a sinner, and who gets to decide? Jesse Lewis thought Cody was a murderer. Annabel Thompson thought so, too. Jesse also saw Annabel as a sinner for her hit-and-run accident with Charlotte Archer. But there were other sinners as well. Eli Birchcraft was labeled as such because he covered up Annabel's accident. The cook at The Mineshaft, Brody Sherwood, was killed because he sold some pot. She began to whisper the names out loud:

"Jesse Lewis.

Annabel Thompson.

Eli Birchcraft.

Charlie Archer, the deputy sheriff." Daisy shuddered. "He may have been worse than Jesse Lewis.

Darin Cloudwater.

Peter Felton.

Levi Thompson.

Cricket Morrison.

Andrew Mills.

River Kelly.

Jeff Bourbon?" The last name stung. It seemed impossible that Bourbon could be on the list, but the Cain brothers were sure he was a sinner. It was his sin that would provide the well with this newfound strength, and by the look of the water pouring toward her, they may have been right.

Now, she worried about the consequences of her actions. She had talked—begged—Bourbon to bring her to the woods. This wouldn't have happened if she weren't so hellbent on getting a story. What now? Would other sin-eaters pop up across Stoneville if this toxic stream rejuvenated the lake?

And how would she explain what happened? *Yeah, hey, so you know that blue goo in Cain Lake making everybody bat-shit crazy and causing them to kill each other? Well, it's kinda my fault. Yup, just wanted a story. Came across some two-hundred-year-old men with a grudge against their sister and wanted to throw me in a magic well. I know, I know, it sounds ludicrous, but Jeff Bourbon saved me, and he fell into the well in the process. Now we're fucked, people.*

She knelt beside the stream, watching the water disappear through holes in the ground and reemerge several yards downhill. In her mind, she traced it back to its source: up the hill, between the split rocks, through the bear traps, into the cliff, and up to the stone well where Bourbon had disappeared.

Since she was already on her knees, she took a moment to say another prayer. This one wasn't for Cody. When she finished, she opened her eyes and watched the stream of water pass by. She wondered if her words would be carried by the stream or diluted by its volume. She stared in fear and wonder at the water as if it were a living thing that would respond to her words. And then she felt dizzy from the water's movement.

She stabilized herself and dunked one hand in the water. It was as cold as melted snow. As the water warmed in her cupped palm, she sensed Jeff Bourbon's presence. Not his physical form, but his life essence in the cool blue water. This is where the water came from. This is how the little micropods came to life—by stealing his.

She thought she'd run out of tears by now. She was wrong. The waterworks continued to stream from the hill and her eyes.

Hetzen licked her ear. She leaned into her newfound friend and gave him a scratch under the chin. Hetzen stretched his neck outward, relishing the attention.

Her fingers felt greasy from the dog's fur, so she rinsed them in the clear water and dried her hands on her pants. Then she splashed some of the cool water on her bloody cheek. For a moment, the abrasion burned worse than when she had first rubbed the skin away. She breathed in and out through clenched teeth until the pain subsided. The refreshing blue water soothed her nerves, and after half a minute, a tingling sensation replaced the pain.

She stood abruptly, squeezed the handle of Jonathan Cain's ax, and followed the water down the hill. Hetzen bound before her, lapping the fresh fluid and jumping from side to side. The glowing stream provided just enough light for her to make it through the forest in the dark.

Above her, Daisy heard a slight thrashing sound, like someone crumpling paper. She couldn't see the source of the noise, but then a familiar voice cawed in the treetops, and she knew Poe had joined her and the dog. Poe's form finally took shape when he descended through an area of paper birch trees. His black feathers starkly contrasted with the bone-white bark of the little trees, even in the depth of night. The corvid flew adjacent and behind Daisy, not in his usual pestering manner but as if he had decided to trust her lead. It nearly made Daisy smile, and she was glad to have the companionship of the two animals.

The stream of water meandered through the dead leaves and rich soil like a blue snake on the hunt. It slithered down the hill, exploring holes and crevices, occasionally disappearing into the earth. At one point, Daisy completely lost sight of the snake, which had dove into a small sinkhole. She found it again fifty yards away. It carried its little blue secret down the hill until finally spilling the truth into the massive lake below.

She'd never been so happy to see Cain Lake. The sky across the lake shimmered with the twinkling glow of Stoneville's lights. She knew that was home, but which direction should she follow—northeast, southwest, or straight across the lake? "Now what?" She asked the dog.

Hetzen just looked at her. His pink tongue bounced over white teeth as he panted in excitement. He didn't seem to have an opinion or an agenda—he just liked being in Daisy's presence.

Daisy watched the stream of blue merge with the freshwater lake. The snake slithered into the lake without losing form, its blue light refusing to be snuffed. The micropods did not disperse in the significant volume of water.

Daisy thought the snake would die when it hit the warm lake water.

It did not.

The blue stream maintained its sinuous shape and continued out of the bay. It slithered to the center of the lake and veered east, traveling toward Stoneville with its own agenda. The phenomenon was strange and unnatural as it turned and twisted. Daisy lost sight of the trail after it exited the bay and turned again. It was going northeast, straight toward the marina.

# 38
# DEATH ITSELF

I thought you could be trusted, Flesti," Cody shouted to the woman at the edge of the lake. "Did you get what you came for, you goddam bitch? Or is there going to be more blood? More death?"

"I'm sorry it came to this," Flesti said. "But I've searched for the Azure Blade since I was a little girl."

"Since you killed your sisters? I saw your memories. I saw what you did."

Flesti was confused until she remembered Cody's interaction with Roshan. "Yes. Yes, that's right. The boy showed you my memories—my childhood. He's proven to be quite the little nuisance."

Cody clenched his fist tighter. If she were threatening Roshan, he would kill her here and now, despite the consequences. "Roshan has nothing to do with this. If you mess with that kid's mind, I swear—."

"The boy is of no interest to me, Savage. I have what I want. And soon, I'll be the last Cain fighting for the power of our lake."

"There's more of your family alive? Where are they?"

Flesti moved a little closer, but Cody didn't notice her taking any steps. She just willed herself toward shore. "I have three brothers who want control of the lake. They live in the woods on the south side of the water. They've been trying to kill me for the better part of my life. But I'm too strong. Too smart for those animals." There was a little giggle to her voice, proud of her strength. "I will no longer be hunted like prey." She looked over her left shoulder, wondering if they were listening from the far shore, hoping her words would carry across the wind and water and fall upon their ears.

Cody stepped to the edge of the water. Eight feet of space separated him from Flesti.

"Cody," Alyse interrupted. "Cody, be careful."

Cody paid no attention to Alyse's warning. "So, go to the south side and find your brothers. And stay there." His words were a warning. "Nobody on this side of the lake poses a threat to you. You have no enemies here."

"Oh, you ignorant boy," Flesti said. "You are too blind to see the truth."

"What truth is that?" He demanded.

"There is one descendant from my blood that remains—stronger than my brothers. More of a threat to my claim to the lake than anyone else."

"You have a living relative here? In Stoneville?"

"A long-lost sister of mine had a family. For generations, her children and grandchildren have multiplied and spread across the country. And now, one of them is right here on this beach, about to die."

Cody studied her in bewilderment. *No! No, this can't be true. Is this why I'm so connected to Cain Lake, why I'm so affected by the little lights? Am I a descendant of the Cain family?*

"You're fucking nuts, lady. There's no way I'm related to you or your bat-shit psycho family." He was spitting the words now. Cody's left fist tightened. He knew the only chance to beat Flesti was if he could draw power from the micropods that coursed through his blood. He stepped into the water, a desperate attempt to recharge his power.

"You're such an arrogant fool, Savage. Such hubris, hmmm? But I was *not* referring to you."

"No way you're killing any of us."

Flesti moved a little closer. Her eyes were wide as she stared deep into his. "I already have." There was something in the way she whispered the statement that sounded like regret or triumph. Cody wasn't sure which.

"Who? Who'd you already kill?"

"Cody!" AJ yelled from behind.

Cody turned to face his friends, fearful of what he'd see. AJ held a hand out, palm facing forward. The light from the streetlight reflected off a thick, dark liquid covering AJ's hand.

Cody's bright eyes grew with terror.

"It's Alyse! She's been stabbed," AJ barked.

Cody sprinted out of the water and back to the bench. He hit his knees at Alyse's feet. "No, no, no."

Alyse leaned against AJ's shoulder. She was on the verge of losing consciousness.

Cody hadn't seen the wound before. He was too focused on her face, trying to read her emotions. But Alyse's black hoodie was soaked in the front. She gently pulled the fabric up, revealing the puncture in her abdomen where the Azure Blade had pierced her body.

She forced a smile, "It's okay. It's okay, I deserve this." She put a bloody hand on his cheek.

Cody looked at AJ, "Call an ambulance."

"I already did."

Alyse slumped a little more as AJ caught her from falling over.

"I was pulled here—to this place," Alyse whispered with broken breath. "Drawn by a desire I could never explain. I was sure it was you. I was sure. Now I know. It was the lake. The lake was calling me."

"You're going to be okay, Alyse. You hear me? You're going to be fine."

She grimaced. "Make sure she doesn't hurt anyone else." And then she collapsed from the loss of blood.

Cody exploded off the ground. He took three long strides toward Flesti, ready to put her evil reign to an end. "If she dies—"

He stopped. His muscles refused to respond to his thoughts, frozen like a well-trained hunting dog. He couldn't move. He couldn't talk. He was helpless.

With a body full of micropods that had been living inside him since he was a kid, Flesti had complete control of his actions. The micropods allowed her send thoughts to his brain and fill him with bouts of rage. That same rage caused him to get into fights, kill his parents, and put a reporter in the hospital.

She was his rage, and he was hers.

Beyond Flesti Thaed, a blue streak of light snaked through the water as if searching for prey. Cody knew what the light was. It was power, and if he could get to it, he could regenerate his strength. But he was helpless against Flesti's ability to control his muscles.

He focused on fighting her off. All he could accomplish was the ability to form broken sentences through a locked jaw and gritted teeth. "I know—my parents' death. You made me. You made me do it. Shut the door. I killed them. You killed them!"

"We killed them—together. You were supposed to be my sin eater. But you proved to be stronger than I imagined. So I found others. And then I found that River girl. She was weak, too—couldn't even kill a fat biker right in front of her. But when your bartender friend picked up the dagger—oh, my. Oh, my....I could sense her strength, even greater than yours. And I knew she would be my greatest ally or my greatest foe. I could use the Azure Blade to control her for a while. But when she came here to give it to me, she tried to kill me instead."

Cody hadn't noticed the wound on her chest until now. The micropods were nearly finished healing the deep cut across her sternum. Diluted blood stained the front of her shirt. Alyse had dealt the first blow, but she was no match for the old witch.

"It's all worked out," Flesti said. "I have the blade. Your friend will soon be dead. My brother's plan to destroy the lake has been foiled, and once I kill them, I'll have all the power of Cain Lake to myself—forever."

The blue snake of light finally found its target. It coiled under her, then exploded upward, erupting like a geyser of liquid light, and swallowed Flesti in one motion. But instead of consuming the woman, it immersed her in power. Cody lost sight of his enemy until the water gave in to gravity's might and fell back into Cain Lake.

*Fuck!*

For a moment—a brief moment—Cody felt Flesti's grip on his body slip. He leaped off the short stone wall, caught her by the waist, and tackled her into the glowing blue water.

When they resurfaced, they were standing in knee-deep water. Cody could feel the effects of the micropods immediately. His fist lit up like a kerosene lantern. Flesti's entire body took a similar appearance.

Six feet of space separated them as they faced off.

Flesti spun in circles and looked at the water. She dropped to her knees, reaching frantically, searching the bottom of the lake with sensitive fingers.

"Looking for this?" Cody gloated as he held the Azure Blade in his hand.

Flesti stood slowly, focused on the blue blade in Cody's possession.

"No! No, give me my knife."

"Come and take it."

They began to circle each other. Cody put himself between Flesti and his friends on shore. Even if it killed him, he was going to make sure the witch of the lake couldn't hurt AJ or Alyse. He didn't want to kill her, but it was his only choice now. The blade augmented his desires, and right now, he wanted revenge for what she'd done to Alyse.

Flesti ran her hands through her hair, pushing it away from her eyes and face. Her skin glowed. Her eyes were possessed by the sins that flowed through the liquid surrounding her, full of black with little crystals swirling in the void.

Cody felt the effect of the microscopic organisms. And then he felt something else—a familiar presence within the lake. He looked to the shore, expecting to see Jeff Bourbon standing on the river-bank. But all he saw was AJ holding Alyse and ambulance lights flashing on the horizon.

He turned his attention back to the deadly psychic. If she were to control him now, with the Azure Blade in his hand, then she could wreak havoc on the town. The carnage would be far worse than the pain Alyse had inflicted on the town. He needed to block his mind. Keep her out.

"You fool," Flesti said. "Now you'll do my killing for me."

Cody stepped forward, opened his hand, and let the Azure Blade tear through the wind. It spun toward Flesti. She raised a hand to stop the blade, but it tore through the skin on her thumb. She shrieked in pain as the blade whizzed past her ear.

"You want the blade?" Cody asked. "I'll plant it in your cold fucking heart."

The blade jetted back toward its new owner, just missing Flesti's shoulder. Cody caught it with the ease of a major league baseball player. And then he felt himself freeze again. He couldn't move his legs. His arms were stuck in place. His mind began to fog. She was taking control.

"I don't need the blade to kill you, Savage. Not when I can make you kill yourself."

Cody's feet were cemented to the lake bottom. He wanted to throw the dagger again, but his hands wouldn't heed his command.

*She's too powerful. She'll kill us all.*

"Drop the blade!"

Cody's hand opened, and the Azure Blade fell. It made a small splash and disappeared into the dark water.

"Turn around," Flesti commanded. Cody's body turned under her command.

He wanted to yell at AJ and Alyse. He wanted them to run before they were in the same peril. The sight from shore nearly killed him. AJ stood on the retaining wall, elevated two feet higher than Cody. The streetlight above reflected off the object in his hand. He was pointing a pistol at Flesti.

*AJ, you dumb motherfucker! You've killed us both.*

A million visions went through Cody's mind. He knew Flesti would take control of AJ and force him to shoot. Then he'd turn the Canik .45 caliber weapon on Alyse, and then on himself. Cody felt as though he was surrounded by bees again. His mind buzzed with images and memories of the two friends. He saw the day they met on the baseball field, the girls they'd chased in high school, the car they crashed, and the parties they attended. He saw AJ standing in his graduation cap the year they finished high school. Pictured him in a tuxedo at his wedding, a suit at Willa's funeral, and finally in a hospital bed after Levi Thompson beat him into a coma. He didn't deserve what was about to come, and for the first time in months, Cody wished he were still in prison—the one with steel bars and glass walls. Everyone was safer then.

"AJ, drop the gun!" Cody yelled. AJ didn't listen. It was too late.

Flesti's hand was up, fingers clenching the air, and pointed toward AJ. "Are you stupid, Timmons? Do you really think I'll let you fire that thing at me?"

AJ held the pistol with one arm straight. Under the street light, it was evident he was shaking with fear.

"AJ, she's controlling you. Drop the gun. Get Alyse to the ambulance!"

"I told you, Cody," AJ said. "This is going to end tonight."

Flesti brought both hands up, attempting to increase her telepathic hold over AJ and make him submit to her will. "You made a mistake bringing a gun here. I control everyone who's ever swum in this water."

AJ brought his second arm up to brace his shooting hand and steady his aim.

Flesti tried harder to control AJ, but to no avail.

AJ looked down the barrel, aligning the small fiber optic sights with his target. "I guess you didn't do your research—I can't swim."

A smile broke across Cody's face. *Well, sonovabitch!*

"Drop the gun, Timmons. You don't know who you're dealing with."

"Yes, I do." His tone was calm. "You're death itself, bitch."

The shot was loud in Cody's face. He felt a blast of air as burnt gunpowder pelted his forehead, but the bullet passed him and struck its intended target. Flesti Thaed fell backwards without a scream. Water splashed upward, engulfing her once more, and when it all came crashing down, she was gone.

Cody felt the buzzing stop. The grip on his body released and his own thoughts returned. Even though he could move freely, he was too traumatized to make a motion. He stared at AJ, who stood with the pistol pointed toward the water in case another shot was warranted.

It was not.

AJ reached out, took Cody's hand, and pulled him onto the seawall.

"Is she dead?" Cody asked.

"I...I don't know. I think...Yeah, I think so." He was trembling like a hunter after his first kill, after the realization of what he'd done finally hit. "Holy shit. Holy shit, I shot her."

At the edge of the lake, a couple of million micropods swirled and tried to follow Cody. Then, they became a dense stream of light and began migrating back across the lake until their glow diminished in the night.

AJ ejected the live round from the chamber and dumped the pistol's magazine. He put the gun back in its hiding place—the front pocket of his hoodie.

The approaching ambulance finally arrived, but it couldn't access the marina's locked gate. It would take them another five minutes to get to the edge of the water, to Alyse. Cody scooped up Alyse and stepped into the water. If Cain Lake could regenerate his hand, then surely it would save a descendant of the Cain family.

"Think this will work?" AJ asked.

"It has to," Cody answered. "It has to." He was trying to convince himself. "Flesti said Alyse was a descendant of the Cains, so this has to work."

They each took a side, holding her back and a leg, and lowered Alyse until the wound in her stomach was submerged. The water glowed in a purple hue as red blood mixed with blue water. The micropods began performing their miracle, just like Cody knew they would. But he wondered where they came from. Hours ago, Cain Lake's power was nearly dead—his psychic ability gone—but out of nowhere, a surge of micropods had found them when they were most needed. He didn't know if it was luck or fate. He'd always confused the two.

By the time the two paramedics arrived at the beach, Alyse's wound was sealed. The bleeding had stopped, but they couldn't be sure what was happening inside. She could have been bleeding internally or have an infection. She was still unconscious, probably from undernourished, fatigue, and stress.

The paramedics loaded her onto a stretcher board and took over caring for her. A couple of additional voluntary EMTs arrived in time to help carry the patient to the ambulance. The ambulance doors slammed shut, and the rescue vehicle raced away.

"Come on, we'll follow them," AJ said as he opened the car door.

"I can't. You go, AJ."

"What are you going to do?"

"There's something else I need to do right now. I'll meet you at the hospital in a little while."

"How? You've got no vehicle."

"Don't worry about me. I'll find a ride. Please, go with Alyse. I'll be there soon."

"What are you going to do?"

"I'm going to make sure she's dead."

# 39

# ACROSS THE LAKE 

Daisy sat on a heavy driftwood log that was half buried in the sand. She couldn't take another step. Exhaustion weighed her down like a cement blanket. Her leg muscles were cramping, and her muscles despised the hefty backpack.

Hetzen lay at her feet, waiting to follow wherever she went. Poe, unusually silent, perched in the dense branches of a speckled alder. The animals' loyalty confused Daisy, and she wondered if they'd leave if they knew Flesti's location. She scratched Hetzen's neck, and the dog's smooth, soft fur eased her anxiety.

"Where's Flesti, Hetzen. Hmm? You gonna follow me home if she doesn't show up?" Daisy wondered if Flesti had abandoned her companions and left the forest. Or, maybe the old lady of the woods was nearby, watching her, even stalking her. She turned to Poe and watched him scour the tree for catkins.

*Bourbon thinks you're a spy for Flesti. Maybe he was right.*

She wondered if Flesti could see her now, through the eyes of the corvid. She flipped her middle finger at Poe, hoping Flesti was watching.

A gunshot rang out from the other side of Cain Lake, splitting the tranquil night air like a meat cleaver. Daisy jumped to her feet. She knew the pistol crack was far from her location—over a mile— but the sound skipped across the water without being muffled. She anticipated a second shot.

It never happened.

She didn't know who had fired the shot or what target was lined up in the gun's sights, but as her heart thumped in her chest, her brain knew—somehow she knew—that Cody was involved. She wanted to swim the distance, but her exhausted body would cramp and tire, giving up on her as she stroked across the water's surface. She'd be lost to the lake—dead by dawn.

She needed to stay alive, no matter what. Sammy and her mother were waiting for her at her apartment, and she had every intention of returning to them with Greenie the Meanie.

She resumed her seat and gripped the heavy ax, which was more a burden than protection. Keeping it in her sight was better than the third Cain brother regaining possession of the weapon. He was still out here—somewhere—hunting her like a bear searching for a wounded deer. He'd be slower now that the steel trap had taken a bite from his foot, but he would be pissed off, too.

She couldn't let him have this ax.

She considered burying the beastly ax, but digging in the earth would be too much work for her exhausted muscles. Throwing it in the lake was an option, but she didn't think it would go far. Heaving it into the water would leave her vulnerable, so she kept it for now, knowing that bearing the weight was her best option.

She searched the sky for Star Cody and Star Daisy. The two lovers were in the same position. Now, they were flanked by two smaller stars on each side that she hadn't noticed before. She tried to memorize their location, hoping to find them on the next clear night. She formed a map in her mind, pinning the two stars halfway between Sirius and Mira.

She stood the ax upside down, the head in the sand, and placed her hands over the handle. Her eyes were so heavy. She closed them as she looked down at Hetzen lying at her feet. She felt secure with him there, his heightened senses ready to alert her to any sound. A choir of frogs sang her to sleep as she leaned her chin on her hands.

Forty minutes passed. She didn't even realize she was asleep until a splash from the water made Hetzen jump. He turned away from Daisy to investigate the sound. Daisy watched his dark shape creep toward the edge of the water.

A small shape pushed across the surface of the lake. She could make out the ripples as they caught the moon's glow.

Hetzen pointed toward the sound and movement. His nose waved in the air, sucking short bursts of air, trying to pick up a scent.

"What is it, boy?" Daisy whispered. "A beaver?" She stood and approached the shoreline. The blue glowing streak of water had returned to the south side of Cain Lake. It carried a small form in its jaws, and as it moved closer, Daisy could see it was not a beaver swimming toward her.

The little waves arrived before the stream of illuminated water and lost their form as they met the sand.

Daisy took two small steps backward as Hetzen let out a single bark.

An arm reached up and forward, pulling water and sand, grasping for solid ground.

Daisy suppressed her urge to scream, afraid it would give her location away to Jonathan Cain. But if he could sense the micropods in her, then he probably already knew where she was.

A female form arose from the water, revealing herself in knee-deep water. She tried to stand and then collapsed back to her knees. She crawled through the shallow water until her hands hit dry sand. Blue, glowing water dripped from her hair and clothes, saturating the sand until an eerie puddle formed. The puddle grew wider, casting a bright glow of azure light that erased the darkness within eight feet.

"Flesti? Flesti, are you alright?"

Flesti Thaed didn't move, didn't speak. Hetzen timidly stepped forward, sniffed Flesti's hair, and gave her a gentle lick.

Flesti put a wet hand on the nape of the dog's neck. Using Hetzen for support, she pushed herself straight until she was sitting on her heels, knees dug into the beach.

In the supernatural light, Daisy could see the wound across the side of Flesti's head. Her brain was exposed, bone and tissue torn away from her empty eye socket to her ear.

*The gunshot. How the fuck is she still alive?*

There was no blood, but the wound seemed to burn with blue ooze as thousands, if not millions, of micropods used their unexplainable power to keep Flesti Thaed alive. They swirled and swarmed through torn flesh, mended muscle, and fused bone.

It was in that moment that Daisy realized Flesti's secret to immortality was all true. Born Marion Cain, Flesti Thaed had lived numerous lives under different aliases to conceal her secret. Now, she'd been exposed. Her brothers wanted her dead because she wouldn't share the lake's power—a power that was fed by the sins of Stoneville's residents. Cain Lake's power came with a price that everyone in town was paying.

Still, here was a woman wounded and in pain. Daisy took a knee beside the gravely injured Flesti. "What? What happened to you? Were you shot?"

Flesti choked on blood and water, spat in the sand, and regarded Daisy in the shimmering blue light with one eye. "A gift from your lover."

Daisy stood, "Cody? Cody did this? He would never—"

Flesti nodded gently.

"He would never shoot anyone. Not even a murderer like you."

"Oh," she groaned. "Well, I guess it was his friend who pulled the trigger. The memory is a bit fuzzy."

"AJ did this? My God, why?"

"You know why, girl. It seems Cody Savage disagrees with my agenda. And now, he has something that belongs to me." She looked back toward the north shore, though it was impossible to see in the night. "I want it back."

"The Azure Blade." Daisy stepped back a half-step.

"I need your help, Daisy. Please. You have to retrieve the blade and bring it back to me. If I survive, I will be weak for days. They'll come after me, you know? They'll sense it. They'll come to finish me off."

"I'm not giving you that goddam blade," Daisy declared. "I know what you've done with it. I know about your sisters and your family. How many people have you killed in your life?"

Flesti fell back onto her palms but waved with her left hand, "Ah, doesn't matter."

"It fucking does matter!" She fell on her knees, head-to-head with the injured woman. "People die so you can have some immortal life. What makes you so worthy? Why do you get to elude death?"

"Because I can!" Flesti barked back while coughing up water and blood into the sand.

"I should kill you myself—"

"After I saved your life? Who do you think sent Poe to untie Bourbon? Who do you think sent Hetzen to guide you from the woods? Hmm? I couldn't stop Cecil and Martin from throwing you into that damn well, but I knew Bourbon could. Or at least, he'd die trying."

Daisy's eyes swelled with tears. "He did die. He died to keep me alive." The thought of Bourbon's sacrifice boiled her blood. "Bourbon was a good man. He made a mistake, and now he's dead."

"What of my brothers? Are they alive?"

"I don't friggin know. Bourbon dragged those two assholes into the well with him."

"You're carrying...," she huffed, tried to catch her breath, and spoke again. "You've got Jonathan's ax—"

"Yes, I killed him," she lied. "That fucker tried to cut me in half."

Flesti wheezed and coughed as she laughed. "Dear girl, if Jonathan wanted to split you down the middle, you wouldn't be here. He's a capable hunter. A fighter."

"Why hasn't he killed you yet?"

"Because I can control them. But not at the same time—only two, not all three." She held up two fingers in a V-shape. "That's why they fear me. And with my blade, they won't be able to stop me. They won't leave me in peace until I'm dead."

"They draw their power—their immortality—from the well and the micropods, just like you. Why don't you just share Cain Lake's gift? Why fight over it?"

"Because they didn't trust me. Nor should they. I killed two of my sisters and one brother already. And if I had the Azure Blade, I'd kill the rest of them."

Daisy locked eyes with Flesti and supported herself with the large ax, "You don't have the Azure Blade, though. Cody has it, and he's the one person you can't get it away from."

"I'll make him give me that knife."

Daisy's head was shaking, "He'll die before he gives it up."

Flesti retorted, sneering, "Oh, he'll give it to me. And once I've fully healed, I'll be unstoppable."

"Why would he ever give it back to you?"

"He'll trade it for his pregnant girlfriend!" She lunged at Daisy's throat with a claw-like hand. The hand hit its mark. Fingernails dug into flesh.

Hetzen jumped to his feet and bolted behind the driftwood log.

Poe fluttered from branch to branch, cawing and squeaking in a strange tongue.

Daisy tried to pull away from Flesti, but her strength was remarkable. Both women came to their feet. The blue micropods covered half of Flesti's face and head. They swirled and crawled through her hair and in and out of her ear.

Daisy tried to scream, but the woman's grip was crushing her throat, cutting off the blood supply to her brain. Pins of light began flashing in her vision, and in seconds, she felt like she was floating. She fell backward, pulling Flesti on top of her.

Flesti's right eye socket glowed as the micropods welded flesh and bone to seal her wound. She stared at Daisy with utter malice. Daisy turned away, or her last vision would be the horrid face of Flesti Thaed. She picked out Star Cody and Star Daisy over her assailant's left shoulder. The two stars had stuck together all night, refusing to leave each other's side. Perhaps they'd always been that way, even since they formed billions of years ago. Maybe that's how they'd be for all eternity.

She wanted to be with her star—her Cody—for all eternity. She was flat on her back, with Flesti mounted on top of her. She felt hapless, and then she felt Jonathan Cain's heavy ax. She brought the handle up and clubbed Flesti's left cheek. The evasive maneuver worked, and Flesti's grip broke as she fell into the sand.

Daisy crunched her abs and sat upright before jumping to her feet. Flesti managed to bring herself to her knees just in time to feel the handle of the ax strike her just below the ribs. The blow knocked the wind from her lungs; now, she struggled to breathe.

Flesti gasped out the words, "I'll kill you if I must. The only way you'll survive is to give in and let me take you to Cody."

Daisy rested on the ax. The head lay on the ground. The handle pointed up. She adjusted her grip and sucked in deep breaths of oxygen to regain her strength. "The only way we survive is by doing this."

Flesti felt the blow. Then, the world around her swirled in a blur of red and blue. When the motion blur stopped, she was looking up at the stars. Star Cody and Star Daisy stared down like a pair of cat eyes. Then she saw her body four feet away. Then she saw nothing.

Jonathan Cain's ax was stuck in the sand where Flesti's head was seconds ago. Daisy fell to her knees, gasping in silent shock. Her lungs failed to work, and her voice buried itself deep within as her eyes erupted with liquid. Tears poured down her face, and she was finally able to suck air.

Shame swallowed her whole.

Paralyzed by her guilt, she was unable to move when she heard movement—heavy steps from behind. She knew who it was. As he approached, the micropods retreated into the lake's depths, taking their light with them and leaving Flesti's lifeless body on the beach.

The steps grew close now. She wanted it to be Jeff Bourbon. She wanted it to be Cody. Anybody would be better than the man it was.

Daisy stared upward, focused on her stars. She waited for her death. She didn't know how it would come. She wished it to be quick.

"Please don't throw me in that well," her squeaky voice whispered.

Jonathan Cain's scent reached her first—a combination of dry leaves, body odor, and old leather. His breathing was heavy, not from exhaustion, but because it took a lot of effort to fill his massive lungs. He paused behind her and let out an inquisitive "Hmph" that originated deep in his throat.

He reached from behind her. His large hand, capable of crushing her skull, gripped the ax's handle, and he pulled it from the earth.

*Oh, God, please make it quick.*

He gently placed his left hand on her right shoulder and whispered with a dry tongue, "You're a tough little one. Well done, little rabbit." He padded her shoulder. "You don't have to run no more. Go home. Have your baby."

*How does he know?*

He turned and limped off into the dark forest.

# 40
# AWAKE

Shari Kapoor tossed and turned in her bed. The hot sun had spent the day warming her house, and now her home trapped the heat in her upstairs bedroom. She wished she had two fans to cool her as she lay beside her motionless husband, who slumbered like a hibernating bear. The oscillating fan on the dresser adjacent to the open window worked back and forth in a rhythm that usually lulled her to sleep, but not tonight.

She leaned over to her nightstand and lifted a cool glass of water to soothe her dry throat. As she sipped, a faint voice caught her attention.

She heard it again somewhere in the house.

Pivoting her feet onto the floor, she stood and wrapped herself in a light nightgown. She stepped to her bedroom door, careful not to disturb her husband. The door was open just enough to let the breeze and her gray and white cat slip through. She gently pulled the door open enough to slide her left shoulder and head through.

Assuming someone had left the television on, she held her breath and listened. The voice came from down the hall, muffled by a closed door, but she was sure it was calling to her.

"Mom. Mom! Dad!"

Shari burst through the door and was down the hall in less than two seconds. She pushed Roshon's bedroom door open to find him sitting on his bed, legs folded under himself, while he held a pillow. A desk lamp illuminated the room, casting his shadow against the light blue wall.

Shari took a big step into the room and fell to her knees beside the bed when Roshan called her again.

"Ro! I'm here. I'm here, baby."

Roshan smiled at the sight of her with an eyeful of tears, "Mommy, she can't hinder my voice anymore. She can't silence me." His words were slurry, like he spoke through with a swollen tongue, but it was music to Shari's ears.

Shari regained her stance and jumped onto his bed. She landed beside him and threw her arms around her youngest son. "Who, Ro? Who can't control you?"

"Marion."

"Marion? Who is Marion, Ro? What are you talking about?"

Roshan leaned into his mother's chest. "Marion Cain. She can't keep me quiet anymore. She's done bad things, and I know her secrets."

Shari was dumbfounded. She was smiling, crying, and confused by his comments. She hadn't heard his voice since he was three years old, and now he was talking about a woman she'd never met—a name she'd never heard. All she wanted was to hold him and make sure he was safe. "Nobody's going to hurt you, sweetie. I promise. Nobody's in control of you." She placed a kiss on the side of his head.

Roshan could sense her confusion, "I wanted to talk to you, Mom. I wanted to tell you so many things. But she kept me quiet all these years."

"Who, Roshan? I don't understand."

"I told you. Flesti Thaed is Marion Cain. She knew I could see her memories. She knew I could see lots of things." His words were slurry. Talking was an unpracticed skill to the psychic child, so he spoke slowly and emphasized his words. "She's gone now. She won't ever be able to control anyone again."

Shari squeezed him, thinking how awful that must have been if his story were true. "Where did Flesti go?" Shari gently prodded. "Was she here? Did she leave?"

"No," Roshan swallowed, and then he glanced out the window,

trying to recall the vision he'd had. "Cody stopped her. Cody and AJ and Daisy—they all stopped her from hurting me anymore, and she can never come back."

"Never?"

"Never ever."

*Good.*

# 41
# TWO STARS

Daisy squatted with her back against the big driftwood log. She was cold and shaking with fear despite the warm night air enveloping her skin. She felt like a hollow shell, numb from her experience and out of tears. Darkness was her only company, a silent alibi that witnessed the heinous murder she'd just committed. Even Hetzen had disappeared into the night when Flesti fell lifeless. Poe vanished in the forest, his black form becoming one with the night.

She couldn't move. Her body ached, and her heart was as heavy as the big ax she'd used to commit her crime. She'd wait for dawn to tiptoe over the horizon, then make her way out of the woods and back to Stoneville. The hike would be too long and dangerous in the dark. Every moment she stayed there, on the southern edge of Cain Lake's forest, corroded her mind like the longest horror movie she'd ever seen.

When she closed her eyes, she could only see the flash of the ax and Flesti's head separated from her shoulders. Blood, purple from the blue light of the micropods, stained the sand and then turned black as the light dimmed. She floated above the scene, taking it all in from a bird's-eye perspective, forced to watch the carnage unfold and shaken by the terror of it all.

She was so tired, but the imagery of Flesti's death was burned into her mind, making it difficult for her to close her eyes.

So, she stared across Cain Lake, watching the moonlight ripple across its surface with a gentle motion that lulled her into a false calm. The numbness of her senses began to wane, and she became aware of the cool, wet earth below her feet. A chorus of frogs sang along the water's edge, resonating from the tall grass growing in vertical patterns. She was sure they were singing about her, good or bad. A cricket chirped stubbornly under the thick grass behind her, calling out to a potential mate. A barred owl sounded off up the hill, then fell silent.

Every sound spooked her and calmed her simultaneously. She was attuned to every living thing around her, all the beautiful vibrations of life flowing through her. And then she'd get a whiff of the corpse, and it would make her aware how easily that life could be snuffed out in a single moment.

She thought about moving to another part of the shore—to escape the scene—but that was a luxury she didn't deserve. No, she needed to stay there and torture herself with the reality of what had occurred.

Another sound stirred her. More footsteps from behind. They were heavy, like a man's—like Jonathan Cain's. She no longer had the ax to protect her, not that she had the strength to wield it. She hugged her backpack for comfort and made herself as small as possible. Maybe he wouldn't see her. Maybe he'd walk past.

"Daisy?" A voice whispered.

She found a reserve of tears. An overwhelming sense of elation seized her, and she had never been so thankful to see a friend.

Jeff Bourbon stepped into the clearing of the beach, into the faint light of the moon. He took three quick steps and dropped to his knees. "Are you okay, kid?"

They both stood simultaneously, and Daisy threw her arms around his waist. His clothes were still wet, and he smelled of sweat, earth, and spring water. His skin was cool as he wrapped his big arms around her like a security blanket.

She leaned against him in silence, nodding just enough for him to feel it against his chest.

She looked up at him, "I'm sorry I left you there, Bourbon. I'm sorry I ran. I thought you were dead."

"It's okay, kid. It's okay. I thought I was, too."

"How? How did you survive? You were in that well for so long."

Bourbon looked back up the hill, then to her. "I don't know. Everything was a blur. I fought and wrestled with those two men in the water. I could feel us being pulled down, surrounded by blue light, and getting tossed around like we were in a washing machine. I held my breath for as long as I could, but then I realized I didn't need to breathe. Those little blue fuckers were breathing for me or something. I can't explain it. Maybe they were supplying me with oxygen. Then, I felt alone. The other two kept sinking, and I was able to swim to the surface."

"What happened to them?"

"Don't know," he shrugged. "When I climbed out of the well, I collapsed on the floor and just rested. I have no idea how long I was there. Then the last quake hit the cavern, and the entire place began to crumble. I got the hell out of there before the ceiling collapsed. I think—I hope—the well was destroyed."

"Those two men...they were Flesti's brothers."

"I know. I heard your whole conversation."

"I thought you were unconscious."

"I was, but when I woke, Poe was pecking and pulling at the rope around my wrists. I had to wait for him to finish before making a move. Took a little longer than I'd hoped."

"Aren't you glad you didn't shoot him?" Daisy asked in a serious tone.

Bourbon gave a slight chuckle. "Yeah, I'm glad." He kissed her head. "I guess that little black bastard had a purpose."

Bourbon didn't let go of her. He turned to the headless body lying in the sand. He was afraid to ask about it. Daisy had been through so much, and he didn't want her to relive the experience. He knew she was in shock and needed time to process what had transpired. She'd have to face Flesti's ghost in time, but not tonight.

Daisy noticed Bourbon staring at the body. Not letting go of her guide, she turned away and offered him an explanation. "She attacked me. She wants her knife back—the Azure Blade that Cecil described. She said Cody had it. I wouldn't let her hurt me, or Cody, or our baby. She's caused so much death and violence. I just wanted it to end. I want things to be normal."

Bourbon regarded her for a moment in the pale moonlight. "This is Stoneville. I think 'normal' skipped out of town a long time ago." He felt responsible for everything they'd been through. He was willing to give his life to protect her before, and he wasn't about to let anything hurt her now. "What do you say we get the fuck out of these woods?"

"I'm not sure I can walk," she whispered.

Bourbon broke their hug. "Then, I'll carry you if I have to."

"What about your foot? Didn't the bear trap break a bone?"

"Good as new, thanks to the well's power, just like the time the lake healed my knee."

Daisy smiled for the first time in days. She was glad Bourbon was alive and okay. She felt safe again. But she wanted to be home in Cody's arms.

"What about her?" She nodded toward the deceased woman.

"Let her rot." Bourbon lifted Daisy's backpack for her, and they stepped over the dead log.

"Which way?" Daisy asked.

"Well, if we go west, it will be too rugged. Let's head east and try to get—"

His thought was cut short by a sound. He turned toward the open water and let the backpack slide off his shoulder. "I'll be damned."

"Is that a boat? Out here in the dark?"

"It sure the hell is."

They listened as the sound grew closer. There was no mistaking the whine of a small motorboat crossing the lake. It was moving slowly, with caution, searching for something.

"Think it's Sheriff Hassett?" Daisy asked.

"I hope not."

"Why not?"

"The last thing we need is for her to see that body. Better that nobody knows about this."

Daisy was uncertain if they should cover up Flesti's death. "There have been too many scandalous incidents in the last few weeks. Stoneville doesn't need another. When we get back, I'll confess to my crime and take responsibility for my actions."

"Like hell, you will. Nobody's going to know about this. You did the community a favor by ridding the world of that bitch. How many crimes has she gotten away with over the centuries? How many sin eaters have been under her control? And for what? So she could escape death? Well, she can't escape anymore. You did a good thing—the right thing."

"I wish it hadn't been me."

"But it was you. You did what needed to be done, what no one else could."

The boat was still out of sight, but the sound of the little Mercury engine grew louder.

"Bourbon?" Daisy started, "Did you really hire that man to kill the Bristol cousins?"

Bourbon's head dropped in disgrace. "Yeah."

"Aren't you ashamed of yourself?"

"Yeah. But I called it off. I called Chavez an hour before it happened and told him to cancel the job. He could keep the money. But he did it anyway, and I can't help but think Flesti had something to do with it. I'm sure she corrupted his mind, like everything else she touches, and forced him to do it against his will."

"But still, you set the ball in motion. How are you going to live with that? You're such a man of honor and integrity."

"Same way you're going to live with Flesti's death—put it behind you; tell yourself you had no other choice, even if it's a lie. We'll never forget what we've done. It's a part of us now. I wanted those men killed because they murdered Andrew Mills. I was going to do it for Andrew and his father. You did it for your Cody and your baby. We can't change what we did, but sometimes..." he paused, "Sometimes, the right thing to do is the ugly thing we don't want to do."

All this talk about secrets and cover-ups made Daisy remember Cecil's words: "Mr. Bourbon has a secret he keeps from his lady friend, the new sheriff."

"Cecil said you had a secret. That was one of your sins. But he didn't know what it was."

Bourbon turned toward the sky, as if he sought Annabel Thompson's permission to tell her what he'd been hiding. When no answer came, he changed his gaze to the ground. "I know who killed Jesse Lewis."

"What? Who?"

Before he could answer, a stream of blue light cut through the water and coiled along the beach. The snake had returned, leading a small fishing boat directly to the bay. The boat's captain steered into shallow water, avoiding stumps and sandbars below the lake's surface. The hazards were lit from below, like a pool light that moved along the bottom of the reservoir. Bourbon assumed the pilot was an old fisherman, casting for walleye along the sunken logs, who'd navigated these waters a thousand times.

He was wrong.

The man steering the boat used his enhanced psychic ability. He could sense the submerged stumps and the boulders that hid just below the surface. And he could sense the location of his lover and his unborn child.

## 42

# HEADING HOME

**B**efore the boat beached itself on the sandy shore, Cody was out and running in knee-deep water. Daisy sprinted with renewed strength and high-stepped into the lake, splashing water everywhere. She met him halfway as they collided in a tight embrace. They squeezed each other tightly as Daisy began to sob.

Cody held her in his muscular arms, lifting her gently until her feet were out of the water. He set her back down, but she refused to let go.

"How," she cried. "How did you find us?"

"That's not important right now. I'm just glad you're okay."

"Did you see? With your mind?"

"I saw you alone, sitting on the beach," he whispered in her ear. "I felt your pain. I'm sorry I couldn't get here faster. You're okay now. It's alright. I'll take you home."

She gave his neck another squeeze before letting go.

After giving the two lovers some space and time to reunite, Bourbon stepped from the darkness into the light swirling around the little motorboat. "Son, we are glad to see you. It's been a hell of a day."

Cody and Daisy walked to the beach and stepped onto the soft sand. Cody stared at the headless body that resembled a pile of wet laundry. He didn't take his eyes away from the corpse, afraid that it was merely a trick of his mind, and if he looked away and back, she would be gone. But it wasn't a trick. Flesti—or Marion Cain—was dead, and her hold over Alyse and himself perished with her.

279

He asked anyway, "She's dead?"

Daisy couldn't speak. She buried her face in his shoulder, hiding her guilt.

Bourbon's tone was cold when he answered for her, "She gave me no choice. She was coming after Daisy and said she'd trade her for that damn Azure Blade."

"You cut her—no, she was already dead. AJ shot her when she attacked us on the north side."

"Not dead enough," Bourbon said. "Why'd Timmons shoot her?"

"She's been controlling Alyse."

"Alyse?" Daisy wondered, lifting her chin. "I thought she was controlling River? It was River that attacked Larry Larson."

"River didn't hurt anyone other than Larry. She's been hiding out at AJ's house. But Alyse has been on a spree. It's been ugly. I'm glad you weren't there. How did you know about the blade?" Cody asked. "Did Flesti tell you?"

"Not exactly," Bourbon shook his head. "We met Flesti's brothers. Real nice guys, even though they wanted to throw us in a fucking well at the top of the cliff."

"A well? Like a wishing well?"

Daisy's head shook, "Nothing like a wishing well. It was in a cave, with beautiful paintings and carved stairs." Then a realization came over her, "My phone! Oh, damn, my fucking phone was in that cave."

"That's okay," Cody assured her. "We'll go back sometime and try to find it."

"I don't think so, Cody," Bourbon said. "The whole place might have collapsed. I think Flesti's brothers were inside when it happened."

"Let me guess," Cody said. "Cecil and Martin?"

Daisy's big brown eyes looked at him, "How did you know?"

"I've had a hell of a day, too. It's a long story," He answered, thinking about Roshan's bee presentation at the church. "Let's talk about it later. Right now, let's focus on getting you two home before someone reports this boat stolen."

Cody took Daisy's backpack and set it in the bow of the little aluminum fishing boat, stopping for a moment to examine the little plastic tag-along. "You brought Greenie the Meanie?"

She almost smiled as she unhooked the plastic toy from her pack. Cody helped her climb into the boat and held it still until she sat at the stern. She payed no attention to the smell of stale beer and dead worms, as she held the plastic monster to her chest.

Cody had never seen her look more exhausted. She was a mess, physically and emotionally, and so beautiful.

"Thank you, Bourbon," Cody said. "I'm not sure what I saw in my vision, but I knew she was in trouble. She was going to come and interview Flesti by herself if she had to." He shook Bourbon's hand. "I'm glad she had you here to save her."

Bourbon squeezed Cody's hand and shoulder, "I wouldn't worry too much about that little flower, Cody. I underestimated her. Don't do the same. She's a hell of a lot tougher than you think. Hell, she's a lot tougher than she thinks."

Cody climbed over the gunwale and sat beside Daisy at the stern. A fifteen-horsepower outboard motor was mounted to the boat's transom. Cody took the control arm and waited for their third passenger to board. But before Bourbon could push the boat from shore, they all heard a crashing noise in the woods, followed by a high-pitched bark. Hetzen bolted through the tall grass that lined the beach and splashed into the lake behind Bourbon.

"We can't leave him," Daisy pleaded.

Cody protested quietly as Daisy grabbed Hetzen's scruffy neck, and Bourbon hoisted the dog's tail into the boat. Hetzen showered them with a spray of water as he shook his coat dry, and Cody saw a momentary smile cross Daisy's face. His protest was diluted with lake water and dog kisses.

Bourbon pushed the boat's bow, then stepped in, letting the watercraft drift away from shore, away from the crime scene, and toward the safer side of Cain Lake.

Before Cody pulled the engine's recoil to fire the piston and start the motor, he gave the beach one last glance.

She was still there. And as the boat drifted away, the glowing micropods followed, slowly losing their intensity. They left the dead woman hidden behind the tall grass along the beach, but Cody observed something dark in the woods—darker than the shadows. It was a man. He had the stature of a linebacker, and a dim light filled his eyes.

Cody didn't mention or point him out, but he knew it was one of the brothers Bourbon spoke of. He hoped this was over. With Flesti dead, maybe the Cain brothers would stay as reclusive as they had been their entire lives. If they didn't? Well, at least he had the Azure Blade.

# 43

# THE BLUE ONION

I t's been three weeks," Cody noted. "You still haven't told me what exactly happened in the woods."

"Yes, I did." Daisy retorted.

"No, not everything. I know you're leaving out some of the details."

"What do you want to hear? What I had for breakfast? Where I peed?" She couldn't help but smirk.

"Ha, Ha, very funny. I just think...well...you've been different since that weekend. You're not sleeping. You skip meals and seem a little... distant. I just want to be sure you're okay."

"I'm fine. Great actually. Maybe I seem different because you're seeing more of me now. Are you having regrets?"

"That you moved in with me? No, absolutely not. I love having you and Sammy there."

"Good. Now, can we just enjoy our dinner?"

They both took a drink of their water and perused the menu again. The Blue Onion was the finest steak house in Stoneville, perhaps because it was the only steak house in Stoneville. As Cody watched the wait staff walk by with sizzling sirloins, grilled vegetables, and decadent desserts, he felt a great deal of shame. He should be the one paying for their meal, not Daisy, but she insisted they give the restaurant a try.

Cody opened the menu and scanned the entrees while calculating the prices in his head, as he tried to pick something cheap, but the savory scent of fresh prime rib teased his hunger. The numbers on the right side of the page reminded him that he'd need to find a job soon, or the monetary strain on their relationship would take its toll.

"What are you getting?" Daisy asked as she fought her indecision. "I'm leaning toward the T-bone. I bet Hetzen would love the bone if I brought it home for him."

"For that price, I'll eat the bone. Hetzen can have his kibble. You spoil that mutt."

Daisy giggled to herself. "He guided me out of the woods. I think I owe him a T-bone."

Before Cody could respond, a strong hand squeezed his shoulder. "Celebrating?"

Cody turned to see Jeff Bourbon with an armful of Jo Hassett. They were dressed as if they'd just left Easter mass, each radiating and buzzing with happiness. Sheriff Hassett's jewelry sparkled in the candlelight almost as much as her eyes. Cody guessed her dress was probably more expensive than his first truck. Bourbon was nearly unrecognizable. His suit and tie starkly contrasted with the worn and torn jeans Cody had last seen him in, and he'd traded his stained green T-shirt for a neatly pressed item off the Men's Warehouse rack.

Cody stood and shook his hand, "Bourbon, Hassett, it's nice to see you."

Daisy stood and hugged the couple. Cody noticed her embrace with Bourbon lasted a little longer. They had bonded in the woods. That was to be expected. But there was something more profound than just a friendship. It was more like a family bond that couldn't be broken by anything but death. He was glad for that. Daisy never really had a father, and Bourbon never had a daughter. The two were as opposite as any pair could be, but that didn't matter. They had a life-altering experience together that would shape their relationship.

"Celebrating the new job?" Bourbon asked again.

"Yes," Daisy answered.

"You must be pretty proud of WKED Television's newest reporter," Jo Hassett said to Cody, smiling at Daisy.

"Very proud."

"You look so beautiful on screen, Daisy," Hassett complimented. "Better than that, B-I-T-C-H Bethany Smart. That woman would talk down to the Pope in an interview."

Daisy blushed. "Yeah, I'm so glad she left the morning news to go to the evening telecast. Being an anchor keeps me at the station—less travel, and Sammy can come to work with me when Mom can't watch him. But it's only been one week, so we'll see how it goes. Plus, I'll be taking maternity leave in about seven months. Let's hope they'll bring me back afterward."

Hassett touched her arm, "Girl, that would be their loss if they didn't."

Cody had wanted to call Jeff Bourbon and ask about River Kelly's fate, but he'd been preoccupied with Daisy moving and her new job. He hadn't been in touch with AJ since the night he'd pulled the trigger, mostly because he felt AJ and River needed time and space to focus on River's predicament.

"What about River Kelly?" Cody asked Sheriff Hassett. "Any word on her charges?"

Hassett looked at Bourbon for an answer. He pulled on his tie as if the noose was cutting into his throat, but he was smiling.

"Larry Larson did not press charges against River. So, without any weapon and a lack of intent, the state prosecutor reduced her charges to a misdemeanor. She's been fined $1,000—pocket change for her boyfriend—and must complete forty hours of community service." Bourbon leaned a little closer to his audience. "I assume it was a little favor for Dale Kelly, too. Being the District Attorney has its privileges."

"That's not all," the sheriff interrupted. "I spoke with the DA this afternoon, Savage. Your criminal record has been expunged, and your probation is over."

"What!" Cody asked. He felt Daisy grab his arm with excitement. "My criminal record? How?"

Candlelight beamed off the sheriff's teeth as she smiled for him and Daisy, "I guess that's what happens when you find the DA's daughter, save her, and stop a murder spree."

*A murder spree? Alyse?* Cody's face went blank with the conflicting news. Had he saved Alyse or ruined her life? He felt sick, and the tantalizing aromas of the restaurant's food were no longer stimulating his appetite. His notions of Alyse's future were as tangled as a plate of spaghetti. Alyse had survived Flesti's assault, but for what? To be locked away for the rest of her life? Should he have saved her? She begged him to let her die that night. Her trial might not be for months or longer. How would she deal with a jail cell when she couldn't bear the confinement of Stoneville?

Alyse was innocent and he needed to prove it. Her actions were controlled by Flesti. But with Flesti dead, how could he prove anything?

"You're a hero, Savage." Hassett's words felt like fiction. Cody didn't want to be a hero. He just wanted to save his friendship with AJ by finding his girlfriend before the police. The only thing that mattered to him now was being a dad and starting a family. His psychic ability was stronger than ever since his confrontation with Marion Cain, but he ignored it, hoping it would subside or vanish altogether. Luckily, things had been quiet in Stoneville for the past three weeks, and he hoped they would stay that way.

His spinning thoughts were interrupted by Bourbon's light jab to the shoulder. "We'll let you two lovebirds get back to your dinner. It looks like our table is ready. We'll get together again real soon."

They said their goodbyes, and Bourbon and Hassett followed a hostess, a short girl with bulbous glasses and a thick waist, to a corner table.

"I'm so happy for you," Daisy said as they resumed their seats.

"Happy for us," Cody corrected.

"For us," she agreed as they took their seats at the table. But as Daisy looked across the restaurant, a woman stared over an open menu at her. There was a line of blood around her throat as if her head had been reattached to her body. She wanted to scream, or run, or both. Instead, she closed her eyes and grabbed Cody's hand. Her heart pounded so hard she could barely speak, and her shaking made the table vibrate.

"What is it? Daisy, are you alright?"

"It's her," she whispered in a raspy voice.

"Who?"

Daisy leaned across the small table. "Flesti. She's here, in the restaurant."

"No, Daisy, that's impossible. Bourbon...AJ and Bourbon made sure...you know." He couldn't explain himself out loud in the serene restaurant, but she knew what he meant.

Daisy nodded toward the woman with the crimson throat.

Cody squeezed her hand. "Honey, that's Mrs. McClesky. You know, Pesky McClesky, the town gossip."

"She's watching us." Daisy looked away, squinted hard, and hoped to reset her vision.

"Yeah, she watches everybody. That's why she's such a gossip."

Daisy's effort to clear her eyes worked. When she refocused on the female patron, it was indeed Pesky McClesky. She looked similar to Marion Cain but carried an extra forty pounds. The red streak of blood around her neck had been replaced with a row of rubies on a silver chain, a cheap costume jewelry piece. Mrs. McClesky gave them a fake smile and returned her attention to the laminated menu.

Daisy's heart idled down, but her hands failed to steady.

"Do you want to go?" Cody asked.

Daisy nodded regretfully. As she stood, her knees betrayed her, and Cody had to support her weight. He knew she'd been troubled by her experience in the woods. He put a strong arm around her waist to stabilize her, and they headed for the exit. As they left, Bourbon caught them at the door. "Is she alright?" Seeing Daisy visibly shaken.

"No, she's not feeling well." Cody leaned toward him and lowered his voice. "Dammit, Bourbon, she shouldn't have seen what you did. She doesn't have the stomach for that kind of violence."

Bourbon sighed, "I know. I'm sorry, son. But like I said before, I had no choice."

Daisy broke from Cody and gave Bourbon one last hug—a thank

you for covering her act of violence. She kissed his cheek and slipped out the door arm-in-arm with Cody.

*****

When Cody and Daisy arrived home, the sun was bowing out over the horizon. The headlights of their little Subaru shone across the lawn, illuminating the front porch. Two tiny faces appeared in the window on the porch. Sammy waved from within while Hetzen pressed his nose to the glass. Daisy laughed at the scene and watched her mother shoo them away from their spying positions. She gave the couple a little wave and closed the curtains.

The lovebirds exited the car, shut the doors, and walked arm-in-arm to the front door.

"What's that?" Daisy pointed to the porch.

Cody followed her delicate finger with his eyes. "Hmm, not sure."

He climbed the three steps to the porch and picked up a paper bag. The two staples that held a note in place also provided a seal for the little surprise inside. Cody held it up for Daisy to read. "Just a little token of my appreciation. Hope you get to celebrate your new life in Stoneville. Thank you!" It was signed D. Kelly.

"It's from the District Attorney." Cody reached into the bag and removed a bottle of Hennessy X.O, the same cognac he'd shared with Dale Kelly the day he visited his home.

"Holy shit," Cody whispered. "A handshake or pat on the back would have been enough, but what the hell, I'll accept it." He handed Daisy the bag while he ran his fingers over the embossed glass, turning it slowly and reading the text.

Daisy stared at him, in awe of his modesty, in love with his character. "You should be proud of yourself. You saved River and stopped Alyse from hurting anyone else. You deserve more than a bottle of booze."

"Yeah, but it was AJ who finished the job. If he hadn't...you know? If he hadn't stopped Flesti, things might have gotten worse. He's the real hero. Him and Bourbon. I can't believe Bourbon took her head

288

off with that ax." He signed and gazed into her eyes apologetically. "You shouldn't have seen that. But I'm glad she's gone."

Daisy swallowed the truth before it drooled from her lips. There'd been so many times she wanted to tell him, but she was afraid of what he'd think of her. "So, are you going to share it with them?"

"Hell no," Cody laughed. He admired the stout, violin-shaped bottle. The smoky, sweet flavor came back to him, and he could almost smell the liquor through the bottle. He wet his lips with a flick of his tongue. "Well, maybe just one glass."

Daisy began to crinkle the bag into a ball when she felt something inside. "What's this?"

"What?"

"There's something else in here." She dumped an envelope into her hand and gave it to Cody. They traded the bottle and the envelope.

Cody opened the flap and peeked inside. "No way." He pulled out a stack of cash and watched Daisy's eyes light up. "Holy shit, how much is that? You can't keep that. Should you keep it? Should we—"

"We should return it," Cody suggested. As he fanned the paper money, the smell of the new bills filled the air, almost as sweet as the scent of the Hennessey X.O. "But he won't take it back." A sense of guilt consumed him, not because he wanted to keep the money, but because they needed it, and because he never thought he'd be in a position where five thousand dollars would change his life. But here he was with no job, living on handouts from AJ and spreading Daisy's wages thin.

He took her around the waist and kissed her passionately. Lost in the moment, Daisy threw her arm around his neck, letting the expensive bottle of cognac slip from her hand. She jumped back and closed her eyes, waiting for the crash to come as the bottle hit the floor. But there was only silence. She opened her eyes to find Cody had thrown his hand behind his back and caught the bottle before it hit the deck.

Her jaw dropped open in shock. "How did you do that?"

Cody pulled the bottle from behind his back and held it by the neck. "Not sure. I just knew it was going to happen and reacted. Must be my reflexes are better than I thought."

He moved in to resume their kiss, holding the bottle safe against his body, but when Daisy peered into his eyes, she noticed something she'd never seen before—little diamonds of light swirling slowly in his pupils. There were just a few, but they were there, floating in the dark. She was instantly reminded of the Cain Brothers and ducked his kiss.

"Come on," she said, clearing her throat. "Let's get inside before the mosquitoes start chewing us up."

Cody walked her inside, feeling like the luckiest man alive, poor as he was. He turned back toward the setting sun to see the orange color of the clouds being squeezed away by the night. The sky was nearly the same color as the cognac. He turned to admire the view inside, as Sammy jumped into Daisy's arms and Hetzen squeezed between her knees for attention, and he was sure that they were finally going to find some normalcy in their chaotic Stoneville lives.

# 44

# THE VISITOR

Roshan Kapoor sat on his bed, knees bent, with his back against his pillow. A Bristol board sketch book lay open in his lap. He'd been drawing with a Konoor graphic pen, his new choice of art medium. He liked the smooth black lines and the stark contrast of black on white. Instead of drawing the visions that flooded his mind, the boy was able to choose his subject matter over the last three weeks. Tonight, he was finishing a drawing of a superhero, a muscular man clad in armor, with a flowing cape and two shields in each hand that could be thrown to attack his enemies or held up to block weapons.

He smiled in satisfaction as he made sound effects and put the final touches on the work of art. "The Rebel Knight," he declared his hero. "Savior of Cain Castle. Hero of Stoneheart, the magical city under attack by the Azure Dragon."

His door creaked open, but his focus was intent.

"Ro?" His mother asked. "Roshan?"

Ro kept the pen working, lost in a world of magic, knights, and dragons.

"Roshan Kapoor!"

"Oh, hi, Mom." Ro finally gave her his attention.

"Son, it's 9:30. You need to put that away and go to bed.

"Just ten more minutes."

"No."

"Come on, Mom, I don't have school tomorrow. I'll do the dishes in the morning."

How could she resist? "And feed the dog?"

"Yup, and feed Sadie, too."

"Okay," Shari agreed. "Did you brush your teeth yet?"

"Done."

"Ten minutes, no more. I'll be back to check on you." She moved across the room, picking up clothes and throwing them into his hamper. Then she sat on the edge of his bed and gave him a tight squeeze and a kiss. She took an interest in his drawing.

"Who's this guy?"

He talked and cross-hatched simultaneously, "The Rebel Knight. See the shields? Those are his weapons. He can throw them, and they come back to him every time. He has to protect Cain Castle from the dragon. That's the dragon flying in the background."

"I see. Very creative. You're so talented, sweetie. Maybe you'll make you're own comic book someday."

He smiled at the thought.

"Okay, lights out in ten."

She rubbed his back with a circular motion, the way she did when he was little and had an upset stomach, then kissed his left temple. She stood, tiptoed across the room in her bare feet, watching for stray Lego pieces, and out the door. She pulled the door closed behind her, leaving a slight opening.

Ro worked his pen for twenty minutes before he decided he was finished. He set his masterpiece on his nightstand, clicked his bedside light off, and climbed under the bed covers.

He thought about his ink hero for a few minutes. And then his real dreams started to become entangled in his daydream. The real dreams had nearly taken over when a tapping sound caused him to erupt from his sleep. He sat up, listened, and decided it was probably Sadie pacing in the hallway.

He lay back, but before he could resume his slumber, the tapping came again. Rain, he thought. It's just rain on the window.

Tap, tap, tap.

The tapping came quicker, but still gently, on the pane of glass near the foot of his bed. He sat up again, then crawled to the end of his bed to look out the window. There was nothing there but the darkness. In the sky, he could see a cluster of stars—a cloudless night. He knew it couldn't be raining.

And then he thought about his older brother. Maybe he was outside, throwing pebbles to get his attention. He slid the sash upward and peeked at the ground below. His brother was not outside.

And then the source of the tapping revealed itself. Roshan jumped back, startled by the black shadow but not afraid. "What are you doing here?"

Without answering, Poe hopped through the window and bounced in front of him on the sill. The crow opened his wings and moved to the wooden foot board of the bed.

Roshan smiled, reached out, and stroked the big corvid's feathers. "I'll bet you're looking for a friend, aren't you? It's okay, I'll be your friend, Poe. Don't worry, I won't tell anyone you're here."

# THE END

# THANK YOU

Enjoyed
## RED DEVIL?

Don't forget to leave a review.


www.TerryFisherBooks.com
Sign-up for announcements and notifications.